LOCK AND KEY

THE INITIATION

BY

RIDLEY PEARSON

HARPER
An Imprint of HarperCollinsPublishers

For Betsy Dodge Pearson,
who loved a mystery
and then became one herself.
—R.P.

Lock and Key: The Initiation
Copyright © 2016 by HarperCollins Publishers
Map copyright © Pomfret School 2015

Library of Congress Control Number: 2016932099
ISBN 978-0-06-239902-1

Typography by Joe Merkel
17 18 19 20 21   CG/OPM   10 9 8 7 6 5 4 3 2 1
❖
First paperback edition, 2017

A NOTE ABOUT JAMES

He wasn't always this way. I think of him as a shy boy who spent time in Father's library and, on occasion, in the cellar practicing chemistry. He is my older brother, James. That makes him a boy, which I can't help, but I don't hold it against him either. And though I could claim "I don't know where he went wrong," it would be a lie. I know exactly where he went wrong: Baskerville Academy.

What follows is a sister's written account of events as witnessed by me and told to me, for you see I was and am my brother's confidante. We have, for as long as I can remember, been best friends.

There was a time he told me everything—and I mean everything! Lately, not nearly as much. I can tell you this, my reader: from an early age

James Keynes Moriarty seemed to understand he was bound for greatness. Not the kind of greatness all would choose, but a kind of greatness just the same. I believe he understood the importance of keeping an objective record, thus I gained his confidence. I became his chronicler, his scribe, his biographer. And now you are the recipient, as I pass along what is perhaps an unwanted baton—the burden of the truth.

I have taken certain liberties in these pages with dialogue, as James's recollections often flow out of him like water from a burst dam. I have developed my own shorthand which I won't bore you with, but suffice it to say I can keep up. Most if not all of the descriptions are mine, as I've been in these places, sometimes with him, sometimes much later as I returned to document what I'd heard took place. On occasion, I've sought out or have endured the descriptions of events from others and have hereby interpreted them to my liking. James has not exactly been forthcoming of late. As you can imagine, in certain instances I have been required to interview others and then rebuild a situation or labor to reconstruct the happening as might the lens of a camera. The emotions expressed are from James himself, though I don't pretend I can keep my own, and even those of others, from entering

these pages. I trust my witnesses to have given me a fair account of situations, language, and emotions. One other secret: my brother kept a journal that, until the start of this story, he did not know I knew about. I borrowed from it then, I borrow from it still. Sisters will be sisters.

Over the course of compiling this, I have learned to accept that greatness comes in all forms. Great evil is as rarely accomplished as is great heroism.

Through the events of a few brief months, my brother transformed. I should have seen it coming, meaning I am not entirely blameless for what happened. Possibly it might have been avoided— though can greatness ever be avoided?

As his sister, what happened to James took me by surprise. It scared me then, scares me still. I submit the events as objectively as possible. Whether beast or monster, messenger or prophet, my brother's transformation was nothing short of mythical.

I was there. So now, dear reader, are you.

MORIA MORIARTY

campus
MAP

CHAPTER 1

LATE AUGUST

TERRIFIED FOR MY LIFE, I RAN FROM MY brother. I was faster. We both knew it. Faster, when outside on grass running toward a finish line marked with two tennis racquets at the end of a stretch of manicured lawn on Boston Common.

Currently, however, I was running down a first-floor hallway in a Beacon Hill home. It was lined with oil portraits of horrendous-looking stern faces, old people to whom I was related: great-uncles, women with hairy moles, a grandfather with a scornful brow and distrustful eyes. The family Moriarty.

At the end of the portraits was a gargantuan mirror with a gilded frame and, in it, someone I knew all too well. The girl I saw had a teardrop face, intense gray-green eyes, tightly formed bow lips. My father called my looks, and my nose in particular, "statuesque," which I hoped was a good thing, given that my eyebrows were unpleasant, narrow slashes with no curve to them whatsoever. My brother and I shared the discolored skin beneath our eyes, something for which I would forever curse my mother, as my father and his ancestors didn't possess that particular trait. The mirror had stopped me for a nanosecond—I had trouble looking away from the portraits. I ran on.

The oriental carpet runner, as old as the faces on the wall, muffled the footfalls of my bare feet. I dodged a black-lacquered table and the frosted-glass cat perched upon it that served as a nightlight when the reproduction gas lamp wall sconces, now electric, were switched off. (Father did not believe in dark hallways or stairs. Each night, he lit the place up like a Christmas tree.) I dodged the hideous stuffed raccoon that stood on its hind legs and, farther down, the some-kind-of-weasel that still scared the gee-whiz out of me. One of the weasel's glass eyes was missing, leaving it looking like it was constantly winking.

My speed advantage did not play out within the house where I was careful of the antiques and my brother more reckless. He knocked over the raccoon without pause. Charged me like a train. I carried his treasured diary in hand. Only its surrender could save me from his wrath. And only then if I could quickly convince him it was all a joke—that I'd never intended to read it—which, as we both knew, was a far-fetched lie. Of course, I intended to devour its contents—I was reading as I ran. I knew if he caught me he was basically going to kill me. I deserved it. I was a thief, even if I preferred to think of myself as a researcher or historian. I felt like a criminal. It turned out I had a lot to learn about that.

James, was tall for his age—fourteen—and, I guessed, already shaving. His pitch-black hair (parted far too high on his head) created a kind of dirty look to his face that recently came and went. By all accounts he had quiet looks: no sharp bones to his round face, darker skin surrounding his sad eyes. If Malfoy was salt, my brother was pepper, and with a Scotsman's perma-blush complexion to his high cheekbones. His sullen dark eyes seemed to be looking everywhere at once and he had ears too big for his head. I didn't know if he'd grow into his ears the way he was expected to grow into his silly clown feet, but if he didn't, he was going to have trouble at dances.

"You are so dead!" he called out. We both knew that was nonsense. He was special to me; we were special to each other. Father didn't encourage social activities for his two children, so James and I had learned to build forts out of blankets, cook unfathomably horrible meals together, act out scenes from our favorite books, and had even created our own language that neither Father nor Ralph, our Romanian driver, nor our cook, the Caribbean "Miss Delphine," understood. Only Lois, our nanny growing up, now Father's rail-thin, gray-haired secretary and the person in charge of our houses and properties, could translate.

Already hiding within, I heard the smooth click of my father's study door opening and closing. It was a room we were forbidden from entering without Father. Naturally, it was where I was hiding. Dressed in rich red-leather book spines, an antique world map globe in a brass stand, dark woods, and thin frayed carpets, it smelled of walnut oil, a fragrance that would stay with me, and make me cry for years to come.

There were limitations to where I could hide. James knew it. Under the harvest table; behind the door; tucked within the plush red velvet floor-to-ceiling curtains hanging on either side of the mahogany bookshelves; in the unlit fireplace; or where I currently was hiding: inside the Italian armoire.

James drew out his search, displaying sadistic tendencies which to my mind had only gotten worse in recent months. Time was when he would have joked with the unseen me, coaxed me into laughter so I'd reveal myself. Playing on our affection, he'd set a bee trap, like the one my father hung outside the kitchen's sink window—all sugar water and inventive cunning. Now instead, James was more the insect zapper variety. If we'd lived in the Middle Ages he'd be in training for the dungeon work where he'd turn the screw on the rack. He was the proverbial kid who picked the wings off living houseflies. Only I was the housefly. He removed my confidence, bit by bit, scheme by scheme. He made me afraid of him and dependent upon him all at the same time. My brother was learning how to be sly, and I didn't care for it one bit.

"'What fools these mortals be,'" he cried out loudly. He probably didn't know I knew he was quoting Shakespeare. That was the other thing: he didn't give me any credit. None. He thought I was a stupid girl. Period. I wanted so badly to shout out, "*Midsummer Night's Dream*!" but kept my mouth shut for fear of the torture I would invite. "You'd have been smarter to go through to Lois's office or into the kitchen. Father's study is a no-no, little girl." He knew I would boil at being called that. I kept myself from screaming out in anger.

A sharp, electronic peal of our home security system drilled through the house. The feature was called "On Watch." It chirped whenever a window or door was opened. It allowed Father to monitor if anyone entered or left the house, effectively making us, his children, prisoners in our own home. It wasn't the way he saw it, but Father saw most things differently than we did. The current warning suggested the front door had opened: Father had returned.

James flung open the antique left door of the hand-carved armoire, the side that contained our father's winter coats, the side that smelled of moth balls, and climbed in atop me. I jabbed him with my finger, believing he intended to drag me out into the room as a sacrificial lamb, but it wasn't that at all. He pulled the door shut behind him and we were two kids in *The Lion, the Witch and the Wardrobe*. Maybe, I thought, if we started clawing at the back wall of the armoire we'd tumble out into snow. As it was, James's right leg was between my knees, as I was sitting down, his knees in my face, and my face in his stomach. I thought he must be holding on to the clothes rod since he was able to remain so steady in such an awkward position. He stole his journal out of my grip. I didn't put up much of a fight.

Father's sixth sense brought him shortly into the adjacent library. "Children?"

Next, he entered his study, only the thickness of an armoire door away. Again, I nearly screamed: my hair—dark brown going on black like my brother's, if you have to ask—had twisted around one of James's shirt buttons. Strands ripped loose with each subtle movement.

I could foresee more than a few serious problems. Father was known to spend hours in his office. He often napped in the chair facing the fireplace. If my brother pulled any more of my hair out I was going to scream. My nose was already running from the tears in my eyes from the hair being pulled. Worse, I heard the sniffing of our two English shepherds, London and Bath. London loved James. Bath was all mine. There was no way the armoire would stay closed for long.

A curious thing: Father did not sit in that favorite reading chair by the fireplace, one that made a particular, and peculiar, squeak when sat in. No, I could picture him standing a few feet away staring at the inquisitive dogs whining at the armoire, or perhaps sitting behind his desk in the chair, which was sturdy and silent. I heard a click, like a fence gate, followed by another, and then, a few moments later, a clunk—as if something heavy had been set down.

The globe wouldn't make such a sound. Neither would any chair in his study. James bumped the inside of my knee intentionally. He was asking me what was going on. This was the unspoken language between brother and sister that only came from endless hours together. A punch in the arm, a flick of a finger on the back of the neck, a hand placed gently onto the shoulder, a ruffle of one's hair, a light pat on the cheek, a strong pat on the cheek. James and I could see each other well enough for me to know he was as confused by Father's actions as was I.

I found myself trying to explain the heavy sound—as if a door had opened. This, in a room with only the one door. Like the study and its door, James and I had only the one parent, and before today, we had liked to think of him as predictable. Maybe that was out of want, possibly out of necessity; single-parent children need stability, I would later be told by the headmaster of Baskerville Academy. We need role models and codes of conduct, a sense of the spiritual and three meals a day. "The rest will take care of itself."

It has since been proved that headmasters can be as wrong as the next person. The "rest" doesn't always take care of itself. It didn't take care of me or James. It abandoned us, just as we'd been told our mother had done. It left us groping for answers, struggling for solutions, and at odds about the quickest road to self-preservation. In short, that brief time spent huddled together in an armoire in Father's study would be one of those wonderful shared secret moments between me and my older brother. As things turned out, it would also prove to be one of the last times I truly felt so close to him.

CHAPTER 2

THE INVADERS STRIKE

Boston is a big city. It spreads out from the bay like a fan, the denser population at the apex where a small brick building marks the start of our country. At night, its streets teem with vehicles old and new, big and small, coughing out exhaust, honking horns (despite ordinances forbidding it), grinding gears, screeching tires, blasting music, covering intimate conversations whispered between pedestrian lovers or the combative rants barked by competing academics.

Our neighborhood, called Beacon Hill, is a world apart, its cobblestone lanes crowded with parked cars, set aglow by yellow gas lamps, quiet, private, and preserved from another epoch. If you were to spill change from your pocket on the way down the stone steps from our front door, half the neighborhood would hear it. Inside the remodeled and refurbished centuries-old brownstones and walk-ups a librarian would be well suited and comfortable. Going to sleep with his window open was a common event for James because Father ran the air-conditioning too low. The open window was not allowed; Father had insisted all summer that the house be "buttoned up" before bed. James could defeat our home security system with a magnet and two wires, as only an older brother could. He did so each night after Father had retired. I often heard his window opening and, when I did, I opened mine. Not because I enjoyed the air, but because I followed James in so much of what he did.

The night of the attack, city sounds called clearly. Beacon Hill was not only charming, given its preservation of the past, it was charmed. Magical things happened here. Costumed carolers sang in its streets at Christmas. Little girls with bows in their hair walked with their mothers. There were neighborhood Easter egg hunts, and everyone dressed in Irish green on March 17th.

James and I had come to know each and every

sound like the face of a friend. He had both a telescope and binoculars at our disposal. On warm summer nights when we couldn't sleep, we would find each other out on the fire escape and stargaze or locate a fire truck or police car responsible for a specific siren. We learned both the geography and the layout of city streets, the Charles River, and the major highways and bridges. We knew this town. Our town. Secretly, we both felt privileged to call it home.

Later, I would discover that three invaders had climbed an extension ladder in order to reach the fire escape. They entered through James's open window, lucky that James was a heavy sleeper.

The sound that awoke James—my brother's telescope and tripod going to the floor in a cacophony of broken lenses—also shook me from sleep.

One moment I was lying down, the next sitting up and throwing my feet off the bed.

While I ran toward his room, James coughed awake. A gloved hand slapped over his mouth as he did. Someone held his legs while the one gagging him pinned his right arm with a knee and his left with a hand. James bucked like a wild horse, and struggled to be free; he screamed, making little more sound than that of an amorous alley cat; he forced himself to sitting, only making things more difficult. The one muffling him switched positions, constraining him from behind, binding both his arms. The guy at James's feet—all three wore balaclava ski masks pulled down over their faces—wrapped a length of rope around James's ankles, the implications of which threw James into a fit. Kidnapping! A third ninja, watching the door, turned to assist his partners. Three against one was unfair; no kind of sport whatsoever. James was quickly subdued.

Don't call me "girly" just because I screamed loudly enough to light a few dark windows on our street. I'd run down the hall and had slipped through James's door without notice. I wasn't sure exactly what was going on but it wasn't to James's liking. After my scream, I turned on the overhead light; after turning on the overhead light, I threw a trophy. It was a first-place science fair trophy: an antique microscope, black metal and brass, mounted on a wooden pedestal with a small brass plaque engraved with my brother's full name: James Keynes Moriarty. The trophy weighed several pounds and was big enough that I didn't throw it very well. Thankfully the three intruders screened James, so that if I hit anyone it wouldn't be my brother. I did hit someone, but good. I heard a "Grumph!" (Actually, it was a word I can't write here.) The three turned toward me. Oops, I thought.

I could claim it was my plan to lead them away from my bound-up brother, but I wasn't that cunning at that point in my life. Their actions resulted from my own: I ran. If a scream could break glass then every chandelier in our home—and there are many—would have rained down like hail. Advantage: Moria. Thanks to my brother's endless chasing of me, I knew how to navigate this house at high speed, no matter how many times it had been strictly forbidden. I planted my bare feet, my nightgown flapping, and sideslipped into and through a turn to the main staircase; I mounted the banister, sliding down backward at a speed Newton would have had to calculate, and dismounted *exactly* at the moment necessary to prevent my bottom colliding with the newel. I quit gymnastics when wearing a leotard became embarrassing—just before my eleventh birthday—but retained enough of my training to swivel, fly through the air, and plant the landing like Gabby Douglas.

My pursuers took several stairs per stride and then jumped, landing with such thunder that I dived, thinking something had exploded behind me. I clambered to my feet. The three stood dead center in the foyer.

"Stop!" shouted Father from the second-floor

railing.

"Father! It's James!" I shouted. "They hurt James!"

The foyer was all gray light and shadowy black shapes. My head was spinning—I might have hit it against the floor while diving.

"OUT!" Father roared. Standing there in his brown satin robe and leather slippers, he nonetheless demonstrated his command over others. Among Father's many gifts were his uncanny authority and resolute confidence. His drawn face and striking, impenetrable eyes possessed in him a bearing that few found the strength to challenge.

Confession: I didn't know if it was fear of Father that caused them to run. It certainly wasn't fear of me. One of them limped, either from the long jump from the staircase or my expert throwing ability. But I was struck by something different. As the balaclavas highlighted the pale flesh contained within the knitted almond-shaped holes, I couldn't see the eyes exactly, but I could make out the direction in which they were looking. It was every direction at once. I felt oddly at sea with them. They were lost, or reluctant to leave. Why hesitate like that? I wondered.

They finally fled into the vestibule and out our front door, forced to unlock its three locks, which bought me time to snag an umbrella from the Chinese porcelain umbrella vase. I cracked it down on the shoulder of the last ninja out the door. It sounds like courage. It wasn't. It was rage. I was boiling hot and prepared to tear the eyes out of any one of them for attacking my brother. I raised the umbrella again, ready to deliver a second blow, but the attackers were long gone. Father caught it from behind.

"It's over," he said, trying to calm me.

"James!" I countered. "They got James!"

Father took off upstairs with the agility of me or one of my friends. I'd never seen him move like that. I'd had no idea he was capable of such speed. He fled across the upstairs hall, slammed a shoulder as he turned into James's room. I was but seconds behind him though it felt like I was in another part of the city I was so far behind. My efforts to climb the stairs cloaked any sounds I might have heard. The silence from within that room could only mean horrible things, things I didn't want to think about. I skidded to a stop before arriving at the room's door, unwilling to take a look inside.

When I heard my father say, "Thank God!" while he was untying James, I slid down the wall, slumped into a crouch, and felt my shoulders shaking and my cheeks wet. I found relief a funny thing.

A strange cousin to grief; it dressed the same, sounded the same, and yet the two were about as far from each other as the north and south poles.

"Moria?" James asked. His first word spoken. "Is she okay?"

Then, I blubbered.

CHAPTER 3

THE GREAT UNSPOKEN

THE FOLLOWING MORNING, JAMES WAS CALLED
into Father's study after finishing off a three-egg
omelet, five strips of bacon, and four pieces of toast.
He washed it all down with a bowl of almond clusters drowning in whole milk. Where it all went, I
wasn't sure, but it had always been this way. I'd
eaten breakfast two hours earlier at 8:00 a.m., the
coffee machine's glass decanter already half empty
by the time I'd arrived into the sunlit room.

The Boston morning gave no hint at the trouble
of the night before. It was a birdsong, sunshine,
scattered cumulus cloud kind of morning. A Mary

Poppins kind of morning. The kind to make me wish we were at the Cape house with its two boats, private beach, and giant lawn that spilled green into the gray blue of Nantucket Sound.

The summons into the study could not be good news. That much was clear from the shock that registered on James's face when Lois advised him of the unscheduled appointment with Father. Such meetings usually made being sent to the school's guidance counselor seem like a party. Made more puzzling by its timing, following the break-in as it did, the directive suggested there was blame to be assigned. No doubt James's wiring of the open window had been discovered.

James entered, his trepidation obvious on his pale skin and grim expression.

"Father," he said, since the man did nothing to acknowledge his presence. Oswyn Bennett Moriarty pointed to the leather chair with the brass-tack trimming while remaining focused on his reading. He continued through to the end of the document, consuming several minutes, which to James stretched for an eternity. He removed a pair of half-glasses used only for reading, a simple enough gesture that put James on edge. If the visit was to be short, Father would have simply moved the glasses down his nose slightly and peered out over them. He'd signaled a seriousness that James wasn't prepared for. Trying desperately not to show it, James remained rattled from the home invasion of the night before.

The house rule was don't speak (to Father) unless spoken to. He had things on his mind; his work filled his head; his children could be a nuisance. James broke the rule, not the best way to start.

"What did the police say?" asked James, improperly.

Father offered no response, not so much as a facial tic. Another several minutes lapsed. He neatened the paperwork to the side of his green leather blotter. "There will be no police, nor any police report." James bit back his disapproval. "I am well aware of the appearance of the events that took place, but appearances can be deceiving, son. It is important to remember this. It's a bit of a cliché, but some of our most important lessons are clichéd, believe me. What I am going to present to you may sound off, James. I expect it may. I ask you to bear with me."

Father did not ask his children for their tolerance or forgiveness, causing James to wonder if the invaders had secretly replaced the man and installed a doppelgänger, an identical twin from a parallel universe. "Of course, Father."

"The issue at hand is Baskerville Academy. Last night . . . that was all about Baskerville Academy."

"I don't understand."

"You have completed your eighth-grade year. You've known for some time where you'd be going to school this fall."

James had a challenge at the ready. Instead, he said what was expected of him. "I suppose, since that decision is not mine to make."

Father tilted his head as if still wearing his reading glasses. "James, please. The time has come."

"So why rub it in? You're not going to allow me to go anywhere but stinking Baskerville Academy." James shuddered. "I'm sorry, Father. That was disrespectful. I apologize."

Father's face went as scarlet as Valentine roses. "As you should."

"Yes, I'm aware of the family tradition. You've explained it since forever ago. I'm aware of our family's history with the school. I just wish we weren't stuck back a hundred years ago. Just because your grandfather and father went there doesn't mean—"

"And I, as well."

"—and you as well—doesn't mean it's right for me. A lot has changed in the past hundred and fifty years that makes some stone castle in the middle of nowhere just a little less appealing. Things like cars and the Internet, and like a hundred more schools to choose from than existed back then." James hesitated. "Grover Cleveland School, for instance."

"That's a public school!" Father said indignantly.

"Commonwealth School, then. It's the best private school in the city and it's practically around the corner! Why do I have to *live* someplace else? Why do you want to get rid of me? What about Moria? Why can't I stay with Moria? Who's going to take care of her?" James had gone too far and he knew it. Like trusting the ice on the pond until you hear it cracking beneath you. "Oops!" he wanted to say, wishing for a delete button. It was like sharing a Snapchat you wanted back. That kind of "Oops."

"Do you think me so incapable of looking after her?"

"I didn't mean that the way it came out."

"Of course you did! And, I just might add, all the more reason for me to disregard your disrespectful suggestion, as it shows a certain lack of maturity on your part that could and would and will be corrected by attending Baskerville. The decision is final, son. If there's one thing Baskerville gives you, it's a chance to both grow up more quickly and to prepare yourself for the years to come."

"I don't want to wear a tie every day of my life."

"Not anywhere near reason enough."

"I love my family."

"Yes. And your family loves you back."

"Some do," James said, well under his breath.

"What's that, young man? Let me explain something here, in case you're missing the obvious. Who do you think that was last night?"

"Kidnappers! Robbers!"

"Nonsense."

"You were as freaked out as Mo and me. You may not want to admit it but—"

"Hazing!" Oswyn Moriarty said. "That was a group of fellows from Baskerville."

"You know this?"

"I suspect it."

"That's reassuring. 'A group of fellas.' That's not exactly how you put it last night. I've heard you cuss about twice in my life, Father. Last night made up for the missing years."

"I was upset. Unsettled."

"You were not yourself. They *tied me up*, Father. Who knows what might have happened if Mo hadn't come along."

"You know how I feel about nicknames. Show some respect, please. It was a prank, a school prank, and that is all."

"And you want me to go live with those Luddites? Seriously? That's your vision of 'higher education'?"

"Watch yourself, James. Tread lightly. Every male Moriarty for generations—"

"I know!"

"—has attended Baskerville Academy going back to our ancestors in England. A dingy Scottish castle it was back then, I'm told. Be happy we're here where we are. You'll be two hours away on a gorgeous campus."

"But I want to stay here with you and Moria."

"As to her, I couldn't agree more. It has been taken care of. Baskerville's coeducational now and has expanded to include eighth grade, what they call a middle; I could have sent you off last year, but did not. I've been . . . well . . . I've been busy. I've arranged it so that she can attend as well."

"How convenient."

"I warned you once, young man."

"They tried to kidnap me. What kind of hazing is that? That's a federal offense kind if you ask me."

"It was a test, is all. A test of your mettle."

"So you getting rid of us has nothing to do with the way you've been all summer?"

"What on earth?"

"You seem afraid, Father. Moria and I have seen the way you check all the locks twice. 'Buttoned up at bedtime.' You turn on more lights than you used to. You draw all the curtains. We're not stupid!"

24

It was true. Our father's typical composure defined the expression "even-keeled"—a sailing reference, I think. It meant he was basically always the same. In his case, stern, quiet, dark, if I'm being honest. Brooding, in a fatherly kind of way. Severe. In short, he was anything but fearful: overconfident, condescending, aggressive. To see him over the past few months hesitate to answer a phone call, or to pull the drapes the moment the sun sank low in the sky, to vary a schedule that at one time I could have set my watch by—these are the things that make a child take notice of her parent. Or his parent, in James's case.

"Nonsense." Our father used "nonsense" like others slammed doors.

"I won't go," James said.

"Of course you will. It's a matter of obligation, James. You *and* Moria will be attending, beginning next month."

"I'll flunk out. On purpose."

"Then I'll send you to military academy until you're ready to transfer back to Baskerville. It'll only take a semester or two. We'll see how you like running four miles before sunrise and crawling through swamps. That'll make a man of you."

He got James with that one. Shut him up like Tupperware. The thing about Father: he always knew what you were going to say—always. He had answers or counteroffers, decrees and disciplines like an archer's arrows waiting on his back. My brother and I knew that he was a businessman on top of his teaching at the university. We'd overheard his late-night discussions, seen the guests—nearly always men, often the same men—who arrived at all hours to the back of the house. He had to be good at it. Even a family fortune needed proper management. His practice at negotiation had come down the line: he was the only son of an only son. The family properties alone were worth millions of dollars, if not tens of millions. We weren't supposed to know that. Which translated, we weren't supposed to open our eyes.

"There's a connection between you and me, James. We are the male heirs. Think of it as I am the king, you are the prince. You will attend and you will graduate from Baskerville Academy. You will take your university in England. Your great-great-grandfather founded the original school there. The continued existence of the school depends on your graduation. I tell you this to emphasize the importance of legacy, your place in this family, and your responsibility to others. It's a burden. I don't deny it. One that all Moriarty firstborn males must endure."

"So you're saying, 'No pressure, James.' Thanks for that!"

"Things are as they are." James heard Father the Fearful speaking. The man we didn't exactly know well. Father the Fatalist, which was light-years from his true self. He usually preached independence, clear thinking, and that to question authority was healthy, to challenge it, something else entirely. He'd carefully taught us not to judge too quickly, to evaluate everything.

"I see," James said. "So that's how it is, and there's no choice."

"Don't expect me to add, 'I'm sorry to say,' because of course I'm not. You are being prepared for greatness, my boy. Baskerville is merely the first step. The years will fly by. I came to love my time there, and so will you."

"You didn't want to go either?" James asked, stunned.

Father grinned warmly, something we typically only saw on a beach or across the dinner table on the rare evening we ate together. "Some of the best years of my life occurred at that school. I trust you and your sister will find it the same."

"You didn't want to go there," James stated, rather than inquired.

"The academics are rigorous, yes. Some of the

bylaws are difficult, but you will come to appreciate them. You will learn things at Baskerville that will serve you well for the rest of your life. If I have my way . . ." He paused, reflective. "I trust I can safely say that these four years will change your life, as well as the lives of many others. They will prepare you to take your role in preserving the Moriarty legacy."

"I don't want to preserve the Moriarty legacy."

"And neither did I, son. Neither did I. Yet look where I am. And here, you will follow, come storm or high water. Here, in this chair, you will sit—"

"Never!"

"—just as my father sat before me."

"It won't happen!"

"It will. You will come to manage the . . . family interests and continue our work. So help me, this is the life that has been chosen for you, for us both. King and prince."

"I vow to disappoint you mightily!"

Father smiled as he spoke. His words and that tone of his did not mix. "I would expect you won't. I don't hold you to these words, James. Talk is talk. You and I will discuss at Thanksgiving and we'll see how far, if at all, this opinion of yours has moved."

"It won't move!"

"It will."

"Even if I could come to understand this for me, how can you possibly make Moria go along? She is neither the next male in the family lineage, nor is she a girl who needs to leave her father right now."

"If I didn't send her," my father said, "she would run away to be with you at the first opportunity. I know the bond between you two, and so do you. I'm saving us all a lot of heartache and trouble. I think you know that. This family is more than a birthright."

"It's a tragedy." James could be quick-witted when it suited him.

"It's a responsibility. One we Moriarty men have no choice but to fulfill. Like it or not. Hate it or resent it right now, each of us strives to make things better for the generations to follow. It was born into your blood, James. Many of us before you have tried to outrun it, deny it. My father turned to drink. His father to war. It's a legacy of pain and suffering over a blood-given position and altruism we not only should never take for granted, but should strive to exploit for the betterment of all. It is who we are. There is no outrunning it."

"So you became a teacher."

"A noble profession. I can afford to teach on my own terms, so I teach part time. Not every man is so lucky."

"And me, am I lucky? Is Moria? Our mother left us. You've never explained that to our liking. You tell us we'll understand when we're older. How much older? Now, our father wants to be rid of us."

"I want nothing of the sort!" James saw Father's color flush red. Our father, who could not be rattled. "I am bound to this decision as you will be to your heirs who follow. It is the most difficult, most repugnant obligation a man can be under: to willfully surrender the one thing—the two things—that mean the most to him."

"Wait!? You don't want me to go?"

"Want?" Father challenged incredulously. *"Want?"* He placed a cherry on top. "WANT?"

The house echoed with it. I heard it upstairs. Possibly, it flew off the cobblestones outside as well. Perhaps it also rumbled down the lane and shook the boathouses on the Charles, the cupola of Faneuil Hall, the Ionic columns of King's Chapel.

My brother took this as his cue to make for the study doors.

"I don't want it! It's required! I have a difficult year ahead, James," Father said. "More travel than usual."

James stopped and turned. "We were attacked. You're scared for our safety here."

"You were hazed. It will happen again if we

30

don't confirm your attendance."

"Then you haven't confirmed?"

"Do you take me for a monster?" Father asked. "We've been having a discussion, you and I."

"One way," James said, immediately regretting it. "Sorry, Father. That was unkind of me."

"Accepted. Now listen, James, attendance at Baskerville is of the utmost importance. I can hardly travel the way I must while leaving you and your sister with only Lois and Ralph to look after you. As it is, you two give Lois nothing but problems. You two are not yet old enough to be left alone. Do you understand?"

"Why all the travel?"

"Don't be impudent." Father broke eye contact with James to look out the window somewhat longingly. "It's not for the university. It's the family interests. Some things must be done in person." He turned from the window back to James. "That's all you need to know. But you raise a point I must address. With any extended travel comes risk. Although Mr. Lowry is in possession of the necessary legal work, should anything happen to me—"

"Father, don't say such things!"

"Listen up! You will trust your sister in such situations. Do you understand? You are a bright, but often stubborn boy. Should anything happen—and

I'm quite confident it won't—*listen to your sister.* Promise me that."

James hesitated, in part because of the shock he was suffering, in part because James *never* listened to me. "I promise."

"Now, go along and send Moria in, if you please."

My turn was next. I was inclined toward timidity when in Father's presence—translation: he scared me. I loved him, respected him, admired him. I was terrified of him. Think of it like owning a pet lion.

Again, the study's oily scent filled my nostrils and swelled my chest. The light caught dust in the air like a million silver fireflies. Father studied me as I entered and took a seat across from him, the desk separating us like a measure of the years between us.

"You will be attending Baskerville Academy with your brother."

"Yes, Father." My heart fluttered. All the worrying I'd been through for the past several months was for nothing. Ended, with one simple statement.

"How do you feel about that?"

I thought it might be a loaded question. I contemplated the right answer, wondering if there was a right answer other than the answer in my heart. "I don't like the idea of leaving you, Father. Can't you come with us, maybe teach at the school?"

A slow and meaningful grin overtook him. "What a lovely idea, Moria. I should think not, but I will always thank you for that consideration. You and James, the same school. What do you think?"

"I like it very much, sir. Very much, indeed."

"And your brother. What do you think of his chances in such a place?"

"I think he'll do splendidly, don't you?"

"His temper?"

"Yes, well, there is that. But I'll be there to . . . temper him."

"Good for you. You've always had the coolest head of the three of us."

I wasn't sure Father had ever noticed me much at all, except as his "adorable Moria," kind of a living toy doll he liked to show off. This comment hit me hard. "Thank you, Father."

"It's because of this I have a special assignment for you. Only you. Do you understand?"

"I . . . I guess."

"I've explained to James that I will be doing a lot of travel in the coming year. All over the world. Things happen. We all know that. Not always good things, I'm sorry to say. Should something happen to me, Moria, you will find the key to this drawer," he said, indicating the top right drawer of his desk, "buried in the fireplace ash, at the back and to the right. You will use it to open this drawer and you will use the benefits of your profoundly curious mind to take it from there. You are perfectly suited for this, Moria. Your brother is not. This is why the task falls to you. The rest will be self-explanatory. If you ever—ever!—open this drawer while I'm living, you will be disowned by me and this family. Do you understand me? I will have nothing to do with you, nor you with me for the remainder of our natural lives. That needs no further explanation. Do we understand one another?"

I nodded, unable to breathe. I'd never experienced such a combination of elation and alarm. Expelled from the family? What could possibly be inside the drawer?

"I need to hear you say it, Moria. And we must shake on it. Man to woman, father to daughter." Father stood and came around the large desk.

I shied from him as he came up out of the chair. Father had never addressed me so matter-of-factly, had never treated me as an equal. As a grown-up. He offered his hand as a bond of promise. I felt . . . important to him all of a sudden. We shook hands. I promised Father I understood his terms.

"Your brother is temperamental. Only under the most dire of circumstances are you to share this with him."

I didn't like the sound of that at all. "Dire, meaning?"

"I will try to mail you both a letter once a week—mail, not email. There may be times they are slow to arrive, but arrive they will. I keep my passport here in the drawer opened by that key. If it's here, then obviously I haven't left the country. Let's say if three weeks should pass without word from me, you will come home and check the drawer." I shuddered. "If my passport is missing, then by all means give it more time. Overseas mail can be absurdly slow. If four or five weeks pass, and my passport is still not here, then you're to assume the worst. I will not hold your actions against you!"

"Father! You make it sound so—"

"A bit melodramatic? I know, dear. I'm asking you to grow up quickly. I understand the problem this creates. If there were another way, believe me . . . but I'm afraid there isn't."

"What happened to James last night . . . does it have anything to do with all of this?" I felt ice cold and slightly sick to my stomach. It felt as if one girl had started the conversation with Father and another was now speaking.

"You always were a smart girl. I've told James it was hazing. You are to do nothing to counter that impression."

"But it wasn't hazing." I tried and failed to sound confident.

"I'm trusting you to keep to the plan, Moria. Any deviation from the plan will have catastrophic consequences, and none of us want that."

CHAPTER 4

OUR UNEASY ARRIVAL

W‌HEN R‌ALPH, A STURDY MAN WITH A FULL head of hair, a slight accent, and narrow eyes, pulled the Lincoln to a stop in the circular drive fronting Baskerville Academy's long line of dormitories, James gave me a terrified look that needed no explanation. No doubt my face reflected the same discontent he was experiencing. Of the twenty or so cars parked tightly together, all delivering a student and his or her possessions—from four-foot teddy bears to camp trunks and Mac computers—only the Moriarty children arrived in a chauffeur-driven black Lincoln. (Later, our arrival would be trumped by a helicopter carrying a retail clothing line heir onto the junior varsity football field, but of course we didn't know it at the time.) We received looks of "who the heck are you?", "spoiled brats!", and both sides of "I want to get to know you." Mostly, the wrong side.

To Father's credit, the campus was everything he'd made it out to be, from the towering sugar maples that shadowed the deep green lawns, to the classic simplicity of brick buildings with white trim. If the Ivy League had a high school, this would be it. A twenty-foot-tall marble sundial stood between us and an ancient-looking chapel, the only structure made of stone instead of brick.

"Wow," I said. "It's like the country club on steroids."

"I promise you," James said, "it won't be as fun."

Father's insistence—i.e., requirement—that I wear a dress had an immediate impact on me, as none—not one—of the other girls was wearing anything with a hem. Thankfully, James didn't wear a dress, but he wore gray slacks, a blue blazer and coat and tie, which is to say he too was miserable. We looked like rich idiots when compared with the blue jeans, running shoes, and Vineyard Vines worn by all the other arrivals. Self-important, condescending, spoiled Bostonians. Father was lucky he had not made the trip with us—not that either of us had ever expected he might see his children off on the next stage of their lives—because James might have taken a tire iron to him if he had.

Ralph was accommodating and wholly embarrassing as he carefully unpacked the back of the Lincoln and then joined us in delivering James to his dorm. Neither James nor I possessed the necessary constitution to tell the man to leave us be and drive off as quickly as possible. Instead, we endured the torture of his accompaniment and assistance with fake smiles plastered onto our unwilling faces. I looked, no doubt, like an American Girl Doll, while James took on a kind of X-Men action figure vibe. It was clear from our first ten minutes at Baskerville Academy we were doomed.

I was delivered to a sorry-looking double room that had been converted into a triple. It possessed all the charm of a coat closet. Its bare gray walls and three bare mattresses, two of them stacked as bunk beds, reminded me of a reality television prison show. Throw in identical maple-veneered desks fronted by formed black-plastic-and-aluminum chairs to complete the joy of my first impression. My name was taped to the top bunk. Ralph sighed as he set down my bags.

"You okay, Mo?" he asked, as if there was anything he or I could do about my situation, good or bad.

"Come back in five years and I'll tell you." I found ten dollars in my purse. I was not the idiot the others thought me to be; I'd been raised in the best city in America. I extended it toward him and he held up his hand as a sign of refusal.

"Don't be ridiculous, Moria! We're family. I delivered your father to this school. Brought him home from graduation as well."

I knew Lois, Ralph, and others were loyal to Father, but I'd never known for how long.

I'd heard an expression once, so I tried it on him. "So you know where all the skeletons are buried!" It meant that a person knew intimate secrets about another. Ralph didn't seem to appreciate it.

He smiled through slit eyes, looking distraught. "You have no idea how much I will miss you both."

"It's all right, Ralph," I told him. "I suppose Father's been preparing us for this for years. It just came a little sudden, at least for me. For James . . . well, if you deny something long enough you begin to believe it yourself. You know? Not that that makes any sense, but it does to me."

"May I?" He opened his arms. We shared a brief, considerate hug, not at all awkward, and I thanked him while holding on just a little too long. He patted my head and, as we separated, said, "You get yourself in any kind of trouble in this place, you call me. Your father doesn't need to know everything." He winked.

I looked at him curiously, having no idea why he would think Baskerville would give me trouble. "O . . . K," I said. With our final good-bye I found my throat tightening. He left. I wanted to call him back. I wanted to run to James and bury my head in his chest and cry. My friend. Maybe my only friend for a long time to come.

Instead, I sat on the edge of the hard mattress. I liked soft mattresses. And spaghetti with no bay leaves, and a television on my wall, not a bunch of old tape-removal scars shadowing another's decorations. I felt like I'd arrived at the party late—like everything nice had just come down.

And me along with it.

James's experience proved altogether different than mine. He arrived to a decently proportioned dorm room, one bed neatly made with a dark gray Pendleton blanket as its top cover and a crisp white pillowcase neatly placed at an inviting slight angle.

One of the two desks held a blue ceramic cup with pens and pencils, a magnetic paper clip holder, a stapler, a Post-It dispenser, and a cheap but effective desk lamp that clamped to the desktop and looked like a shipping crane.

As to the shared closet, one half of which held all of two pairs of pants, a single blue blazer, two ties, a worn pair of hiking boots, and an unworn pair of dress shoes, James was able to stuff his shelves, fill his hangers, and borrow a foot of empty hanger space that technically belonged to his roommate. He hoped the boy wouldn't mind him also putting his large suitcase in the adjoining space as he, James, had too many shoes to leave room for the bag. It was too thick to stow under his bed with his three duffels. It was while dispensing with the under-the-bed duffel bags that he caught a glimpse beneath the Pendleton. He saw only a single overnight bag—cracked leather—and, alongside it, a long and narrow box that might have contained a shotgun or telescope. Curious to the point of agitation, James nearly allowed himself to investigate its contents, but swore off starting a year-long residency with his roommate by committing a criminal act. Still, the temptation proved mighty enough that the only solution was to leave the room immediately and pace the dormitory hall while awaiting the boy's return.

It wasn't long before a slender silhouette of an unnaturally tall boy appeared at the end of the hall, backlit by the window in the dormitory's door. The hem of his sport coat floated behind him like a cape, the light distorting his limbs into the thickness of pipe cleaners. He was something of a specter. James had no doubt—none—that this was his room-mate. He would wonder for months—years—how he could have been so certain. The boy walked in long, confident strides, though with all the grace of a freshly born colt. He wasn't comfortable in his body and was working hard to appear otherwise. James understood the pressures of this arrival day to Baskerville; he felt them himself. Every new boy and girl was on display, both to each other and, more importantly, to the returning students who quickly judged them on appearance alone. There was noth-ing fair about such things. Middle school had been the failed testing ground for many of them—the cliques, prejudices, abilities, attitudes, insecurities all fueled by strange changes to their bodies, and moods that came and went as quickly as changes in the weather. James had no taste for being on display, wanted nothing to do with it. The boy came toward him, strutting with overconfidence. James found his stride and posture off-putting.

The boy walked past James without a glance and

turned into their shared room, stopping abruptly. He turned with a deliberateness and appraised James. Looked back into the room. Back at James.

"Aha!" the boy said. "So you are James Moriarty!"

"You're English!"

"British. Isn't everyone? You may try to hide behind that American accent, but I reckon if we were to pluck a hair out of your head and run its DNA you would find you and your people were once cradled in Great Britain yourselves. It's not shameful to be an outcast. I forgive you, although others of my ilk still find it trying to do so." While James struggled for words, the other boy continued. "You're from Boston, someplace impressive, I assume. Beacon Hill? North Shore? You have a sister." He looked back into the room. "She's a year younger than you. You're the only son, or at least the oldest. You play lacrosse; you're quite good at it, bravo! You came in from the front of the school, a mistake you won't make next year, and one I avoided, I'm pleased to say. Much faster to park in back and use the stairs. You've been engaged in a wrestling . . . uhhh!" He stepped back and bumped into the doorjamb. "A struggle. Not wrestling. Was it life-threatening? You've flushed just now and—"

"Shut up!" James roared, pressing his hands to his ears, then catching himself and yanking them down. He walked past his roommate and into their shared space, which suddenly felt much smaller. "How could you possibly . . . ? Who are you?"

"I'll take your questions in order, if I may. As to my deductions, they are just that. Nothing more. No hocus-pocus, no divination, just plain old observation, I'm afraid."

"My sister? Beacon Hill? You Googled me."

"Did nothing of the sort, James."

"Prove it."

"I'd rather not," the boy said somewhat sheepishly. "I can be a bit pretentious, I'm told. Especially when I'm nervous. I have been looking forward to meeting you, you see? Mine was a long trip from London. The interim days have been tedious, if you must know."

"My sister?" James pressed unconditionally.

"Very well. As to your name, it's on a tag on a duffel bag beneath your bed. The same bag is an athletic bag marked as Northeast Regional Champions—bravo, again. The sticker on the lid of your laptop is crossed lacrosse sticks, simple enough. Boston, because of the tag still on your brand-new belt. Messersmiths is a highly upscale haberdashery native to Boston, hence Beacon Hill or similar neighborhood. Only male child because all of your clothing is new. Nothing passed down from an older brother. Lucky guess, if I'm correct."

"My . . . sister!"

"Easy enough. A pink ribbon on your other bag, used to identify it in luggage claim, yes? You do not strike me as a pink-leaning boy. It's from a sister's birthday or Christmas present. She must be a younger sister, because they grow out of pink fairly quickly. I know you arrived to the front of school because you tracked grass clippings onto our shared floor. If you come in from the back, as I did, not only is it a shorter distance, but there's no lawn to cross." He allowed a moment for James to respond. When that failed to happen, he continued. "Nothing more than the art of observation, I promise."

"A real charmer with the ladies, I'll bet you are."

"You are projecting hostility toward me because you feel inadequate. You mustn't! I'm quite certain you possess a good number of skills and abilities in your own right. That I have no interest in lacrosse or team sports in particular is a matter of personal preference. I prefer to swim and run track, where I don't have to rely upon the poor performance of others."

"Of all my luck," James mumbled.

"I am quite adept at detecting sarcasm, James. I might remind you: opposites attract. I would estimate there's a high probability we will establish a keen and lasting friendship."

"I wouldn't count on it."

"But I must. The alternative is unthinkable."

"I suppose I don't have any choice but to hear it," James said, bordering on nasty.

"Isn't it obvious? If not dear friends, then, given our differences, sworn enemies. I don't think that would suit either of us." The boy smiled, his pointed face and big ears reminiscent of a Russian wolfhound. "Certainly not me."

"Sworn enemies, eh?" James made a point of making it sound as if he found this an attractive possibility.

"What would be the point of that?"

"Are you going to tell me your name, roomy?" James asked.

"Have I not? What a foul-mannered friend I am. Sincerest apologies, James." His movement sharp, angular, and yet oddly graceful, the boy placed his long-fingered hand dangling in space, awaiting contact. James reached out and accepted it warily. The boy had a milky handshake that left James squirming. "I'm called Sherlock Holmes."

CHAPTER 5

BELONGING

Baskerville Academy was new territory for James, and like many pioneers, he found himself ill equipped for it. In the effort to scale the wall of sharing, he lacked the proper rope—since our mother's departure from home (I'd been six, my brother, seven) we'd been raised by my father in an insular existence; trying to navigate the cliques and class hierarchy, James was without an accurate map, stumbling through things like greeting upperclassmen when school tradition forbade such advances from "unders"; addressing teachers by "Mr." or "Ms." when the proper terminology was "Proctor,"

"Master," or "Doctor." So much was new.

My experience was slightly different than my brother's owing in part to the talkative nature of girls, and the fact there were only eighteen eighth graders, compared to sixty or more in each of the high school grades. The grade names themselves required a translator. I was a middle—I suppose for middle school. James was third form—ninth grade. Then came fourth form, which was tenth grade, fifth form, and sixth form or seniors. I made friends with two girls immediately, my roommates Natalie Sekulow and Jamala Lytner, well aware (from my experience in *real* middle school) that they might backstab me at any random moment. It came down to this: I accepted I was alone from day one, and it turned out I was not. Though James strived (too hard, in my opinion) to belong and be included, he and I at least remained cordial. We didn't see much of each other the first few days—different classes, sports tryouts, and the evening study hall required of all newcomers. I saw him at meals, usually across the dining hall—for a boy to be seen spending time with his little sister no doubt signaled the coming of the apocalypse. For all that peer pressure, James still managed to flash me a smile, or throw me a wink. And I, back at him. I wasn't going to push things. I knew I would be better at this than James.

My position and standing were in fact enhanced by my relationship to an older, decent-looking boy; already a few on my dorm were asking for introductions to my brother. Nothing doing, said I.

Though remote to the point of being scary, the Baskerville campus remained as gorgeous as upon our arrival. The ivy-covered brick buildings (the dorms were called "the Bricks"), the cupola clock tower on the four-story school building "Main House," the ancient chapel with its gray stone with a peaked slate roof and lavish stained-glass windows. The well-kept lawns and playing fields. The sugar maples. The tall marble sundial surrounded by hexagonal steps that made the perfect gathering spot. Idyllic, unless you factored in 350 teenagers, most of whom believed their school seniority, their parents' wealth, or their family history entitled them and required others to look past their zits, their eating disorders, and their bad table manners. So many of us were trying to outrun our parents' concept of what our lives were supposed to be, that we paid little attention to anyone but ourselves. Me-me-me-me wasn't just the way the chapel choir warmed up; it was also the prayer each of us uttered every morning as we got out of bed. This was my impression as of day four, which felt about two months into my residency. If days passed this slowly and with such difficulty, I was convinced I'd be in my early twenties by the end of my first year at Baskerville Academy.

James wasn't faring much better in Bricks 3.

"They aren't being mean," Sherlock said, looking up from his desk at James. "I mean, of course they are, but I don't believe it's intentional. They just aren't smart."

"I didn't ask." James kept his head down, not wanting to hear another word.

"Your upper left sleeve is stained, suggesting you wiped your face. That implies drying tears, ergo, crying. For the past two days I've watched the upperclassmen be rude to you, James, and by your own admission you were placed onto the junior varsity soccer team when you're good enough to deserve varsity. I thought that was vanity on your part, or wishful thinking, until I heard Clements and Ismalin, both fifth formers, saying basically the same thing."

"You did not."

His roommate looked perplexed. "Why would I tell you what I heard, if I had not heard it."

"You're lying!"

"My dear friend—"

"Do NOT call me that!"

"—you clearly have no sense of the British, and for that I feel badly for you. We will lie to trick the enemy; that much is duly recorded as history. But to a friend? A comrade? Heaven forbid! It's just not on. Plain as the nose on your face. Bob's your uncle."

"Shut up."

"The manners on the boy!" Holmes said, as if talking to a third and unseen person in the room.

"And don't do that. It gives me the creeps."

"We are roommates. That, by definition, makes us, well, if not friends, partners. We look out for each other. Do I mind that you treat me so poorly outside the confines of this room? The sneers? The snickers? It doesn't feel good, I'll tell you what! But I accept it, of course, as the ritualistic traditions of a boarding institution. You are trying to separate yourself from me. To impress others with your rude-ness. But within these walls, my de—" He sighed. "James, we are two peas in a pod, you know. We are roomies, and like it or not, we need each other, if for nothing else than for our own survival."

"What on earth are you talking about? I do not need you. I do not like you. I find you strange, odd, and even a little frightening at times. I've asked, not once, but twice for a change of rooms. Twice in four days, you understand?"

Holmes went quiet. Returned to his studying without so much as a wince of ill will against his roommate. Ten minutes passed. Fifteen.

"Which one is Clements, and which one is Ismalin?" James asked, breaking the silence.

"You must improve your ability to remember people, James. In a place like this, the more familiar you make the stranger feel, the sooner he or she will befriend you. Clements is remembered by a shortening of his name to Clem, which sounds like 'phlegm.' The boy practically gargles snot; blond, dull blue eyes that give the impression he was dropped one too many times as an infant, thick hands. Ismalin is shortened to Slin, for 'slim.' Norwegian or Swedish by heritage I'm guessing by his coloring, a whiter blond than Clements, thin hair and eyes like ice. I'd be careful with that boy; he knows far more than he lets on."

"Do you ever skip the details and just answer the question?"

"Why would I ever do that? The details make the thing. Without details we're all the same. What's the fun of that?"

"Ugh! Never mind! What did you mean about our survival?" James asked.

Sherlock not only did not react, he didn't seem to hear James. James tried again. Same nonreaction. It was as if Sherlock was wearing headphones with the music up really loud. Exactly like that, except his hairy ears were exposed. (Sherlock Holmes was hairy to the point of disgusting in James's opinion. James being a young man who had to rub his arms vigorously to spot any of the few thin hairs that lived there.)

"I said—"

"I heard you, James. I won't contend with belligerence. Figure it out. If you bully me and treat me like dog poo, I will not return the compliment, but I also will not honor you with my presence and intelligence. If you treat me with anything less than respect, I will disappear. Perhaps not visibly, but intellectually, socially, and in every other pragmatic way. Completely and totally. Try as you may to break the bubble around me, you will find it impenetrable. Not only now, but when you need me most. And believe me, James, you need me badly, just as I need you. I did not choose you any more than you did me, for your information. But unlike you, I deal with my current situation, not some hypothetical dream or fantasy that's carried forward from a trivial youth of what I perceive as too much pampering and days at the beach and

on the tennis court. Some of us were less fortu-
nate, I'm proud to say. Some of us appreciate the
opportunity here at Baskerville, even if thousands
of miles and an ocean away from our brother."

"You have a brother?"

"If that is all you took away from what I said, I
feel even more sorry for you."

"I get it. I get it! What about our survival?"

Sherlock had retreated into his bubble, and
proved true to his word. James couldn't pop it no
matter how many ways he tried. The roommates
returned to their studies. Four days into residence
at Baskerville Academy and they already had no
fewer than three hours of homework. Two of those
hours, for all newcomers regardless of grade level,
were spent in organized study hall in the art room
in the main hall. The remainder of their studying
could be in the library or a dorm room. Rumor was
that the course load would double by the end of the
month. By midterms, in the middle of October, it
was said nearly 10 percent of each class would flunk
and the students be suspended and sent home. This
option would have appealed to James had it not
been for Father's warning of military academy.

Making no headway with Sherlock, and not
in possession of his cell phone (illegal on campus
and a first-offense mandatory community service),

James headed to the school post office and placed a collect call from one of five pay phones there. Sherlock's mention of his brother had made James homesick to speak with Father.

He ran into Ryan Eisenower on the stairs down and was being chummy with the boy as I spotted the two. Ryan's dark hair was shaved close to his head; he had wide shoulders, a weight-lifter build, and a big, goofy smile. His father taught government; his mother worked on the headmaster's staff, making Ryan a faculty brat, the sorriest of designations for any student.

I'd beaten James to the phones by ten minutes. I called out from below. James ignored me completely, though Ryan looked down and smiled.

"He's not home!" I informed my brother. "I've just tried calling for the third time." Either James had gone instantly deaf, or he'd elected to pretend I didn't exist. "He must be traveling!" I called more loudly. "James, he's not going to—"

"I heard you."

Apparently, I was a nonperson. I wasn't used to being invisible to my brother without a game involved. In fact, it was shocking and I certainly was not comfortable with the idea. I felt a fist to my heart.

James did not know of my arrangement with

Father. I was anxious to hear from Father given the instructions he'd left me with. But my worry about Father took a backseat to my brother's avoidance.

I cried harder that night than I had since the night James had been attacked, my face stuffed into my pillow so my roommates wouldn't hear.

CHAPTER 6

HEADMASTER

HEADMASTER DR. THOMAS CRUDGEON CALLED a special school assembly on a gray Monday morning with a wind blowing strongly enough to move the wig on Mrs. Furman's head. Crudgeon's secretary looked like a grandmotherly birdlike waif, but when she spoke it was with the bearing of a military drill sergeant. She was one of those cute little frogs that turns out to be poisonous. She called the assembly to attention like a morning crow outside your bedroom window. She took herself and her job seriously, acting more like Dr. Crudgeon's bodyguard than his stenographer.

When the auditorium quieted—faculty in the front two rows, then seniors, fifth form, etc., all the way into the balcony seats where I sat, scanning the heads of hair for sign of James—the impeccably dressed Dr. Crudgeon spoke in a commanding tone without need of a microphone. Though photos in the hall showed a sloping hardwood floor with rows of chocolate brown wooden seats, it now resembled a theater in a multiplex with a theatrical stage and closed curtain that bore the Baskerville crest in gold: the head of a wolfhound (the school mascot) surrounded by a circle of words, not in Latin but ancient Greek. The students had five or six translations for the inscription, most of them containing language that is not repeatable here.

Word had spread quickly that such special assemblies were never good. They suggested trouble either national or international (politics, wars, disasters) or internal to the school (a violation or suspension or expulsion of one or more students).

"Before I arrive to the topic at hand, because it's related," Crudgeon began, "Baskerville would like to welcome into our ranks two fourth-generation legacies—yes, you heard me correctly!—and direct descendants of the founder of Baskerville Academy, Eldridge L. Moriarty. James is in our third form, and his sister, Moria, a middle. Please stand up and be recognized."

James and I stood up for all of a tenth of a second, embarrassed, humiliated, and no doubt as red as lollipops. I knew that James would be seething. A new school was hard enough; it seemed an unkind act to the two of us, one bordering on harassment, to be singled out. Tepid applause mingled with the voices of students exchanging what could only be rude, underhanded comments. I was certain I didn't want to hear any one of them repeated. Only as Crudgeon, whom I now hated, continued his address did our introduction make any kind of sense beyond some kind of cruel hazing ritual.

"The reason I mention James and Moria and their famous relative here at Baskerville is because of a grave situation that has come to my attention, and that is the theft of the school Bible from the Wing Chapel. The significance and importance to this institution of that particular volume cannot be overemphasized. If I hear one more snicker, that student will be a guest in my office following this meeting . . . Mr. Thorndyke!" The auditorium quieted immediately. "Lest you doubt the gravity of this situation, until and unless the school Bible is found—the Moriarty family Bible—there will be room inspections each morning prior to breakfast, and imposed study hall, beginning tomorrow night, no exceptions, for the entire school. Hush! Silence! Mrs. Furman will post the details of the location assignments for study hall following seventh period this afternoon.

"I strongly urge whoever took the Bible to take advantage of the next roughly thirty-six hours of amnesty to alert a proctor or master or myself as to the location of the volume. Under no means touch the Bible! I repeat: *do not touch* the Bible, as any contact could destroy its delicate condition. Do you hear me?"

Crudgeon waited.

"YES, HEADMASTER!" said the entire room except those of us too new to know the tradition.

"Very well. If the Bible's location is passed along during this approximately two-day period, there will be no effort made to discover the identity of person or persons responsible." He cleared his throat. "Past the amnesty period you will all find things a bit more difficult for everyone here. When this prank comes to an end . . . at that time, and not before, the morning room inspections and evening study halls shall also come to an end." He paused. Mrs. Furman stepped forward and whispered into his left ear. "Ah, yes. Thank you, Mrs. Furman. Some of you, many of you perhaps, will be invited to speak with me in private in my office in an effort that we may resolve this little mystery all the more quickly. I caution students not to assign guilt or suspicion to those who are summoned. The process will include members of student government, leaders in our community, and randomly selected students as well. We have no prior knowledge or suspicion of the students involved, and any speculation on your part to the contrary would suggest a student susceptible to rumor and one grossly misinformed."

The auditorium stirred with several hundred restless bodies and feet, but there was not a peep from anyone. A few students had involuntarily placed their hands atop their heads in frustration once the mandatory study hall had been announced, but they pulled them down as Crudgeon paused.

"The missing edition dates back to the first day of our charter as an institution. Its historical importance alone makes it of the utmost cultural significance. There is, believe me, little if any remunerative value to the Bible. If it was stolen by someone hoping to sell it as an antique or any such notion, you have been woefully misguided. Again: any contact with the volume is dangerous—hence our keeping it under lock and key. However, its value to the Moriarty family, from whom it has been on loan for some one hundred and thirty years, and therefore its value to this institution, must be considered. If meant as a joke, the humor is lost on me. I offer you amnesty before bringing in the local police to clear up this matter." The comment drew a loud mumble of voices. Crudgeon pretended he hadn't heard it. If he'd been saving this tidbit for last, he'd gotten the reaction he'd sought. Astonishment.

"When we dismiss, we will do so in an orderly manner, front to back and finally the balcony. You are to go directly to first period. We will stay on normal hours today. No one—I repeat, no one!—has permission to return to the Bricks, as inspections are currently under way." Another roar of murmur. Before he had to cite someone for disobedience, Crudgeon dismissed the students. The exit was anything but orderly, though that was to be expected.

James found himself in the clogged aisle leading to the back of the auditorium. He was alongside Bret Thorndyke and Clay Richmond. "Thanks for everything, Moriarty," Thorndyke said.

"Do you have any idea how much stuff they're going to find in these inspections?" Richmond said. "Guys are going to get tossed because of this. Our friends. You cooked us!"

"But it wasn't—" James caught himself. Whining wouldn't help his situation.

"He's been waiting for this," Thorndyke said. "Crudgeon has. All this is is an excuse to lower his dictatorial hammer and turn this into a fascist state."

"Oh, shut it. You're always finding a conspiracy in everything, Bret. Get real! He doesn't need an excuse to call for a school-wide inspection, and you know it." Natalie Sekulow, my roommate, was standing just behind James and eavesdropping. She was clearly trying to align herself with James, a fact she supported by shooting him a quick but sympathetic look. Middle school is so trying. I couldn't wait to be in high school. "Is it a pain in the you-know-what? Yes. But it's not as if James stole his own family Bible." She hesitated, reconsidering. "Is it, James?"

"I didn't know we had a family Bible," James answered her. "I didn't know it was here at Baskerville, and I didn't know it was on display in the chapel. I hate study hall, and I hate the idea of room inspections. I happen to have a half-dozen bottle rockets hidden in my room. I suppose if they're found, I'm out, which wouldn't be bad except my father has threatened me with military school as the next option."

Like several other middles, Natalie looked older than her age. She had a wide, interesting face, flat hair, and currently smelled like a barn because she'd already been out for a morning ride on her seventeen-hand gelding at the orchard. She had a full figure for a girl our age and a creamy slur to her words arising from a Georgia upbringing.

Bret Thorndyke brightened with mention of the bottle rockets. "Class B or Class C?"

"These things put the rock in rockets," James answered. "Class B as in bi—"

"Don't say it!" Natalie cut him off. "Being heard cursing will get you Saturday-morning detention, in case no one told you."

No one had told James, but he didn't admit to it.

The line moved slowly but steadily toward the auditorium's exit. "You're a bad influence, Bret Thorndyke," said Natalie, causing the boys to laugh.

"Mr. Moriarty, a moment please." Mrs. Furman looked like something out of a wax museum. She could talk without her teeth showing like a mechanical figure from a Disney World attraction. Her wig hair looked glued into place. I stood by the hallway water fountain, backing up to stay out of the stream of students allowing me to eavesdrop, which, as we've established, is any girl's inalienable right. "You and your sister will be among the first students to see Dr. Crudgeon in his office. This, so no one might accuse Headmaster of playing favorites. I wish to advise you, Mr. Moriarty, that

Headmaster is honored—perhaps the word does an injustice to his emotions—to be serving at a time not one, but two Moriartys are in residence here at Baskerville Academy. I tell you this because he may not. Dr. Crudgeon is . . . well, officious and acutely aware of his position here at the school. You understand? A man must do what a man must do. I'm not sure if anyone is famous for having said that, but they should be, don't you think? Anywho . . . it is best not to skirt the issue. Nor is it advised to answer in too longwinded a fashion. You understand?"

"No, not really," James said.

"Well, that would be why I'm the secretary and he's the headmaster!" She giggled at her own failed joke. "He will ask you questions. He will likely take a fraternal tone with you. Do not take that as an entreaty for you to pontificate or elaborate upon your explanations. No! Be precise. Be truthful. And be quick. He will admire you and appreciate you for such behavior."

"And you're telling me this because?"

"Why, because you're a Moriarty, dear boy. You're here for four years, your sister, five. Best foot forward and all that, yes? I don't want you making a fool out of yourself the first time you meet the great man."

"I appreciate your confidence."

"Consider me something of a social engineer in this instance. Do you follow?"

James appeared totally and utterly bewildered. In spite of himself, he nodded. Perhaps just to get it over with. "Thank you. I think," he said.

Mrs. Furman cocked her head, puzzled by the response. "Always address him as Headmaster, never Dr. Crudgeon. And of course you may thank me, my dear. Today, and for the next few years, thank me all you wish! The board and Dr. Crudgeon make the policy, James." A frank and telling snarl revealed her ultrawhite teeth for the first time. "I put that policy into action." She reached up, took a twist of James's hair, and tucked it behind his ear. He shivered and his neck flushed a brilliant red. "At the end of first period, James. The front of Main House, ground level. Whatever you do, do not be late." She collected herself and marched off, somewhat feminine, mostly military, her low heels stabbing the mauve carpet and leaving sharp impressions behind. No lightweight, our Mrs. Furman.

CHAPTER 7

THE LEGACY ISSUE

"SIT DOWN, SIT DOWN!" THE HEADMASTER looked bigger than he had in the auditorium, not taller but stout like the former rugby player he was. The photos on and behind his desk, along with those hung throughout the spacious office, told of an athletic family man who liked to travel, especially to jungle temples and ancient ruins. He'd apparently spent much of his life seeking out such places, for he aged on the walls. One of the man's many degrees filled in the blanks for James: a PhD in archaeology; a master's degree in religion; yet another master's in education. He looked to be in his forties, but there was too much history spread around; he must have been much older.

Once James had settled onto the green leather cushion of the dark hardwood chair, Crudgeon took his place behind his desk.

"Welcome to Baskerville, James."

"Thank you, Headmaster."

"I trust I didn't embarrass you and your sister too badly just now. It's important the students understand the severity of the crime involved. That Bible—your family Bible—is an essential historical artifact here at Baskerville. Why, we can't exist without it, quite honestly! This is why it's kept under lock and key at all times. Upon its return—and it will be returned, Mr. Moriarty—we will be forced to reconsider keeping it on display in the chapel, which is nothing short of a crying shame." His direct address of James made him feel as if he were being accused of the theft himself. He wasn't sure if he was supposed to defend himself or not.

"Tell me about yourself! Please!" The man expressed far too much enthusiasm to be taken for real. Why put on such a show? James wondered.

"I don't know," James said.

"You don't know about yourself? That's telling in and of itself. Or you are uncomfortable talking about yourself?"

James shrugged. "I don't know."

"Yes, I believe we established that. Let's try again: Tell me about yourself, James."

The man was unhappy with James. His eyes were unrelenting and powerful. "I live in Boston with my father and sister. Our mother . . . left us, or something like that. She's not around."

"I'm sorry to hear that."

"Father says she's not coming back. Moria and I think he does that to protect us. He won't actually tell us she died. You know. Family stuff. It's just weird."

"Your father's a good man."

"You know him?"

"I knew of him. He's a Moriarty. But I was two years behind him."

"Here?"

"You sound so surprised."

"I guess I am."

"How is he? Your father. Doing well?"

"I don't—" James caught himself. "I suppose. I'm not sure what you want me to say."

"That's better than 'I don't know.' Worlds better! He's teaching, isn't he?"

"He is. He likes it."

"Everything's good at home?"

James hesitated before answering. It sounded

like one of those required things to ask, and he didn't feel like gratifying Crudgeon by answering every single thing. "Why am I here, talking to you? Not that I'm complaining."

"It sounds as if you are."

"Not at all. Is it about the Bible?"

"It's about you, James. Likes, dislikes? Strengths, weaknesses?"

James nodded. "Yeah, okay. Sports. Video games. Food; I like food. Cape Cod in the summer. Movies; the action ones." Crudgeon said nothing, awaiting more. "Dislikes? Long winters. Idiots. Being bored. Indian food. My strengths? Seriously, Headmaster, I think that's for others to say. My weaknesses? That's a long list, I'm sure. I can't sing a note but wish I could. I can only do six pull-ups, which su— which is pathetic." The headmaster nodded, holding back a grin. "I have endless patience for things I like, like computer code and tech stuff. I'm incredibly short on patience when it comes to reading my homework assignments and writing papers."

"You see? Not so difficult." He sized up James. "Why Baskerville?"

"Excuse me, Headmaster?"

"Your aspirations? What do you hope to get from your time here? How will you be different on graduation day from the young man you are now?"

James had no clue what an aspiration was. It sounded like something bad, maybe something to do with breathing. "I hadn't really—" James caught himself again. Talking to the headmaster was a steep learning curve. "I suppose I want to be smarter. Get into a good college."

"Was it your idea to attend Baskerville?" the man asked bluntly.

"Well, no, not exactly." James hung his head. "I'm kind of a city guy, Headmaster. My father . . . Baskerville . . ."

"The legacy issue."

"Yeah, something like that."

Crudgeon took a deep breath of either consideration or restraint. "Our heritage, our history is everything, James. It shapes who and what we are. What we are to become. Acceptance is a hurdle hard to fly over gracefully. Most of us prefer to smash into the hurdles several times before allowing ourselves the strength of will to carry us over. It may become difficult for you. For your sake, I hope not. I encourage you to make the best of your situation here at Baskerville. Will I put you in detention, suspend, expel you if I need to? Absolutely. You will get no special treatment from me or the other teachers or coaches. None. But, at the same time, you and your sister are family here. Your name means a great deal here at Baskerville, and I'm sure your father would join me in encouraging you to keep that in mind at all times. Heavy a burden as that may be, it is also a badge of honor. It's your choice how you deal with it."

"Yes, sir. Headmaster, sir."

"I will ask you this only once. Did you have anything to do with the disappearance of your family Bible?"

"What? Me? No, sir! I didn't know we had a family Bible, Headmaster. Much less one here at Baskerville."

"Very well. Unless you have any questions I may answer, we're done here. You may leave."

"There is one question I have," James said, standing.

"Speak."

"My roommate, Headmaster. Do we . . . ? Is there . . . ?"

"No."

"The whole year?" James asked, exasperated.

"The terms are seventeen weeks, separated by vacation. During a student's first term there is no opportunity to change roommates. From then on, rooming situations can be applied for every eight weeks, every half semester, both by room and residents. Seniority is given precedence in every such decision. Mrs. Furman can answer that kind of question for you."

"Yes, sir."

"I would have thought Mr. Holmes would suit you."

James wondered how the man could possibly know the name of his roommate. Perhaps, he thought, it was contained in some of the paperwork on his desk. He hoped so.

"No. I mean, he's okay, I guess. Just a little—"

"British."

"There is that, but he's—"

"Mr. Holmes was my personal choice for you, James. I rarely am involved in the selection of roommates, but in your case—"

"I thought you weren't going to treat me special."

The headmaster's eyes flared.

"Be careful, young man. You're on thin ice."

James recalled Mrs. Furman's warning about being too casual.

"I'm sorry for interrupting."

"I believe we're done here." Head down, unpleasant.

"I'm sorry, Headmaster."

"You can see your own way out. I trust you will

make every effort to enjoy the academy, James. I trust you will come to think of us as a home away from home."

"Yes, sir. Thank you, sir." James made for the door, his hand slick on the doorknob.

CHAPTER 8

THE FIRST NOTE

Sherlock Holmes had filled the dorm room with fog in an apparent attempt to brew a cup of tea. Upon entering, James hacked his way through the mist.

"It's like you took a shower in here! Ever heard of opening a window?"

"That's a rhetorical question, I presume. I rather enjoy an atmosphere reminiscent of London. Good for the lungs, you know!"

James threw open the window with a flourish. "Well, this is Connecticut, so get used to it! Steam enough in the summer to press your shirt.

You'll just have to wait."

"Or you can learn to enjoy a good cuppa."

"Cup of what?"

"No, it's one word: cuppa. It means 'cup of tea.'"

"Then why not just say 'cup of tea'?" James was exasperated. "Why can't you Brits just say what you mean?"

Sherlock harrumphed indignantly. "Yanks," he exclaimed derisively.

"What's this?" James held up a red envelope with his name on it, gleaned from his desktop.

"A red envelope."

"Where did the red envelope come from?" he said, petulantly.

"Your desk. It was there when I arrived following the assembly."

James turned it over in his hand. "Looks like a valentine."

"I wouldn't count on it. From your sister, perhaps? I would also remind you that given the absence of mobile phones, notes and letters are our only means to communicate. I assume we will all be using these methods quite a bit."

"I hate the phone rule. So stupid."

"It's intended to level the playing field," Sherlock said, "and reduce distractions. Hating it won't change it. Acceptance puts the mind at ease."

James glanced hotly, encouraging Sherlock to shut up. He tore open the envelope and read:

Aloft in the middle of the seven ribs you will find it, but only by night.

The message had been printed from a computer, or possibly typed using a typewriter. James turned it over and over, rereading it each time.

"The love note you anticipated?"

"Mind your own business."

"Something involving the missing Bible perhaps." Sherlock sounded so sure of himself.

"How . . . Shut up! I said it's none of your business."

"Hey, Jamie, hey, Lock." I waved my arms to dispense the fog. "Mind if I leave the door open? It's like a sauna in here." I realized immediately that I'd interrupted a strained conversation or discussion. The tension between my brother and his roommate was thicker than the mist.

"Just what I was telling him," James said, quickly stuffing the card and red envelope into his back pocket. "You two know each other? What's that, a nickname?"

"We do, and it is," I answered. "Sherlock introduced himself at dinner two nights ago.

You wouldn't have noticed," I said, putting as much sting into it as I could. "We became instant friends, didn't we, Lock? The nickname just kind of happened."

"I like it," James said. "Lock. Not bad."

"My name is Sherlock Holmes. I don't respond well to nicknames—from either of you—but if you're going to insist, since your brother's middle name is Keynes, he could be called—"

"Don't go there!" James declared.

"Where?" Sherlock said, goading him.

"Lock and Key?" I said. Both boys groaned. I grinned. "Adorable. And as for your snooty demand of no nicknames, I nickname everybody, don't I, Jamie? And Lock it is. Don't ask me why, but it suits you."

Sherlock huffed and returned to his job at hand: studying a campus map included with the orientation folder.

"Did you even know we had a family Bible?" I asked James.

"First I've heard of it."

"How weird is that? You know? We get a shout-out from the headmaster, which I could have done without, and then he brings up some family heirloom we've never heard of."

"I think Baskerville is filled with stuff we

haven't heard of," James said.

"Meaning?" I asked.

"It's hyperbole," Sherlock said. "He's exaggerating to make a point, in part because of the note in his back pocket."

James turned to Sherlock Holmes as if ready to decapitate him.

"Jamie?"

"It's nothing. And I said cool it with the nickname!"

"We can assume it has to do with the missing Bible," Sherlock said. "And because of the way *Jamie* responded to it—bewilderment with a dash of curiosity—we can further extrapolate that whatever is written there is not entirely clear. A puzzle, perhaps? A clue?"

"Moria's the only one calls me Jamie, *Lock*. You'd better remember that!" He stabbed his sister with his eyes. "And not here at school ever again. Got it?"

"Easy, Dexter. I get it."

"Another middle name?" Sherlock asked.

"TV show," I said. "Cultural reference. Serial killer."

"Ah," Sherlock said. "I love a good mystery. Doesn't everyone?"

"What's the card say?" I asked.

"It's for me, not you. Forget about it."

"If it has to do with our family Bible, then it's for me, too."

"It doesn't."

"If I read it, then I'll know you're right," I said.

"If he knew what it meant," Sherlock interjected, "he'd be more willing to share it. Your brother is embarrassed because he has no idea."

"As if you'd know!" James barked.

"Why do you suppose I'm perusing a map of the campus, *Jamie*? For my entertainment? Do you actually believe I don't know every building on the campus? There are fourteen total. What's interesting is that if that note contains a clue to the whereabouts of the Bible, as I believe it must, and if it suggests a campus location or a specific structure, or perhaps an element of one or more structures, then isn't such a map the first place one should, would, turn to?"

"As if I've had time! And where do you get off acting like you know about my note? You don't know anything."

"Let me see it, Jamie," I said, offering my outstretched hand. "Seriously." I shook my open palm.

He was stuck on Sherlock's meddling comments. "How could you possibly . . . What *is it* with you?"

"Am I close? Warm? Warmer?" Sherlock was pointing to various buildings on the school map. "Let's see. What do they have in common? Windows. Floors. Doors. If I were directing you in a kind of scavenger hunt, it would need to be more specific. Chimney? Clock tower? Ivy covered? Something else structural? Contents? There are books in the library and Main House. A lab here and there: language lab, science lab. Also hymnals in the chapel. Music? Marble in the chapel. An organ. A piano in the common room and in the music rooms. This is fun, don't you think! Give us a clue, won't you, *Jamie Keynes*?"

"Shut . . . up!" he hollered.

"Is he right? Has Lock guessed your note? Seriously?"

"He's a freak! I don't get him. I don't get you!" he said, shouting in Sherlock's ear. I pulled him back.

"James! Come on! Back off! What is it?"

James looked as frightened as Sherlock looked amused. "He's just . . . It's just . . . plain weird, is all."

"Because I'm painfully close?" Sherlock asked

James. Then to me he declared, "Because I'm painfully close."

James stomped out of the room, slamming the door behind.

I looked over at Sherlock apologetically. The English boy grinned back at me. When he lifted his hand slowly, I saw he held a red envelope and a small white piece of notepaper.

"You picked his pocket! How clever, Mr. Holmes," I said.

"Let us get to it before he realizes he's lost it. Afterward, I think it best if we leave it on the floor, don't you?"

"Clever and mischievous!" I said, drawing James's desk chair to Sherlock. "We're going to get along great, you and me."

"You and *I*," he corrected. "You Yanks have butchered the use of 'me' to the point it's barely recognizable."

"Whatever," I said. "Show me the note."

I read the note my brother had received.

Aloft in the middle of the seven ribs you will find it, but only by night.

"I can understand why Jamie went nuts," I said to Sherlock. "You were right about what it said. That is uncanny."

"Lucky guess."

"You're not psychic or something, are you?"

"I am something," he said, and I laughed.

"Yes, you are." I didn't mean to smile as widely as I did. It felt like I was flirting, which was definitely not the case. "'Ribs.'"

"Only at night."

"Is that significant?"

"It's interesting, certainly."

"Because?"

"Because there's either something waiting there, or there isn't. Right? It's a curious choice to add night into the equation, given that the entire school is now in required study hall followed by an imposed curfew."

"A prank? Someone angry at James because of Dr. Crudgeon's assembly, and trying to get back at him by getting him into trouble? Oh my gosh! I'll bet you're right!"

"I didn't say anything of the sort," Sherlock said, "though it is an intriguing theory, that."

"What else is there? Why else tell him it has to be done at night?"

"Why else, indeed? For that, one first must assume it is not a prank. So let us take that position, shall we?" The boy had a curious way about him. I got the feeling his mind worked at supernatural speeds, that he was somehow five steps ahead of me. I didn't appreciate such arrogance, even if unspoken, and realized I would either have to admire it or, as James had done, resent it.

"You won't make many friends if you're always like this, you know."

"Always like what? Myself? Then the friendships aren't worth making, dear Moria. Would you have me a chameleon, always changing myself to fit the color of those around me? To what purpose? Am I to be six people? Nine? And what if I'm one color with one friend, another with another, and suddenly those two and I are together? What color then?" I'd hit some nerve, a dentist with a probe. "No! Better to know than to not know. A pillar of wood split into toothpicks won't support a thing."

"That is so random. Forget I said anything."

"That's an impossibility. Of course I can't forget what you said. How is one supposed to forget what has already been heard? You realize scent and sound are the only two senses we cannot control. We can elect not to touch, to taste, to see. But once you say something, you'd better be able to live with it, because it can't be forgotten."

After just ten minutes with Lock, I was

beginning to understand why James had fled the room. I admired the boy greatly, I even felt drawn to be in his company in order to see what might come out of him next, but the idea of not being able to turn him off like I could a confusing TV show was indeed somewhat terrifying.

"I've bothered you," he said, sounding anything but sincere. "My apologies."

I snorted. He understood I wasn't buying the apology. Later, I would look back and realize this was one of those moments we'd connected in ways two people always hope to connect, but rarely do. "Why do you think 'night' is part of it?"

"It's a test, of course."

"Of course?"

"A test of your brother's determination. His will. Fortitude. Daring. Resolve."

"Enough!" I said, stopping him. "Just because one is a know-it-all does not require one to demonstrate it at every opportunity."

"Noted."

"You're saying he or she wanted to make it as difficult as possible on James. But what if the person sending this can't get to the place, can't leave the Bible until—"

"Study hall, when everyone else is accounted for."

"Oh, you are the devil, Lock! Of course!" I thought about it for a moment. "But actually, no. I mean, who could do it if we're all accounted for? Besides, you can't take a bathroom break, run to your room in the Bricks, grab the Bible, put it some-where else, and get back to study hall in any kind of believable time. The proctor will come looking for you."

"If you're a student."

The way he just dropped that into my lap star-tled me. "What? You think a proctor is going to play a prank like that? Why?"

"The logical deduction is that it cannot be a student to place whatever it is, wherever it will be, *if* we accept it can only be placed during study hall. You must agree with me here. There is no other way to see it, Moria. Since, as you have so astutely pointed out, a fellow student's role in such an act is unlikely to the point of impossible. And, since it is also highly questionable a proctor would engage in such activity, it leads us back to where we began: that the requirement for James to accomplish this task at night can only be seen as a challenge. A test. Someone is daring him. More to the point perhaps, he or she—or they—is also overly confident he won't take the note to a proctor or the headmaster himself. That's an interesting confidence. James is known to this person, I should think."

I sat there in rapt attention, in awe of the boy I faced, yet desperate to appear only vaguely impressed. He had laid out the options like stones in a footpath, so easily followed. His was a mind capable of much faster processing than mine. I found it seductive; I wanted to hear more, I wanted to be around such brilliance in spite of the boy's poor manners.

"A friend or close associate. But one willing to put James at risk of expulsion, should he be caught in the act. An interesting dichotomy, that. I suppose we must consider persons or a person who perceives James as a rival; but how has he gained a rival so quickly? We've only just arrived! So no! More likely a student, short-tempered or quick to judgment. Ah!" Sherlock went silent, staring into space as if able to see through walls. "Or . . ." He allowed the word to hang in the air, a day-old helium balloon unable to rise or fall. "Let's consider the possibility of an adult behind these clues. Yes." He was talking to himself, thinking aloud; I was no longer in the room. "But how, if at all, might the clues connect to the missing Bible? Perplexing, that." He spun his chair to face me with such lightning speed that I tipped back and would have gone over had he not reached out to catch my hand—again, with a quickness more reserved for a striking snake. He righted me, returning me to balance. "As improbably and slightly foolish as it may sound," he giggled girlishly, not at all becoming, "and with no possible motive I can discern at this exact moment, I do believe I may have hit upon it. Let's say, for argument's sake, an adult stole the Bible, wanting James, and James alone, to discover its contents. Thus, the clues are here to lead him to it! So I ask you this, Moria: What information is contained in this family Bible of yours?"

"I . . . ah . . . have never heard of it before." I hated to sound so stupid and, more than that, did not want to appear ignorant, especially of things having to do with my own family. "Dr. Curmudgeon said family records and stuff like that."

"Clever nickname. Yes, typically, lineage," Sherlock said. "Birth dates. Who begot whom. A family tree of sorts if not literally. Perhaps cause of death?" he inquired to himself. "Hmm. Intriguing. It has a role here at Baskerville since its very presence here must be of some significance."

"What is it?" I could perceive a veil of discouragement.

"Plainly, not enough, Moria. Sorely lacking, we might say. Hmm? There's something there." He shot his arm out in front of himself, fully extended, and rubbed his fingers together as if feeling grit in the air. Only a frost of mist remained, wafting like dissipating smoke. "Yet . . . nothing. As ephemeral as a ghost. There, but not there." His dark eyes darted about. "More data points are needed. Perhaps the Bible and the clues are related, perhaps not. The timing would suggest the former, but one can be fooled by coincidence. You and I require two things, Moria. They are . . . ?"

He'd put me on the spot. I wanted so badly to prove myself his equal. "For one, what it is that's been left for James. This note he got."

"Brava!"

I bit back a grin of satisfaction. "Let's see . . ."

"Get on with it! Haven't got all day!"

"Shh! I'm thinking!" I felt hurried, disrupted, unsettled. I resented his interruption. "I've lost it," I conceded. "You shouldn't have hurried me, Lock. That wasn't fair."

"Whosoever it is who must yet venture into the prescribed location in order to leave said clue for James to find."

It was so obvious, I felt the idiot and tried to talk my way out of my mistake. *The person behind it in the first place.* "Unless it was put there last night, or the night before," I said.

Sherlock slapped the desk. This time, I did go over backward, right onto my head.

"Of course!" He jumped over the fallen chair and straddled me from above, feet on either side of me. He looked about nine feet tall from where I lay on the floor. "Moria," he declared loudly, "you're brilliant!"

CHAPTER 9

BONES AND RIBS

Thankfully, I received a postcard from
Father that afternoon, putting to rest my concern
over his silence and resetting the waiting period
before my anxiety would begin to creep back in.
The image on the front of the card was the Capi-
tol Building in Washington, DC, but the postmark
carried the zip code of Atlantic City, New Jersey,
a contradiction I found curious if not intriguing. I
congratulated myself on the fact that not everyone
would have bothered to study the postmark; I am
frightfully smart.

Nearing the end of mandatory study hall in

the school library, I saw James react when he felt a hole burning in his back pocket. The red envelope wasn't there! He stabbed his hand into the pocket for a second time to the same result, an overwhelming sense of panic and loss taking hold. He would never admit it to Sherlock Holmes, but he'd spent some of the study hall looking over the same brochure containing the campus map. He'd used the library—a first for him—to read up on the design of the school buildings, along with Baskerville's vast art collection, trying to make sense of the reference to ribs in the note. For him, it all came back to the note:

Aloft in the . . . center? no . . . *middle of the seven ribs* . . . he? no . . . *you will find it, but only by night.*

He thought that was right. He would have exactly fifteen minutes between the end of evening study hall and the first room check by his hall master, Mr. Cantell. That gave James only a few minutes to check out the chapel. He'd read that it had a Hammerbeam roof with exposed trusses. He'd also found a very old black-and-white photo of the chapel being reconstructed, below which the caption quoted the architect saying "the bones of the superstructure will last a millennia." Bones, as in ribs, he thought. Trouble was, the chapel wasn't in the direction of the Bricks. To be seen in the vicinity would invite questions. The only students walking near to the chapel were other middles like me, some of whom lived across the street near the faculty housing. James, a good head taller, would need to blend in if he were to have any kind of chance to avoid being spotted and cited for not going directly to his dorm.

I need you to make a distraction, he wrote in a note, sliding it stealthily across the table to Clay Richmond.

Why would I help you? Richmond wrote back on the same note.

James had to think long and hard on that one. *So study hall can end.*

You know where the Bible is?

I think maybe. Do you?

I wish. OK. But you owe me.

As study hall dismissed, Clay Richmond wiped out on his skateboard and cried painfully for help. Seemingly everyone turned at once in his direction. All but one person.

Thus began James's life of conspiracy. If I'm honest, which I most often am, he and I occasionally collaborated as brother and sister to deceive Father or Lois, Ralph or our cook. We told fibs. We embellished upon the truth where necessary to protect one or the other, or the both of us. I consider such behavior "expected" for siblings, though the only sibling I have is James, so I lack a proper reference point. But here, in the hallowed halls of Baskerville Academy, James Moriarty reached out to a known ne'er-do-well for assistance in an act that violated school rules and therefore made each boy beholden to the other in that they were now accomplices. James had discovered strength in numbers; he'd discovered others would do things for him when he had something to offer in return; he'd discovered that with the proper cover a person could accomplish things previously believed impossible.

He reached the chapel—the "bones" and ribs— without a hitch.

Late at night, the empty chapel morphed into a cavernous, echoey place that announced and reverberated James's every movement. The sounds sloshed around like pool water after a cannonball. The tap of a heel or sole striking the marble floor pinged off the stone walls and dark stained-glass windows, repeating itself in slowly fading reflections until covered by the next errant noise. The squeak of a door, a sniffle, the pop of a knee joint. The century-old, inward-facing pews were crafted from wood so dark they looked almost ebony, a wide marble aisle separating them. The aisle reached a marble statue of a kneeling knight with sword and shield, whose back was carved as a lectern. Past the knight, a single step led up to the inward-facing choir pew opposite a grand pipe organ, all of which terminated in a semicircular apse that hosted a long linen-covered harvest table holding a matched pair of candelabras, their silver tentacles reaching for the ceiling forty feet overhead.

The ceiling was supported by seven carved beams. *Seven ribs* . . . James counted them twice just to make sure. The back row of the center-facing pews was fixed to the chapel's stone walls beneath the towering stained-glass windows. He thought he could probably climb from the back-row seats to the stone windowsills. From there to the beams would be far trickier and more dangerous. His eye traveled back toward the balcony, above the chapel entrance on the opposite end of the building from the apse. There, the final truss was nearly at head height. Equally intriguing, on either side was a narrow stone ledge upon which the trusses rested. If he climbed up on the last of the trusses he could reach the ledge and tightrope-walk his way to the center of the chapel. Problem was, if he fell he'd probably crack his head open.

He heard the clock tower above the Main House toll the first of its ten strokes. Curfew! He'd spent a substantial bit more time in the chapel than could be explained. The diversion of Clay and his faked fall was long past; there would be no more distraction. James knew he would have to move carefully to go unseen on his return to Bricks 3. He turned toward the impressively large main door. Leaving by that entrance would make him much too easily seen. He sprinted to the far end, turned left at the pipe organ, ran through what was a choir room—an upright piano, some choir robes—and left through a side door. He cut around the back of the chapel beneath towering trees and moved building to building in order to reach the Main House without crossing open lawn. The last of the bells rang. He was now officially past curfew.

Slipping around the front of the Main House, he ducked into a darkened staircase that led to the back playing fields and the lowest level of the Bricks. If he could just manage to sneak into the first of the lower dorms, and use the bathroom, he could invent an excuse of stomach problems and buy himself a pass to his own dorm. He was two steps from a door when a hand jutted out from shadow and grabbed him by the upper arm. James gasped, but managed not to scream.

"Mr. Moriarty," came a man's voice. It was far too dark beneath the breezeway for James to make out a face. "Technically, you are past curfew."

"Yes . . . sir."

"What are you doing prowling around the grounds instead of obeying curfew?" The authority in the man's voice and his knowledge of school rules identified him as one of the many proctors who took turns handing out demerits in the evening hours.

"I wasn't prowling. I . . . dinner didn't exactly agree with me. I was stuck in the library bathroom after study hall. I had to throw out my underwear. Do you want to check?" He had no idea when, where, or how the proctor had spotted him. He couldn't see the man's face, didn't recognize his gravely voice. Didn't know what he'd do if the proctor took him up on his offer to check for his underwear. "It's embarrassing, sir. So is being late to my dorm and having to explain it in front of my roommate."

The grip relaxed and released him. "Go."

James opened the door to Bricks Lower 1. With it came a flood of hallway light and James turned to see who'd apprehended him. The space was empty. James hadn't heard the man depart, and for a moment he wondered if it was his own sense of guilt and imagination that had invented the incident. He pulled the door shut quietly behind him and headed straight for the nearest bathroom, now trusting his excuse more than ever.

"Has the room check happened?" James asked anxiously upon entering.

"Five minutes ago," Sherlock answered. "The hall master did not ask after you, which I found most curious. I was about to tell him to check the bathroom when he informed me he'd received a call that you'd be along shortly. And here you are."

James stood there. "A call?" The man who'd grabbed him? he wondered.

"Judging by your reaction, I will assume that comes as a surprise."

"Dinner didn't agree with me."

"Indeed. The food here wouldn't agree with a goat. So that was your excuse? And it was accepted?"

James's eyes roamed to the acoustic tile ceiling, dotted with black holes from pencils being stuck there in previous decades. "I got trapped in the bathroom."

"Of course you did. And what did you find?" Sherlock asked.

"What are you talking about?"

"I'm talking about the red envelope. The clue to the missing Bible. What did you find?"

"I . . . ah . . . I told you: dinner made me sick to my stomach. I was on the toilet this whole time."

"You were either in the gymnasium or the chapel, both of which have seven roof trusses. They are the only two buildings that qualify for that unique distinction." Sherlock pointed to James's bed and the red envelope lying there. "You dropped it on your way out. Not the best spy. You want to learn to hold on to your clues."

"You stole it!"

"I didn't. Ask Moria. We found it on the floor. But never mind that, was it the gym or the chapel?"

James didn't say a thing. He snatched up the envelope and stuffed it into his back pocket. "You stole it," he said.

"The problem is this," Sherlock said. "The gym beams are approximately eight inches wide, whereas the chapel's are closer to twelve. I've researched the Bible in question and it is oversized, more like an unabridged dictionary in relation to a standard dictionary. The chapel makes much more sense as a hiding place, both for the wider beams and because that was the building from which it was taken. If it is simply relocated in the same building, it's a much easier prank, a much easier task. To remove it, transport it to the gym, and place it there is a far more ambitious undertaking."

"I have no idea what you're talking about."

"Then you're a fool, and neither of us believes that, James, now do we? Has it occurred to you why I like you?"

"Am I supposed to care?"

"We all care why people like and dislike us, James. It's part of what makes us human. You're clever, that's why. I've watched you do your assignments. Your math comprehension is impressive. You clearly have a quick mind, as do I. When you read, you read carefully and, judging by the deliberateness with which you approach your English papers, you choose your words carefully—another sign of high intelligence. I like people who at least come close to my own level of deduction and analysis."

"You are so full of . . . yourself."

"It's true, I'm impressed with myself, almost daily. If I don't impress myself then how am I ever to feel accomplished?"

"Who cares if you impress others?"

"Indeed. Others' opinions hardly matter, but one's own sense of accomplishment is paramount, is it not? The point being, you said I have no idea what you're talking about, which is simply not the case. I know exactly what's going on, James. And

I promise you, you are going about things entirely wrong."

"Is that right?"

"It is. Let us assume you just visited the chapel and not the gym." Sherlock raised a finger. "Uh-uh! Deduced from your dry shoes. They water the upper playing fields each night at eight. We were in study hall until nine forty-five. Your shoes would be wet, even if you went on the paths between here and the gym, and they are not wet. So it was the chapel. You determined there are seven spans, as the note suggests. Did you happen to visit the balcony? I should think you did because you have dust showing on the right sleeve of your sport coat. I collected the same; they need to clean that staircase better." He pointed to the arm of his sport coat that was hung on the back of his desk chair. "So, during your visit, did you happen to actually *look* at the center beam? Hmm? Did you see anything approximating the size of a family Bible? No, you did not. Nor would you have had you visited the gym. Not there, either."

"I suppose you've already checked?"

"Of course I've checked. How else could I speak so definitely?"

"You never speak anything *but* definitely."

"Because I happen to know what I'm talking

about before I open my maw, a rare if not nonexistent quality in these hallways." He sized up James, which James didn't care for in the least. "I further suspect you were attempting to come up with a solution as to how to reach that center beam, an act that I daresay involved some degree of climbing and balance. Am I correct?" He didn't wait for James's answer. "This, I imagine, is part of the challenge— oh, yes, challenge, for had you bothered to get a good look at the center beam you would have not seen a family Bible. You might not have seen anything at all." He indicated a set of binoculars on his desk. "For bird-watching, but most informative in this case. What you would have seen is yet another envelope. This one also red. You are being led on a scavenger hunt, and therefore: a challenge. You are being tested or hazed, my dear friend—"

"Don't call me that!"

"'Dear' or 'friend'?"

"Both. Either! Neither!"

"Part of that test, I should imagine, is your approach to solutions. The challenge, I'm talking about. It's not just what you accomplish, but how you accomplish it. Or, and I shudder at the thought, you are being set up to fail. In this case, to fall. To hurt yourself. Perhaps badly. I don't think any of us has been here long enough to make such enemies, but this is the work of either an ally or an enemy, and you seem precious short of allies at the moment, having insulted your sister and this room-mate only hours ago."

"You are so strange," James said.

"Rather than thinking how to retrieve it, ask yourself this: How was the envelope placed atop that beam in the first place? And before you make some critical or slanderous statement about me or my personality, let it be known Moria was the one who prompted this thought, not I."

James sat down on the edge of his bed, tempo-rarily without a comeback.

"This is important information, the placement of the second envelope. Did someone actually climb all the way to the middle of the center beam and leave an envelope there? When? It's no easy task. And why require it be at night? I'll tell you why—"

"I never doubted it."

"Study hall. It had to be when no one would wander into the chapel and catch whoever's behind this while in the act."

"But we were all in study hall."

"Interesting, isn't it? Do we suspect a proctor? Perhaps! Given the school-wide study hall, if a student, he or she would have had to work quickly. A bathroom break during study hall? That's what you'd think, but you'd be wrong. Moria again. The envelope has been there at least since this afternoon, when I discovered it. It didn't have to be found at night; whoever put it there *wanted* it to be found at night, wanted you to miss curfew or get caught. In any event, wanted you in trouble. That leads me to wonder if the envelope contains anything at all. It may not, you know? It may just be there to make you go get it." He raised his dark eyebrows inquisitively on his chiseled, pinched face. "But again: to the placement! No one went out on that beam, James. It is dust covered, that beam. It would show shoe prints, or might have been wiped clean by someone sliding out there. The envelope was placed there without such an effort, and can be retrieved in like fashion with no risk to life or limb."

"And of course you have figured out how." James sounded as disgusted and discouraged as he was at that moment. "Who asked you? What gives you the right?"

Sherlock threw his head back as if slapped. "Is this your gratitude?"

"Shut up! Zip it, don't lip it. Clap your trap! Keep your nose—your beak!—out of my business and stay away from my sister. If you don't, I'm going to smash that beak into your face."

"Clay Richmond and the skateboard," Sherlock

said. "You two were passing notes at study hall. That little stunt of his was to help you slip away, correct? Do you think I'm the only one capable of drawing parallels, James? Do you honestly think some proctor was not watching you from the moment you left study hall?" Sherlock saw a spark of understanding or recognition in James's eyes. "What? What is it, James? You saw someone? You were approached? By whom? This is a most important piece of data, James, I assure you!"

"I said . . . shut up!"

"And I shall, for I need to hear something only twice, I assure you. Once can be out of emotion, but twice requires forethought. Consider the matter closed. But if you try to walk out on that beam, James, we will be shoveling what remains of you into a dust bin. So I'd get another plan if I were you. And believe me, that's rhetorical! I have no desire whatsoever to be you."

CHAPTER 10

CRYING SHAME

MY ROOMMATES, NATALIE AND JAMALA, ONE A girl at home on a farm, the other a sleek African American girl from the Upper East Side of Manhattan, accompanied me to the dining room. We were heading there early because there are any number of card games played in the common room before dinner. It was a place to meet people, though none of us admitted that was her reason for going early. The maple, elm, and oak trees on campus were ginormous, their leaves clattering and swaying in the hilltop's constant and often chilly wind. A few were tinged with color, signifying the premature arrival of a New England autumn that was by far my favorite season. I couldn't wait for it to arrive, and I didn't want it to arrive—because of the cold that followed. I felt caught between the like and dislike that pretty much described my daily sentiment since arriving at Baskerville. I had turned into a bit of an emotional yo-yo, loving the school, hating the school; loving my new friends, being scared of so many kids; overwhelmed by academics, secretly liking what I was learning. In Boston I'd had such a routine, most of it dictated by Father; here, I had to set a routine, find a routine, decide what mattered, and it all felt a bit out of my grasp.

While passing below the auditorium I overheard a single sniff of someone's nose. I stutter-stepped. I felt a deep, resonating connection to that sound; it triggered all sorts of images from my childhood.

"I'll catch up," I told the others. "Deal me in." I turned and hurried back to the twin doors, scurried up a staircase, and reached the auditorium. It took me nearly a minute to find James in the balcony, slumped down in the second row.

"Hey," I said, when he refused to acknowledge me.

"Shut up!"

"What's wrong?"

"This is the last time I'll ever cry over him."

"Father?"

"Nothing. He doesn't answer the phone. No letters. Emails. Nothing."

"Not true! I got this!" I dug into my backpack and showed him the postcard. He read it and flipped it over several times.

"Atlantic City."

My brother didn't miss much. "Traveling, like he said."

"It's like he got rid of us, and that's it." He wiped off the smeared tears. "I am so sick of this! We've never mattered to him!"

"He said he was traveling and he is," I reminded him, feeling a knot in my throat. Father, not care? Impossible. "He told me we'd hear from him, and we have."

"*You* have," he said, emphasizing it to sting me.

"I would have shared it, but you treat me like I don't exist half the time. The same way you treat Sherlock. What is it with you? Why are you so mean to me and him?"

"He is such a jerk!"

"It's like you're someone else, and not a good someone else. It's me, Jamie. You and me, we're a team, right? We've always been a team. I hate the way you treat me like I'm nothing. And so randomly! I never know which James Moriarty I'm talking to. Since when?"

"Go away!"

"See what I mean?" I sat down into one of the padded seats across the aisle from him, and began to cry. All my fears I'd kept contained and out of sight from my roommates came pouring out. James was familiar to me. He was comfort. My tears ran of their own accord. I didn't want to be crying.

"Listen, Mo . . ." He reached across the aisle toward me. It was an olive branch, a peace offering. It was my brother, not the James Moriarty of Baskerville.

"Moriarty!?" It was the voice of Bret Thorndyke from down below in the main part of the auditorium, but where we couldn't see him.

"Up here," James called out, withdrawing the offer of his hand. His eyes darkened and I felt a chill up my spine. If my brother had been connected to that outstretched arm, a different James Moriarty was now looking at me. His entire demeanor had changed—he was another boy; not one you would want to meet in a dark alley.

I gasped his name, but the coldness of his rebuke sent more tears running down my cheeks. I felt isolated and afraid. A number of boys were thundering up the stairs. As yet unseen, Thorndyke called out, "This meeting was your idea. You didn't have to hide from u—"

There were three boys. Bret, Clay Richmond, and Ryan Eisenower. Despite only a few weeks living here, I knew these were not the best-behaved boys in the school.

"Sorry," James said to the others. "My sister is sniveling about how homesick she is." He looked at me so intensely as if daring me to contradict him. I would be punished if I did, of that I had no doubt. "I'm trying to tell her it's going to work out. But look at her! What a child."

The ache in my heart tore me into pieces, rendered me a blithering mess. My tears came harder than ever. I covered my face, came to my feet and pushed past the snickering boys, nearly fell down the stairs, and found my way outside. The deadness in my brother's eyes, the cold, calculating way he'd threatened me without a word. Me, his sister. I never made it to cards or dinner. I cried myself out in my room, alone, and fell into a poisonous, dreamless sleep.

CHAPTER 11

DIVERSION

"HAVE YOU RECONSIDERED MY OFFER?" SHER-lock asked James confidentially during a chance encounter in the lunch cafeteria line.

"Shut it."

"These hooligans you entered with . . ." Sher-lock said, indicating the three boys currently kicking other kids out of their seats at one of the dining room's many large circular tables. They shooed the younger classmen away, clearing four seats together. "Is this the group you hope to use to . . . you know . . . go treasure hunting?"

"Don't know what you're talking about. You're

holding up the line. Are you going to eat or not?"

Sherlock moved down the stainless steel bins of hot lunch offerings, avoiding the rubberized chicken and motor oil gravy. He built himself a pita sandwich from lettuce, hummus, and tomatoes. Took hot tea as a beverage.

"You eat like a girl," James said.

"Do you mean the manner in which I consume my meals, or the portions, or the content?"

"Forget it."

"Oh! You simply meant it as a disparaging comment. I understand. Sticks and stones, and all that, James. You should know better." He added cream to his tea, while James poured himself a fountain soda. "My offer, James, precludes the necessity for the . . . present company you are keeping. It involves," he said, lowering his voice further, "a distraction such as flooding the girls' washroom, thereby removing our hall master, Mr. Cantell, and buying us time to investigate this properly."

"You can't go into the girls' dorm," James said, suddenly sounding interested.

"It's a matter of negative water pressure, my dear frerrrr—" Sherlock caught himself from using the term of endearment that his roommate abhorred. "If my calculations are correct—and when are they not?—a simultaneous flushing of the boys' toilets and urinals, from the upper-level restroom, should result in an expulsion of sewage on the floor below. It's a venting problem. With too little vent air available, the downstairs plumbing will pull from the drains, and thus . . . Disgusting, but effective, I should think."

"I don't need your help. I didn't ask for your help. You are strange to the point of annoying, Sherlock. Keep to yourself and stop bothering me. And change your socks or do something about your feet. I can hardly enter our room without gagging."

"I didn't expect a personal attack," Sherlock said, dismayed. "I'll forget I heard that."

"Please don't," said James, bumping Sherlock intentionally and spilling the boy's tea, soaking and disintegrating his pita sandwich.

CHAPTER 12

RUNNING LIKE COLD HONEY

A SECOND DAY PASSED WITHOUT THE BIBLE'S recovery, meaning a second night of all-school study hall and curfew. The gods of the Main House had extended the curfew by thirty minutes, allowing us to check mail or phone home before returning to our rooms. This was intended as a form of leniency when in fact it only served to remind us students that we remained on a tight leash.

Somewhat friendless, expecting no mail, and having no one to call, I headed to Samantha's room to borrow her calculator. Samantha and I shared math and science. (My calculator had disappeared into my backpack, which at times resembled a fabric beast with a constant appetite; it remained unfound.) The stop included a sample of something called gooey butter cake, sent to her by an aunt from St. Louis, which lived up to its name by coating my fingers in a layer of a viscous, sugary substance that no matter how many times I licked, would not leave. I headed to the girls' room. I ran into a field hockey teammate, Latisha. Her dark, creamy complexion was the envy of all the girls, including me.

"You know," I said, the two of us engaged in our mirrored reflections, "if I were Hannibal Lecter I'd just skin you and wear your face around so I could be seen with skin like that."

"Who? That's gross." Latisha looked at me and I realized I'd frightened her. I was learning the hard way that conversations James and I might have had did not work at Baskerville. It turned out that one's sense of humor is a personal thing; James and I shared a love of the grotesque. Not so apparently with Latisha.

"A serial killer. *The Silence of the Lambs*?"

"I've heard of it. Never saw it. You can have my skin."

"I wish."

"No, you don't. It's black, in case you didn't notice."

"It's gorgeous."

"If you are black at this school you are considered either a charity case, or the daughter of a professional athlete."

"You can't be serious?"

"Believe it or not, my father is not a rapper, nor is he an artist. He happens to be a three-star general in the army. He's at the Pentagon now, but my parents and I chose Baskerville to get me away from our home in Virginia. My father's mother is living with us and she's out of her mind—like, literally, *stark raving mad*—and I just couldn't handle it anymore."

"That's hard." I considered bringing up my lack of a mother, my lack of any contact with grandparents, but kept it to myself.

"My father went here. So did my uncle. My father's on the board or something. He comes here a couple times a year."

"Mine, too. I think."

"I thought you owned the place."

"Not hardly."

"How many names of people of color at this school do you know, Moria?"

"I . . . ah . . ."

"It's 'the Chinese chick' or 'the black guy,' or 'the skinny Indian kid,' right?" She didn't give me time to answer. "But you don't say 'the white kid with the big head,' when you're describing Robby Knight, do you? Of course you don't. See? It's like that."

I laughed. "Robby Knight's head looks like a pumpkin, it's so big!" She laughed. I liked her.

"How long have you played field hockey?"

"Two years. You?"

"You're way better than I am," I admitted. "You should be JV."

"Not as a middle. Never going to happen."

"How many kids have parents who went here?" I asked. "Like us?"

"Legacies?" Latisha said. "A lot. A very lot. An extreme, very lot. This place is like an exclusive club or something. My dad acts like he still goes here sometimes. It's kinda weird. It's like even after all the time in the army, this place is more important to him, you know? But his friends, a whole bunch of his besties, are from his time here at Baskerville. They're thick as thieves."

"You know . . . now that you mention it, my father has friends like that, too. From here. I wonder if they know each other, our fathers?"

"Probably. My dad is totally dedicated to this place."

"Let me ask you this: Does your father happen

to have these group meetings with businessmen and lawyer-types late at night?"

"How could you know that?"

Memories flooded me. "Like, four or five at a time? Expensive suits? Your dad all secretive about it?"

"My dad is in the army. He's secretive about what he eats for breakfast. It's just the way he is."

"How long do the meetings last?"

"I don't know. I'm never awake when they leave."

"Never? Never once were you curious?" She looked as if I'd caught her shoplifting. "Latisha?"

"Maybe. What about you?"

"Of course! Always! My brother and I are secret agents. We spy on Father constantly!"

"What about your mom?"

"I don't have one," I said. "At least I don't think so. It's complicated."

"That's awful."

"You?"

"My mom might as well be in the army, too. She does everything my dad wants. All the time."

"That's good, right?"

"It's too much, if you ask me. She says I know nothing about marriage and that when it's my turn I can have the marriage I want."

"Snap!"

"Yeah, you got that right."

"I kinda feel like—"

I was interrupted by what sounded like a burp, or something you'd hear from one of the stalls, except it was only Latisha and me. We both looked at the drain as a second, throaty belch emanated from below—a dragon fart, maybe? The toilets gurgled like boiling teapots. Something happened in the three showers that sounded like snakes hissing. Then the sinks chimed in, spinning the two of us around. We moved toward the door instinctively, but too late. The room's central drain erupted like Old Faithful spewing raw sewage in a blast of brown mist quickly followed by a stream of the unmentionable. Gobs of it. The drain itself broke free under the pressure and danced atop the vertical column of sludge like a tin hat. It splashed to the floor, which was already an inch deep and rising for our ankles. The stuff was filling the sinks, gushing over the rims of the toilets, and shooting from the shower drains.

It stopped. Latisha and I were brown and wet all the way through. We stumbled into the hall, where curious girls screamed at the sight and smell of us. Revolted, they hollered as a mob and pointed us back into the bathroom, where the tide of excrement was already subsiding, though with the speed of cold honey at the bottom of the jar. We headed for the showers, disgusted by the slop under our shoes, and soon were standing beneath streams of warm water, washing the goop off our faces and out of our hair. I was so beyond disgusted that I threw up. My clothes were maybe 50 percent free of the stuff, but I could feel a layer of it between my clothes and skin and so I undressed right there in the shower. Hearing Latisha's clothes slap to the tile, I realized she'd had the same idea.

"Towels and robes!" she called out loudly to the girls in the hallway.

I lifted and lowered first one foot, then the other, unable to face the swirling goop I stood in. I heard proctors and a hall mistress and all kinds of adults shouting for the right to come in, but Latisha and I let them know only the women could enter and we needed robes and towels. I think half the school was in the dormitory by the time Latisha and I finally emerged, our hair up in towels, our feet still icky. Some teachers took us away and moved us along to a neighboring dorm and got us into clean showers there. I stayed under the water for over half an hour, washed my hair five times. Then twice more. The whole time, I thought about what Latisha and I had discovered about our fathers. I was haunted especially by her telling me how many legacies were at the school. How many of them, I wondered, had fathers or mothers who visited late at night, making trips to places they disguised with postcards, warning their children what to do if they disappeared? What was going on at Baskerville, and how were the Moriartys involved?

What I remembered more than anything was this: Sherlock standing halfway down the stairs where one dorm connected to the other, his face serious, his eyes locked onto me. What he lacked was any look of surprise, any curiosity—his hallmark. As I'd been shuttled between dorms, Sherlock had stood there above me, knowing and purposeful.

It was, I thought, almost as if he'd expected this.

CHAPTER 13

OUT OF REACH

Jᴀᴍᴇꜱ ᴀɴᴅ ʜɪꜱ ᴛʜʀᴇᴇ ᴀᴄᴄᴏᴍᴘʟɪᴄᴇꜱ ᴡᴀʟᴋᴇᴅ calmly around the back of the library through a series of connected parking lots that included the dining room, and across a section of treed lawn to behind the chapel. From there they entered through the choir room door and into the chancel, their steps reverberating inside the cavernous structure.

James pointed to the ceiling's center truss. "That's where it is."

"That's a tricky climb," said Clay.

"I know. There's probably another way to get out there, but I don't see it." James sounded somewhat confounded. "We'll use the rope Bret brought to make sure I don't croak. The girls' dorm is only going to buy us so much time, so we'd better get to it." With that, James took the rope, moved up the pews to the wall, and tried to throw the rope over the overhead beam. It took the boys five tries to realize they had to tie a series of knots in the end of the rope to make it heavy enough to carry the rope over. Finally, they got it, but they'd wasted a good five minutes.

Tying the end around his waist, James instructed the others, "I'm going to climb and the three of you are going to keep the slack."

"Like having you on belay," Clay said. "I rock climb in the summer."

"Whatever. Wait a second! If you rock climb . . ." James took off the rope and handed it to Clay. "You just volunteered."

Clay didn't like it, but he accepted James's delegating the job to him.

"Do any of you fools know anything about belay?" he asked.

"I'm good to anchor," said Bret, the stockiest of the four.

A minute later, Clay was climbing, the rope held taut by James and Bret. He slipped twice trying to reach the lower lip of the inset stained-glass window. He bounced against the rock wall but his team kept him aloft. Once he was standing in the recess of the tall window, he took a breather.

"A little light wouldn't hurt. I feel like I'm cave climbing."

"How about . . ." James made sure Bret had the rope. He hurried over to the kneeling Sir Galahad and turned on the small electric light used to help the minister when preaching.

"No, you idiot!" Bret shouted a little loudly. "Turn that off! It'll throw his shadow! We talked about this!"

James switched off the light. "Oh, right."

"Next time," Bret said, "try thinking. Or better yet, leave the thinking to me, and ask before you act."

"Shut up!"

"I'm serious."

James took his place back on rope crew, but he wasn't happy and let Bret know it.

The attempt to climb the distance between the stained-glass window and the beam failed miserably. For such a short distance overhead, it remained unattainable. Clay fell twice. Returned to the window, he was then hoisted by the three, but his weight and the friction of the rope prevented him getting within reach.

"You've been seen," came an indistinguishable voice from the balcony. James thought it could have been a man or an older boy—a fifth or sixth former.

Startled, the boys holding the rope let go. Clay zoomed toward a disastrous reunion with the pews. Only Ryan saved him, by sitting down. Or maybe God intervened, James thought, it being his house and all. Clay bounced inches from injury.

"The light, I assume," said the balcony voice.

"Who's there?" James called out. He helped get Clay to standing, and untied the rope.

"You have less than two minutes," decried the voice.

There were bad words spoken, mixed with anger. James explained this was his roommate. There appeared a silhouette standing in the darkness of the balcony. The figure, likely a boy, wore something over his shoulders that looked like and behaved as a cape or Ulster overcoat.

"Behind the choir," the voice instructed, "you will find a telescoping pole used to replace the chandelier light bulbs. It's heavy, and will require two of you to hoist it. If you hurry, you should be able to displace the card on the beam with just enough time remaining to put away the pole. I'd act quickly if I were you, and for heaven's sake— forgive the pun—don't forget your rope. Good luck, gentlemen." The figure took two steps back and disappeared entirely.

Another volley of crude language that has no place in these pages, nor in a chapel. James acted upon the advice. He located the pole; it took two strong boys to handle it when extended. Within a matter of seconds they knocked the note off the beam. It fluttered like a wounded bird.

James and Ryan lowered the heavy pole. It clanged loudly to the marble floor just as the chapel's heavy front door groaned open, prompting a wedge-shaped slice of light to spread across the floor.

James raced to retrieve the note. He snatched it from the floor and took off running.

"Who's there?" called a gruff voice as the door opened.

The other three boys raced through the choir room and, according to plan, separated once outside. James took the same route that had gotten them there: through the trees as fast as he could possibly run, behind the dining room, across the parking lot, to behind the library.

James reached the brick wall of the lower dorms, and moved window to window, staying out of sight. A hundred yards later, he reached Bricks 3. He arrived to his room sweating and out of breath.

Sitting at James's desk, unruffled and seemingly at ease, sat Headmaster Thomas Crudgeon.

CHAPTER 14

A VISITOR

Sherlock arrived to the door, pulling to finish zipping his fly. "Oh, sorry, Headmaster. Am I interrupting?"

"Out," Crudgeon ordered Sherlock, pointing.

James turned and pressed something made of paper into Sherlock's hand. Sherlock crossed his arms, hiding it. On his way out, Sherlock moved past the arriving Mr. Cantell, their hall master. Cantell entered wearing a decent imitation of Crudgeon's obvious displeasure. Sherlock slipped what turned out to be a red envelope into his back pocket as he slid down the wall and sat out in the hall, his ears attuned to the conversation inside his own room.

"Mr. Moriarty."

"Headmaster."

"You will stand when addressing me."

"Yes, Headmaster." James stood, though begrudgingly, which proved to be a mistake. Body language and the conveyance of Attitude—capital A—it turns out, was everything to Dr. Crudgeon.

"You visited Upper Two," Crudgeon said, naming a boy's dorm closer to Main House, "earlier this evening. You were seen there."

James said nothing.

"Do you deny it?"

"No, of course not, Headmaster. I didn't hear a question, that's all."

"That sharp tongue of yours will not carry you well, young man. To whom were you paying a visit, and with whom, since as I understand it you were in the company of at least two others?"

The truth was that James and his pals had not visited anywhere other than the boys' bathroom. But James was learning his way around the truth, or at least becoming adept at manipulating it to his advantage.

"Clements and Ismalin, Headmaster. A failed attempt, I'm sorry to say."

"Is that so?"

"I guess they weren't back from study hall. At least I couldn't find them. They were going to talk to Coach about getting me onto the varsity soccer team. I wanted to hear how it went."

"Were they?"

"Yes, Headmaster. I very much want to play for varsity."

Mr. Cantell leaned forward like a tree bending in a strong breeze and whispered into the headmaster's ear, which, judging by Crudgeon's face, was an unpleasant encounter. Mr. Cantell was known in the dorm as Mr. Can't Tell due to his general cluelessness, strained eyesight, and poor hearing. Crudgeon found him about as welcome as a horse finds flies.

"I'm looking for volunteers, Mr. Moriarty," Crudgeon said. "There's been a small plumbing problem in the girls' dorm, Lower Two, and I'm looking for real leaders to jump in, to pitch in. What do you say?"

"Plumbing problem?" James struggled mightily to contain his grin.

"Something appears to have adversely affected the pressure in the system. Can you believe that? As a result, there's been some spillage, some overflow. If you have rubber boots, what the Brits call

Wellingtons, I would keenly suggest finding them."

"Volunteer?" James asked.

"Then it's settled! Excellent! I'm glad to hear it," Crudgeon said. "I knew you were a leader, Mr. Moriarty. Well done!"

"I was only asking—" James stopped himself, realizing Crudgeon wasn't going to take no for an answer.

"And let me just say that anyone found to be responsible for the mishap will not only be immediately expelled from school, but will be held financially liable for any damages, and the case will be referred to local authorities as vandalism. If—and I only say 'if'—any of the persons is caught it will be a black mark on his or her résumé for years to come. May I just add that, in all my years of association with the school, I have never known of such a prank being perpetrated. It required calculation, coordination, and planning. Were it not so loathsome an outcome, one might applaud such resourcefulness." The headmaster's mixed message had James's head spinning. On the one hand he seemed ready to lynch James from the nearest tree; on the other, to celebrate the kind of mind that could conceive of such a thing.

"O . . . K."

He approached James and whispered, to keep

away from Cantell. "Mr. Moriarty, a word to the wise: if you are endeavoring to retrieve your family Bible; that is, if you know of its location, you and your associates are advised to leave a note with that location. I spoke of this, did I not? Remember: no questions asked. The clock is ticking for such amnesty. Know this: the Bible must not be handled. This is imperative! It's why we keep it under lock and key."

"Why would my family's Bible be dangerous, Headmaster? Is it the contents you're worried about?"

Crudgeon gestured for Mr. Cantell to leave the room. The hall master did so and closed the door.

"I said: watch that tongue!" Crudgeon's face went a fiery red.

"You know what I think?" James asked rhetorically. "I think there's something in it. A document folded up in its pages? Or maybe it's that our genealogy is off. We can be traced back to some revolutionary, or slave owner or pirate or something. The point being: you don't want anyone to see it."

"I cautioned against handling it. I will say no more on the subject. This, for the health and well-being of the handler. Do you take my meaning? I do hope so!"

"I don't know anything about the Bible's location, Headmaster. But if you don't want us looking for it, why did you tell us about it and then add that until it's found we'd all be in study hall? You *must* have wanted us looking for it."

The two conducted a short but meaningful staring contest.

"I think we both know better. Listen to me, James. You would not be the first Moriarty to make trouble in hopes of being free of Baskerville. But, as it is said: be careful what you wish for. This school, this administration, has your best interests at heart. Your future in mind. At this point in your development the outside world will prove far less tolerant and a good deal more demanding. Mark my word."

"My father said nearly the exact same thing to me." James did not appreciate the coincidence. "What's going on here? What's with this Bible?"

"Mr. Cantell!" the headmaster called loudly. The hall master returned.

"I thought," Crudgeon said, addressing Cantell, "perhaps we might enlist Messieurs Richmond and Thorndyke to assist Mr. Moriarty with the cleanup, since the three are so often seen in the company of one another. A caution, James: be careful of the company you keep." Raising his voice again to conversational, Crudgeon offered James a snarl masked as a smile. "Guilt by association can prove as damning as willful participation."

Mr. Cantell stepped forward, sensing he was allowed to speak. "I'd dig up some rubber gloves and goggles, if I were you, Mr. Moriarty. The science lab would be a good place to look. You'll be doing a little exercise in the study of bacteria for the next few hours. You might want a face mask as well if one can be found. You may expect a particularly noisome environment." The two men departed, snickering. James quickly Googled the word "noisome"—*causing or able to cause nausea; a sickening stench*—and understood why the men had been moved to amusement.

CHAPTER 15

HEATED INTEREST

Receiving a note from a boy was something new to me, and not at all unwanted. The hand that had penned my name onto the school envelope was strong, precise, and the writing therefore closer to calligraphy than cursive. I opened it with trepidation, Natalie and Jamala watching me the whole time. Determined to keep the contents private, I swiveled from time to time to prevent either of them looking over my shoulder. Natalie had shed the horse barn smell thanks to wearing her school uniform. When Jamala craned to see what I was reading I was forewarned by the tinkle of ceramic beads woven into her hair that turned her into a wind chime.

I assumed the note was from a boy and not a proctor by the simple fact it was addressed with my first name, Moria, not Miss Moriarty. Never mind my woman's intuition; I was still growing into it, along with everything else about womanhood. It not only informed me of the fact, but suggested the identity of the boy as well: Lock.

For one thing, I could imagine Sherlock sending me such a note. For another, it was written in a wide, flowing ink that I was pretty sure belonged to a fountain pen. Sherlock and the headmaster were the only two persons on campus I could imagine using such an instrument. For yet another, neither I nor my roommates had seen it delivered. Mystery surrounded Sherlock like his bizarre wool cape. I found that mystery stimulating, like I imagined a cup of coffee (a beverage I had no desire to try despite its availability in the dining hall). Pulse-elevating. Capable of flushing me with warmth and a kind of giddiness new to me. Considering my high degree of intellect—and all who met me did, as far as I was concerned—such physical and emotional responses rarely visited me. I spent a good deal of my time in my head and only now and then remembered it attached to my often uncoordinated and awkward body, one I didn't understand or particularly even want to understand.

So, as I slipped the stout card from the envelope, sheltering it from view with cupped (trembling) hands, I read it with heated interest.

> *Observe the darkness as it is caught.*
> *The extraordinary when it is fraught,*
> *alight in random symmetry*
> *and spend some time with me.*

$$\sqrt{BEACON\ STREET}$$

I uncupped my hands and placed the note onto my well-organized desktop. (My roommates kept their space about as organized as a rat's nest.) Natalie and Jamala heaved me aside to get a look at it.

"Huh?" Jamala gasped ignorantly, which, being exactly what I'd expected, was the reason I'd allowed them both to see it.

"It's a poem!" gasped Natalie. "How incredibly romantic!"

"It's not," I said.

"Of course it is. Incredibly romantic."

"What's it mean?"

"Who knows?" I said, trying to sound oblivious, which was not easy for me. I was rarely if ever oblivious. Foolish. Childish. Girly. But oblivious? Please!

"It's an invitation. There's no doubt about that whatsoever!" Jamala was the smarter of the two, Natalie the endless romantic.

"I promised Susan I'd help her with her geography maps. When I come back, I want a full explanation." Jamala grabbed her books and was off, leaving me alone with Natalie.

"You know, even if you figure it out, you can't go alone. You can't meet a boy in some secret location all alone. I won't allow it."

"That's a hideous thought," I said. "No boy in this school would hurt me or any girl, and you know it."

"You remember what they said in orientation." Natalie, something of a pseudo-know-it-all, wasn't asking. "We girls practice the buddy rule. The poem's not signed, which is both intriguing and mysterious. Who doesn't sign an invitation like that? Right there it smells of trouble."

"You're right," I said, thinking that by agreeing with her I could shut her up.

"That's better." Natalie handled the note to read it. Her touching it annoyed me. I wanted it all to myself. "It's a pretty poem, but in a weird way. Don't you think?"

"Very weird."

"But not exactly mental maniac weird, unless that's a ploy to lure you."

"You watch too many horror movies," I said. "Not all boys who write notes are serial killers."

"But we agree it's from a boy?" Natalie asked.

"Could be a clever girl, I guess. But, yes, I think it's a boy."

"Do you know who?"

"I might."

"Tell me!"

"No way! At the moment it's a meaningless poem, so what's it matter?"

"It is, isn't it? I can't make it out."

This was a test I was giving her, though she remained blissfully unaware of it. She passed the test by failing it. She had no clue of the meaning while I'd already pieced together some of it.

The word "symmetry" told me to see the poem as a reflection of itself. Therefore "meet with me" referred back to "darkness as it is caught." Darkness was caught at night. The square root clue had me puzzled. I climbed up onto my top bunk and lay down with my head on the pillow and my eyes on the ceiling. Thinking. Reading. Rereading. Memorizing.

A girl in a previous year had attached those glowing plastic stars to the ceiling. Maintenance, or some other girl, had removed them but they left behind a brighter paint color where they'd once covered. I had the stars without the phosphorescence, an impression of the sky without the annoying illumination keeping me awake. I allowed my eyes to roam the eleven stars and the curving moon, interrupting my vision by slipping the card between my eyes and the hideously textured surface and reading the lines over and over. I was pretty sure she'd not stuck them up there randomly. Their shadow selves looked familiar to me—some constellation I didn't know the name of. The term "Seven Sisters" came to mind, though I didn't think that sounded constellational. I'd learned a number of the clusters from Father when standing barefoot in the sand by the edge of the water, Nantucket Sound lapping at our feet, or lying down on towels to save our necks from getting tight. He'd rattled them off like they were the names of neighbors. I sensed he'd made friends of them, which had opened up more than the sky to me. I had left the time of having dolls as friends and was still too shy or overly protected to have the real kind. I had James. I had memories of Mother I wasn't sure I wanted. I had this deep ache in me that cried out to fill it, a place where knowledge was stored and a sense that if I didn't fill it quickly I'd run out of time to do so; that I'd forget before I had the chance to remember. So, where my father filled his place with names of constellations, I filled mine with books. He opened that world, giving me permission to use the library in our Boston home, the one in our summer home and, by far most important to me, the library in his office—so long as he was in the office at the time of my selection.

This was like being given an award. Or maybe a family sword dating back centuries. The offer represented hope and trust; the hope of discovering worlds as yet unknown, the trust of a man I admired very much. Maybe he'd planned the trip to the beach in the dark to coincide with the offer. Maybe it had just slipped out of him. Maybe he'd identified something in me that told him it was time. I'm not an adult, so I have no idea what triggered the invitation. But it changed me. Stars and constellations will forever fill me with a sense of awe and expectation, of another's belief in me, of a kind of timelessness that only the blindness crafted by a night beach, the salt smell, and the sound of licking waves can create.

Observe the darkness as it is caught . . .

My choice of a place to observe the darkness would have been a beach on Cape Cod, a bit too far away at a hundred miles or more. Where would a boy like Lock catch the night, watch the stars? I wondered. Was it even Lock who'd left me the note? And then it hit me. *Observe* the darkness . . . The school observatory! The telescope would allow me to see the "extraordinary when it is fraught, alight in random symmetry." A lush and gorgeous description of the stars. I'd never been to the school observatory but had a vague understanding it was poised atop the hill opposite ours, with the hockey rink, another place I hadn't visited, in the valley between the two. The story I'd heard was that the observatory was attached to what had once been the grandest estate house between Hartford and Boston, one that had burned down a generation earlier, leaving only its celestial observatory unscathed. At some point the entire estate had been acquired by Baskerville Academy—or quite possibly, the other way around—and the observatory restored and updated.

I jumped out of bed with far too much enthusiasm and, if I must say, far more gracefulness than usual, landing like a gymnast and hurrying to throw up the window blinds before I thought to consider my actions.

"What?" called Natalie, who was busy writing a paper she'd put off for days. "Is something out there?" She jumped out of her chair. "Should I call Mistress Grace?" Our hall mistress was as close to a fairy godmother as anyone I'd met. Smart. Unflappable. Fluent in three languages. But she wasn't my first go-to in a panic, which was clearly Natalie's current state.

"No. I'm just hot is all," I said, hoisting the large window up and throwing it open. One thing the dorms had not been so far was hot. We practically froze each night, in the middle of September, for heaven's sake. Opening the window was tantamount to insanity by any definition. I had committed a roommate atrocity and worse, I knew all this before I ever did it, making it all the more insane. The blinds clattered behind what the proctors called "the night breeze" but the Weather Channel would have assigned a number to. The room went from cool to chilly to icy in less time than I had to realize my mistake and pull the window shut again.

"You . . . opened . . . the . . . window!"

"I'm sorry. I'm sorry!"

"I think my nose just froze off!"

"I'm really sorry. Really! It's just—" I had a choice to make; I decided to include her, though only slightly. "'Observe the darkness . . . alight.' The sky! He, if it is a he, is talking about the night

143

sky. He's telling me to observe the night sky!" I tried to temper my excitement, but found myself overly carried away once again.

"Oh my gosh! You're right. You're absolutely right! OK, I forgive you." She pulled open the window herself, oblivious to the chill. If anything, we relished it.

Our hair blew back as we leaned out the window, craning our necks upward where ghostly clouds raced like Death Eaters. The unseen moon fought a gauzy haze that burnished its edges, bent and twisted like smoke in flight. In between it all, stars sparkled in a nocturnal brilliance. Such sights could only be seen from isolated, lightless places like Baskerville Academy. Or from the beach at our family compound, a place that called so close to my memory I could actually mistake the wind for the faint cough of waves uncurling at my feet.

It came to me around 2 a.m. I might have been dreaming or maybe not. The square root of Beacon Hill! What a dunce! I suddenly couldn't wait for tomorrow to be almost yesterday. I would have to slip away halfway through school dinner in order to find out who had left the poem, and why. One of the longest days of my life.

CHAPTER 16

HIS OPINION MATTERS

"How difficult was it to figure out?" Sherlock sat beneath a beautiful curving spiral staircase that coiled around the outside of the round observatory. I stopped, walked back down a few steps, and peered through the metalwork. The sun had set behind the ridge a few minutes earlier, bringing a quick and early dusk.

"Is that you, Lock? What are you doing curled up in a ball in shadow? Other than hiding, I mean."

"Staying warm. You're late."

"It's ten minutes past seven. I'm quite proud of

myself, actually. A girl has a right to be a few minutes late, after all. It must be two miles over to here. I had estimated one and a half. Besides, it's a steep climb past the hockey rink. It slowed me down."

"How difficult?"

"I didn't know it was from you, if that's what you mean. I struggled a bit. It took some missing stars on my ceiling—those glow-in-the-dark kind—to remind me of the Seven Sisters—"

"Pleiades," Sherlock said, interrupting. "Middle-aged hot stars in Taurus."

"Show-off."

"Always."

"Seven squared is forty-nine. We live at 49 Louisberg Square in Beacon Hill. I came at the clue backward. Missed it entirely until the number forty-nine occurred to me. The square root of Beacon Hill? I mean, *really*! You could have thought up something better than that."

"Not really. That was my best at the time."

"And if I hadn't showed?"

"I'd have been here tomorrow. I'm in no great hurry." He uncoiled himself. The act struck me as snakelike, and gave me a shiver. He passed me on the stairs and I followed him. He had a key, a single key on rabbit's foot keychain, which he pulled from his pocket. To my complete shock the key opened the observatory door and we went inside.

I felt small, like I'd been shrunk as part of a special effect. It was all the telescope's fault. It was so big yet well proportioned that it put everything around it into a different perspective. We found a pair of chairs on rollers. We sat down. Lock passed me a red notecard.

"How did you get this?" I asked.

"Your brother is careless. He'll have to work on that. First, he handed me the note while he was occupied with something else. I'd read it—without opening it, I might add—before I handed it back. More importantly, he keeps the notes in his desk drawer. Or, I should say the envelopes. He doesn't bother to check if the envelopes contain anything. Currently, one does not. It's the second clue. It was left in the chapel."

"Did you know James had to clean up the—"

"Yes. I heard. And I smelled. He came back filthy. I can't live in that room a day longer. At least not without the window open, which means your brother and I are constantly in our winter coats."

"You didn't let me finish my question," I said.

"No need. I often know what a person is thinking before they do."

"Really, Lock. You take things too far."

"That's not my name."

"It's what I call you so get used to it."

He muttered to himself. I took that as a good sign; he wasn't chewing me out, at least. The card's message confused me.

> *Where what is seen is not*
> *I forgot*
> *Remembered then again and again*
> *In the company of so many friends.*

"That's it?" I asked.

"Ummm," he groaned.

"The auditorium? Its stage? Some kind of performance?"

"No."

"See something with friends. Remember your lines. Multiple performances—again and again. You sure?"

"I don't need you to *solve it*!" He snorted derisively.

"Well, pardon me," I said.

"Accepted." He was serious!

"Well, you conceited, stuffy, pseudointellectual! You don't need to be rude!"

"I need you to confirm my interpretation."

"I'm flattered." He hemmed and hawed a moment, his eyes wandering. "You wanted to see me!" I said, blushing at my discovery. "You wanted to impress me."

"Ridiculous!" he said, though I noted he didn't deny it.

"Then why?"

I knew immediately Sherlock was searching for an explanation himself. "He won't listen to me. If he can't figure it out, then the jig is up."

"Why do you say such a thing?"

"Because this is about him: James. It's not about any missing Bible. It's a test and I want him to pass it. It has to be him. It *must* be him. I want you to leave it in his cubbyhole or mailbox, something like that. A note: I know what this means. He'll wonder how it found its way out of his desk, of course. We don't want to make trouble between you two, so you'll say that it arrived in your mailbox by mistake. Its theft will fall onto me, but I'll deny it. He hates me anyway."

"You want me to tell him I found it in my cubbyhole and it had his name on it."

"His name isn't on it! Is it? No! So you tell him you thought because it looks exactly like the first clue, this might be intended for him."

"What's going on, Lock? Why so complicated?"

"I need someone to talk to him about the note. It can't be me. I trust you. He trusts you."

"He and I aren't speaking. He was horrible to me."

"I'm sorry, but you'll be speaking about this. He needs to figure this out, not bury it in a drawer because he's too ignorant."

"That's harsh."

"If he thinks you stole it from him, that's bad going forward. You see? If I try to talk to him about the puzzle, he won't listen. I'm making this up as I go."

"Why does it have to be him? You said that. What do you think is going on here at the school? Our family. All the legacy students. I was talking to . . . a friend," I said, deciding not to name Latisha just yet, "and come to find out, her dad and our father . . . they both have these groups of men visit them late at night. Secret stuff like that. What do you think?"

"Interesting."

"Why?"

"It might explain the attention James receives from Dr. Crudgeon, as well as the clues. The family's connection to the school is obvious, but you're right, a bigger, wider connection between graduates might suggest—"

I was quite aware he'd stopped himself. "What?"

"A cabal."

"A what?"

"Originally, a secret political faction. I reference it more as a secret group with a common aim."

"Like a clique."

"Precisely! Very good!"

I wondered why Sherlock's opinion of me mattered so much, but it did. I wanted him to like me as much as I liked him, and that was without knowing why I liked him in the first place. He was a stuffed shirt, an arrogant boy with an inflamed sense of his own importance. But he was also brilliant, quirky, and fun to be with. Worst of all, he had kind eyes.

"What's this mean?" I said, indicating the clue.

"I'm counting on you to tell me."

"Because you don't know!" I shouted. My voice sounded amazing in the enormous structure: the voice of God!

"Exactly. Because I never know anything," he said, thick with sarcasm.

I was hoping to shame him into telling me the riddle actually meant something. I couldn't make any sense of it, even on my fifth reading. I stretched. I shouldn't have. It wasn't smart to try to outsmart or match wits with Sherlock. I would learn that soon enough.

"The stars!" I said excitedly. "'In the company

of so many friends.' 'Where what is seen is not.' By the time we can view the light of a star, the star itself is often long dead. I'm right, aren't I? No wonder you wanted to meet here."

"Clever girl," Sherlock said, causing me to swell with pride. "A nifty theory, actually." Nifty? I wondered. "Completely and totally one hundred percent wrong, but nicely conceived. I'll give you points for that."

I could have struck him.

"Shall we take a peek?" he said, offering the telescope with a sweeping hand.

"I suppose you know how to work it?" The panel along the wall looked like the console for a nuclear power plant.

"No, but how hard can it be? Have you met any of the fellows from the astronomy club?" Fellows? "Not close to the temperature of tea water."

"The expression is: Not the sharpest knife in the drawer. Not the brightest bulb in the bunch. Tea water? Seriously?"

"Those are your expressions, not mine," he said disdainfully. He worked the telescope's controls like a man with four arms. A panel groaned open overhead. It was just dark enough that a few stars twinkled. I worked hard to keep from appearing impressed. It required great concentration. The telescope moved. "There we go. Saturn. Wrapped in rings, with its moons: Titan, Enceladus, Mimas. A thing of beauty."

"So you actually figured out how to turn it on, and aim it?" I sounded incredulous, which was a mistake. It's one thing to feed a controlled fire, quite another, a wildfire blaze.

"No more guesses?" he asked, as he tested his eye to a smaller telescope mounted like a toy to the giant. "Splendid!" he said, checking the larger device's optical and then stepping back in a gentlemanly fashion and urging me to step up. That was the thing about Sherlock: he could seem forty years old at times. Most of the time, actually.

I put my eye to the big telescope. The closeness of one of Saturn's moons hit me in the chest, literally stealing my breath. You don't really see a person's face in a crowd; you don't see the stars in the sky, only flickers of light. The immediate presence of the thing filled me with a childish glee; I wanted to squeal. I contained myself. I didn't like learning to act older.

"Have you figured it out yet?" he asked. "And do not tell me the telescope or I have distracted you and you're not thinking, because if that's the case I'm wasting a lot of valuable time."

"Illusion," I answered, for I had been

thinking about the enigmatic poem in the second clue. "'Where what is seen is not. I forgot.' Like being inspired and thinking you have it right there in hand, only to have it slip away. 'Remembered then again and again' is the creative part of our mind catching on to that lost idea, like a hangnail hooking a sweater. Lost ideas. Lost friends."

"I so enjoy the way your mind works, Moria. Where do you come up with these things? You and your thoughts are like spit and polish, salt and pepper, French fries and ketchup. Antithetic, but uniquely paired. Just one problem: you leave logic far behind, hungry, stubborn, and sometimes cruel. You must learn to tame your ambitions if you're to get any good at this."

"You're suggesting I'm not—any good at this? Thanks a lot! You stuffed pepper."

"Once more. Try once more."

I didn't like to be tested and teased for my answers, but I didn't enjoy being excluded either, and Sherlock would most certainly exclude me if I failed him.

"'Where what is seen is not,'" I quoted. Like the stars, I thought. You see one thing; it's really something more, something different. A building suggests rooms, and reveals rooms; it wasn't buildings. The night sky and stars qualified, but

Sherlock would never give me such an easy clue. A school suggested learning and that's what you got.

"A book," I said. "It reveals little of what's inside. You must open it to know it."

"Go on."

I took this as a good sign. He hadn't mocked me. "'I forgot . . . Remembered then again and again.' If you forget something, you can consult a reference book and remember it again and again. I'm thinking a nonfiction book, but stories are pretty much the same. You can forget a story, or parts of it, and rereading helps you remember."

"Interesting."

"You don't want me to succeed! I've just realized that."

"Nonsense!"

"You want me to fail so you can show off how smart you are. I'm close, aren't I? And you know it!"

"There is no close or far in matters such as these," Sherlock said. "Truth is as sharp and pointed as a needle. It's not blunt or fuzzy."

"'In the company of so many friends.'"

"I must compliment you on possessing a splendid memory. Memory is key to gifted intelligence. You show great promise, Moria."

"You pompous, self-righteous, conceited boy!"

I caught myself shouting. "How dare you talk down to me like that! Who on God's green Earth do you think you are?"

"I know exactly who I am, what I aspire to, my basic strengths and weaknesses. You won't see me battling for a spot on the football pitch, though I do enjoy a pickup game from time to time. Left midfield suits me. I'm not a striker and I'm too lightweight for defense."

"It's a library, if you must know," I said calmly. "In a library there are books and many feel like your friends. Being in a library makes me feel surrounded by people I've known and liked."

He clapped slowly, the sound reverberating through the observatory. He made sure it sounded pathetic.

"You're so elitist!" I said.

"I am anything but! No inheritance, no family. I'm a commoner. For your information, my older brother, Mycroft, and I are the only family we have. I am attending Baskerville on full scholarship, emphasis on scholar, meaning I must rely solely upon my wits. No wits, no opportunity. It's quite simple. If I display a certain amount of debonair charm, I can't help it, it is the product of my British education prior to this, and nothing more."

"Listen, charm*less*, your so-called charm is

about as effective as a bug zapper." I paused for dramatic effect. (I know a thing or two about drama.) "It's a library. The clue is pointing my brother to the library. There, I expect, he'll find another envelope, another clue, but it's a very big library and my brother's brilliance is not bookish. And he is brilliant, Lock, mark my word. Don't underestimate him; never underestimate James Moriarty. He'll conquer and control the world before he'll allow someone to feel superior to him. Did I say 'someone'? I meant *anyone*!"

"As to that, it's a matter of gravitational force. In the sky, objects with the larger mass control objects of a lesser mass. The one and only binding law of dominance is mass and gravity. On earth, among humans, humans with higher intelligence control those of lesser intelligence. Intelligence is therefore gravity. I doubt very much James Moriarty possesses the requisite reasoning to control himself, much less the world, so I dismiss your threat—or was it a caution?—out of hand."

"You are so strange," I said.

"That's a relative evaluation. What are your reference points for comparison?"

"See? That's what I'm talking about!"

Confusion was not a look that lived happily on his narrow face. I wanted to like Sherlock Holmes, but just when I thought such a thing might be possible, he would say something so repulsive I was uncomfortable even being in a room with him.

"My expectation is another red envelope. The odds are astronomical," he said, gesturing to the telescope, "it would be anything but. In a room of dark-colored book bindings and white paper, how long do you think it would require to spot the edge of a red envelope protruding from a volume?"

"You've already found it."

"Goes without saying. But your brother has not. And he must. It's time we get the game afoot!"

"It isn't a game."

"It is most definitely someone's idea of one. The question remains: Whose idea? This leads logically to: Why or what for? Which in turn presents a panoply of possibilities still too vast at this point for us to begin to catalogue. As vast as the night sky."

"Us," I said, my breath catching.

"Oh, yes. Most definitely us."

CHAPTER 17

BLOOD CONNECTION

Sherlock knew little of James and me as brother and sister. His elaborate scheme to get me talking with James about the second clue was overwrought with problems, all of which could be overcome by a simple act.

I tapped lightly on the window to their Lower 3 dorm room. James was lying on his mattress, rolling a miniature football in his hands. He saw me and opened the window. I offered my hand and he pulled me through and inside.

"What's up?" he asked. "You're not allowed in here without Cantell's approval."

"So shut the door and we'll talk softly," I said.

He turned to close the door, his back to me. "Is it Father?"

"No. I wish. Nothing new." I slipped open his desk drawer. I slipped the red clue into the drawer as I reached inside. "Have you got a pen I could borr— Hey! What's this? Another clue?"

I pulled out the empty envelope and held it together with the notecard I was delivering. This was little sister putting her nose where it didn't belong. This was the Moria my brother knew oh so well. This was so much easier than Sherlock's convoluted strategy. I read the clue.

"Put that down!" he said, too loudly, and practically flying across the room.

But of course I didn't. I turned my back to him and feigned reading. He reached around me. We wrestled, and he came away with it.

"That's mine!"

"It's another clue! Why didn't you tell me?" I snatched at it, because that's what little sisters do. There was no way I was getting it without him handing it to me.

"None of your business."

"How do you know? I'm a Moriarty too! Maybe it is my business!" I eyed him up and down. "You don't look well, brother." He sat down at his desk gazing out the window, a slump to his shoulders. He tapped his fingers to accompany his slow, shallow breathing.

"If you're choosing sides, Mo, I'd rather it be with me."

"Excuse me? If you mean Sherlock, I would never, ever choose him over you. I barely know him, Jamie. You and I . . . we're the team, right?"

"Was it him in the chapel?"

"What are you talking about?" My heart was about to explode. I did not want to lie to my brother. Not ever. Best not to answer, I decided. "Why were you so mean to me in the auditorium? I was being nice to you! That was so cruel, so mean and unfair."

"That's . . . ridiculous."

"You won't own up to how you treated me? Since when, Jamie?" He didn't fight me over use of the nickname with only the two of us present.

"OK. I'm sorry. OK?"

"No, it's not OK because I can hear you don't mean it. All we have here is each other. That's all we have for certain."

"It was wrong. I'm sorry."

"It was. It was horrible." I didn't know how far I could push things. "You're different. You're changing."

"I'm growing up, Mo. It's something you could use a little of."

"You have *no idea* what girls go through! The looks boys give us. The way we're treated like inferior underlings. We grow up a lot faster than you because of that. We go through stuff you could never handle. Not in a million years! We actually talk. We don't just kick balls and swing bats. We hurt. We change. We ache. We grow up light-years ahead of you cavemen!"

"You switch allegiances."

"That's not true, and you know it! No one will ever take the place of you, James. Not ever. No way! But, if I see you hanging around with the wrong boys, doing bad stuff, am I supposed to line up like a cheerleader? Not going to happen! My job as your sister is to help you see when you're messing up, because others don't know you well enough to know, much less have the *guts* to tell you. It takes guts to be your sister, for your information!"

"He's the reason," James said, his eyes darker and more brooding.

"He's helping!"

"He's a flyspeck. He's distorting your vision of things."

"Is not!"

"The toilets in Bricks 2? That was his idea to

flush those toilets! He set me up."

"Sherlock figured that out?" Now I was impressed.

"I should have seen that coming!"

"But it worked. Why did you do it?"

He ignored me. "You know who needs to know about him? Mrs. Furman. Crudgeon, maybe. It's time someone does something about him."

"James, no! He's been *helping* you."

"I didn't ask for his help. I don't want his help!"

"You see what I have to deal with? You see who you're becoming? It's not you, James. This isn't you! Sherlock can . . ." I shouldn't have mentioned his name. For James, it was like I'd invoked the name of the devil.

". . . go rot for all I care," James said.

I stepped closer to him, somewhat taken aback by the intense heat coming off of him. It was like he was glowing hot. Our blood connection was not entirely lost. My brother took a long minute to calm down. I ran my fingers through his hair, something I knew he enjoyed.

I quoted the clue's poem. "'Where what is seen is not, I forgot. Remembered then again and again.'"

"I'll figure it out," he said softly.

"Things remembered that repeat. Music repeats. Television shows." I didn't want to jump to the answer too quickly for fear of revealing my agreement with Sherlock. "You see something, but not what it's about, not what's in it. If you forget, then something is there to remind you repeatedly. What else fits that description?"

"Clocks. Time. You don't actually see time, you see something counting time. Clocks go around and around, repeating."

"True. Very good!"

"Dance steps."

"Interesting," I said. "And we dance with friends, like it says."

"Is there a dance coming up?"

"I don't think so."

"Waking up. Going to sleep. Sunrise. Sunset."

I hadn't thought of any of these. I wondered if Sherlock had. Suddenly steering James seemed far more difficult. I felt I had to play along. "Good ones! 'Where what is seen is not.' We see the sunlight before we see the actual sun."

"I don't know . . . That's pretty abstract."

"What else?"

"Calendars . . ."

"That's time, again."

"Words. Wait . . . books," James said, staring at a stack of them on his desk. "'Where what is seen, is not.' You see the book but not the story inside."

"Of course!" I tried to sound surprised, stunned by what a good job I did. I'd always known my brother to be smarter than most, if not all of his friends. Smarter than me, if I dare to admit it. "'In the company of so many friends!' You don't read as much as I do, Jamie, but I'm telling you, books become like friends to me!"

"The library," James mumbled. "It's the school library."

"A book? The Bible's hidden in the library?"

"I don't know," he said, standing. "But if there's one place Mr. Cantell will allow me to go after curfew, it's the library."

"You're brilliant! My brilliant brother!"

"Get out of here. And tell me the moment you hear from Father. I'm worried about him."

"Stop treating me like leftover cheese, would you, please?"

"No promises." He sniffed the air. "You do kind of stink."

I punched him. Hard. We'd been insulting each other this same way ever since I could remember. "Your feet should be licensed as chemical weapons."

He slugged me back.

I'd never been happier.

CHAPTER 18

A SOLDIER, A GUARD, A SPY

JAMES DIDN'T GO TO THE LIBRARY. HE MADE HIS way across the commons and the quiet state roadway that separated faculty housing from the school's main campus.

He found the headmaster at home reading from a pile of business letters and reports of every kind. Crudgeon, who made a point to the student body that his "door is always open," welcomed James and sat him down in the sitting room across from the man. He offered him something to drink and James declined, though he accepted a home-baked oatmeal cookie when offered.

The sitting room had walls painted gray-green

and white crown moldings; ornate lamps perched on side tables on both ends of an aqua-blue love seat and alongside where the thickset Crudgeon sat in a chair facing an unlit fireplace. The room felt homey and lived in and James would have moved in if it had been offered.

"Headmaster, sir, you assigned me to clean up that mess."

"Master Cantell did, but yes, James." He closed the book he'd been reading and gave the boy his full attention. "What of it? Do you feel it undeserved?"

"The first I heard of such a plan, it was from my roommate, Sherlock Holmes. I didn't tell you that, and I should have."

"Is that so?"

"He'd figured out the volume capacity of the sewer ventilation pipes. That if that capacity proved insufficient, water would be sucked into the system, rush to the lowest level, and flood the lowest bathroom."

"He told you this?"

"He did. Just before it happened."

"I see. And how do you feel about reporting your roommate, James?"

"I . . . ah . . ." James had not anticipated being challenged on his decision. "I thought you'd appreciate the truth."

"Indeed. But you could have written me a note, an anonymous note, for instance. And you didn't, which means you wanted to take credit for turning him in." He paused, waiting for James to say something. "Did you want to take credit, James?"

"I guess."

"Instead of settling it between the two of you."

"You mean like a fight?"

"Not at all. That's never the solution. Conflict resolution. Verbally. You'll recall Mr. Holmes wasn't the one spotted in Upper Two. It was you, James."

"Well . . . right."

"Where do you stand on loyalty, James?"

"To a cause or to a person?"

"Very good! You see the difference. You tell me."

"In video games, sometimes if you go against your sergeant's orders, you end up shot by the enemy no matter how well you're doing."

"In life as well."

"But the sergeant's orders might not seem right for the mission."

"In your example, is it the infantryman's 'job' to decide what's good for the mission?"

"If my sergeant tells me to shoot a bunch of women and children, do I do it?" James countered.

"Very good! So what's the determining factor?"

"Ethics, I guess. Values."

"You guess, or you know?"

"I know there are certain things I won't do for anybody."

"And that's fine, until you're the sergeant." Headmaster let the comment hang in the room like smoke.

James's head was spinning. "If my men won't follow orders, I'll disarm them and leave them behind."

"You'd kill them? For you're certainly leaving them to their deaths."

"You keep changing the rules!"

"Do I? Aren't the rules laid out to the sergeant and his men back in basic training?"

"So what are you saying?"

"I'm not saying anything. I'm asking you about your loyalty."

"To Sherlock."

"To the school, you said. I appreciate your loyalty to the school, James. It's imperative, a fine quality. I'm wondering about Sherlock. He'll never trust you again."

"What do I care?"

"The sergeant cares. He can't have his men not trusting him."

"I'm not a sergeant."

"Not yet, you're not."

Now in the air hung something unmentioned. The pointed way Crudgeon looked at him confirmed this to James, who wondered what it could be. Something to do with the requirement of his attending the school. It connected Father to this place, and his father before him. And now James himself. The Great Unspoken was no accident— Crudgeon wanted James thinking about this: *Not yet, you're not.*

"Meaning?"

"You're new here. How do either of us know what role you might play in the coming months and years?" Crudgeon dodged the answer; he wasn't going to explain the Great Unspoken, but make James come to it himself.

"I should have left you a note. An unsigned note. Anonymous."

"Still leaves Sherlock in trouble."

"It was his idea!"

"While there are still places in the world where it's illegal to have ideas, this country is not one of them. Executing ideas, now that's a different story. You see the difference, I'm sure."

"You're testing me," James said. "Why? What for? I don't get it."

"Here at Baskerville you will begin to solidify your beliefs, James. This is the age young women and men start that process. Once you know what you stand for, who you stand with, you will never go wrong by giving that cause or those people your all, your everything. Even your life, as the infantrymen must sometimes do. Whether or not others understand is far less important than that you do. Commitment to ideals is that to which the great men and women have fashioned and dedicated their lives. Do you want to be a Great Man, James?"

Did he? James hadn't given it any thought whatsoever. He wanted another cookie; he was always hungry. He wanted to be living on Beacon Hill with Father and spending time with what few friends he had. He wanted his driver's license and money and freedom. He wisely shared none of this.

"Yes," he said, having no idea of the origins of his answer. It rose out of him like a belch.

Upon hearing this, the headmaster relaxed his shoulders, unclenched his fists. It was like watching all the air go out of a Christmas Santa. His tone changed as well to a more friendly and collegial spirit.

James left the meeting after four more cookies and a glass of milk to wash them down.

Leaving the headmaster's house, James briefly

felt accomplished, upstanding, and valued, about as good as he'd felt since arriving at school. He stood on the headmaster's elevated front porch looking out across the road at the school's lighted brick buildings, feeling a part of something.

Why his impression changed, he had no idea. A noise? A scent carried on the light breeze? The distance between him and the Bricks suddenly appeared cavernous, an inky, foreboding emptiness; a river of black with no bridge across. He actually considered returning inside and asking for a ride across the street, just the thought of which made him feel like such a coward. It was a few hundred yards of darkness, he told himself. What was the big deal?

Perhaps it was the lack of streetlights on the state roadway that gave him a chill. The lack of any cars. Or maybe it was the sound of the breeze like a low, indistinguishable note. He placed his foot on the first stair tread like a person testing the lake water for temperature. He descended, crossed the roadway, and climbed over the stone wall rather than walk up the road and enter the school's horseshoe driveway. He unexpectedly preferred the idea of remaining in the dark with an eye toward the lighted areas rather than making himself seen and an easy target.

The trees between him and the varsity soccer field rose like soldiers at their posts. He found their company intimidating. From an open window in Bricks 4 came the din of pop music. He had no taste for it. He kept his interest in opera a secret, to avoid being teased to death, but he found Puccini arias to be as close to perfection as any sound he'd ever heard. He had his father to blame for that; the man had been dragging us to the theater, symphony, and opera for all our childhood. It was a curse, no matter what James had been told to the contrary.

Each tree came alive for him, a soldier, a guard, a spy. But he also saw them as columns behind which to hide. He moved one to the next, picturing himself a Navy SEAL on a mission to infiltrate the brick fortress ahead. He slapped his back against the bark and waited, heart pounding.

A hand grabbed his arm, yanked him around the tree, and gripped his throat to keep him from calling out for help. James's knees went weak. He couldn't swallow.

"You listen to me, boy, and you listen good." The man's voice sounded like a wood rasp. He wore a black baseball cap with no logo, its bill shadowing his face to obscurity. Dark clothes, including a black T-shirt despite the chill night air. "You want to be like all of them, fine. You want to be with us, solve the clues. Quickly! That is your path, your rightful future that some would try to keep from you." He loosened his grip. "Easy, now!"

"The . . . clues . . . are . . . for . . . the . . . Bible . . ." James choked out. "Right?"

"Solve them, and you will find your future."

James lowered his head, relaxing. Then he chopped up with both hands, tearing loose the man's grip and blasting the man's arms high overhead. The T-shirt rode up just for an instant. James saw a small tree-and-key tattoo. His attacker wrapped up and subdued James, spinning him around. He whispered warmly from behind. "Fools follow the other hunters. Winners follow the fox." He shoved James forward and down onto his knees in the damp grass.

When James recovered and looked back, the man was gone.

CHAPTER 19

THE PHILOSOPHY OF TRUTH

Sherlock believed being called to the headmaster's office was a reprimand of the worst kind; being called to the man's home had to be worse, especially late at night. At the time, he had no idea James had been there only twenty-four hours earlier.

It was not an invitation Sherlock could refuse or reschedule. Mrs. Furman made it exceptionally clear Sherlock was not to be tardy. "Headmaster does not tolerate tardy," she said.

Sherlock arrived to the Victorian's front door precisely at 9:45 p.m., as instructed.

"Come in," said Dr. Crudgeon. He wore a cardigan sweater over a shirt and school tie, pressed trousers, and tasseled loafers. He received Sherlock in the sitting room, as he had James.

Sherlock wore a black bow tie, a black shirt, blue jeans, and a navy blue school blazer. He accepted the offer of tea. The most interesting accessory in the room was a leather globe that had to be several hundred years old. It was cradled in a brass floor stand that was dressed in a charcoal-flecked patina of old age. Sherlock couldn't take his eyes off the thing, mainly because what he could see of Europe, the Mediterranean, and Africa had it all wrong.

"Funny," Crudgeon said, catching Sherlock staring at the globe, "how we think we know something so well, only to find out later we barely knew it at all. I try to keep that in mind when I'm thinking about the education of my students. As critically important as is the truth, it is always in a state of constant flux. For decades Pluto is a planet; then it's not; then maybe it is. Eggs are bad for you; eggs are good for you. It's the exploration of, the pursuit of the truth that matters. It's learning how to learn more than it's learning any particular fact."

"We could debate much of that," Sherlock said, unintentionally stridently. "It's highly debatable if truths altered as a result of improved technology were ever truths at all. You are mixing fact with truth, a dangerous though not uncommon practice. The very notion of the existence of absolute truth is debatable. Stated fact, on the other hand, is often disproved by subsequent studies or examination."

"Thought a lot about this, have you?" asked Crudgeon flippantly.

"Not really. But it is an interesting topic and I think one worth exploring more deeply. Have I, Headmaster, been summoned to enter a discourse on the philosophy of truth?" Sherlock sounded relieved and delighted.

"As to the first thing," Crudgeon said, "I recommend the *Stanford Encyclopedia of Philosophy*, an online resource I think you might enjoy."

"And here I was thinking you would suggest *Unifying the Philosophy of Truth* by Achourioti, Galinon, Fernández, and Fujimoto," Sherlock said, searching the headmaster's eyes to see if the man had ever heard of the volume, much less read it. The surprise displayed on the man's face forced Sherlock to assume the negative on both counts.

"As to the second thing, no. You are here for quite a different purpose altogether. One that I doubt you will find pleasant in any way, shape, or manner."

"Oh," said Sherlock. "More's the pity."

"The subject is James Moriarty."

"I could feign surprise, but what would be the point? I know *for a fact*," he winced a grin, "that James was called to your office. Later, you visited our dorm room in person to speak to him in private. You asked me to step outside, which I did. As James's roommate, I am a quality source of inside information. Am I to spy for you? I'd like that, I think."

"Quite the contrary," Crudgeon replied. "I believe you are either guiding the boy or providing direct encouragement for him to step outside the lines of our rules and regulations. Following my interview of him, I doubted very much he was clever enough to have come up with that bathroom prank. I won't ask, because I don't want to know. I don't want to expel you, son. You have a place here at Baskerville. I urge you to leave him be, Sherlock. Allow him to make his own decisions, mistakes, and accomplishments."

"We were paired intentionally," said Sherlock. "James and I, as roommates."

"He told you," Crudgeon said.

"He did nothing of the sort!"

"You will address me properly or your backside will see my closed door, young man."

"Now that you've confirmed it, I am forced to interpret the pairing as a matter of benefit for

James. You believed I could be of assistance. Now that I am of assistance, you'd rather I step back. Is that about right?"

"I've warned you once about civility. I'm not taken to repeating myself."

"Did you plan for a good number of students to seek out the missing Bible when you assigned full-school study hall? A brilliant stroke, Headmaster! On the record you've told us all to stay away, but at the same time you instigate motivation for the Bible to be found as soon as possible."

"Ridiculous." Crudgeon's denial sounded hollow.

"To the contrary," Sherlock said, "I'm impressed!"

"I'm forbidding you to advise James to break the rules of this academy. Are we clear?"

"You wish to protect him. From the danger touching the Bible represents, or something beyond that?"

"The trouble with students who think they're so smart is that they never are."

"Never or seldom?" Sherlock asked. "Something to do with his lineage as a Moriarty." He corrected himself, a rare enough event. "As a *male* Moriarty, since you are in no way cautioning against my advising Moria."

The red flash of blood rushing to the surface of Crudgeon's skin, from shirt collar to behind his ear, informed Sherlock he'd scored a direct hit. "I don't mean to be bombastic, Headmaster, or rude or disrespectful. I'm quite at a loss as to what exactly your message is to me."

"I won't have you advising James to break the rules. Scholarships come and scholarships go."

"Understood."

"Do not take this lightly, young man."

"No, Headmaster. I do not. Not at all. Which begs the question: Why is it of such importance to you for me to leave poor James to fend for himself? He is woefully inadequate."

"He's brilliant—one of the highest-scoring students in your class."

"They must not test for common sense."

"Impertinence, Mr. Holmes, is a fast track to expulsion. Am I clear? Do not blur the lines at this academy. Students are students. Proctors are proctors. And the headmaster is very much the headmaster. Do not for a moment assume we are on equal footing."

"No, Headmaster. There are few proctors at this school who are on an equal footing with me." Sherlock stood, without being dismissed. "I am indebted to you and the school for the opportunity you have provided me. However, I will at no time compromise my principles, for you or for anyone.

A person in need is a person, indeed. If James, my roommate, needs help, be it on algebra or solving a puzzle, he will have it. If that gets me thrown out of this school, then I didn't belong here in the first place. I'm tired now, and I'll be going, Headmaster. I will take your suggestion under consideration. Goodnight, Headmaster."

Sherlock left the man still sitting in the chair in front of the unlit fire. He let himself out, and did not pause for a moment as he fled the property. It was only once he was into the dark of the soccer field that he bent at the waist and threw up his dinner.

CHAPTER 20

A MOST UNEXPECTED
MOMENT

I MADE THE INVITATION A PUZZLE BOTH FOR
secrecy's sake and because I knew Lock appreciated such things. I waited inside the girls' dining
hall washroom, the door open just wide enough to
peek through. Both washrooms, a custodial closet,
a computer lab, and a number of school offices
occupied the dining hall's lower level. Most of
the building was left dark at night as part of the
school's green program.

Two long days had passed since Sherlock
had been summoned to the headmaster's house.
They had been uncomfortable days with little

communication between us. Homework was getting much harder. Our first field hockey game was coming up on Saturday.

Being confined to a dark, stinky bathroom gave me time to worry more about the lack of correspondence from Father. Each day I opened my school mailbox I caught myself holding my breath. I didn't want to ever have to follow the instructions he'd left me—the key in the ashes, his desk drawer. Send me another postcard! Anything!

Sherlock arrived to the bottom of the darkened stairs as a specter. The hallway floor of gray vinyl tiles and the dreary gray-green walls reminded me of French class from my former middle school.

Sherlock seemed to float, rather than walk, toward the computer lab. He produced what I took to be the same rabbit-footed master key I'd seen him with outside the observatory.

"You may come out now, Moria," he said softly.

I had not signed the invitation, nor had I so much as breathed a breath upon his arrival. "But do be a love and bring me a damp face towel with you."

I was so annoyed, so humiliated I'd been discovered, that I considered not responding at all. I could wait it out if need be. Anything but admit defeat to Mr. Pompous.

"Come on," he said, "it was a good effort."

I wetted a paper towel and brought it to him. I didn't bother asking how he knew where I was; I didn't want to give him that satisfaction of acknowledging his superiority.

"Over here," he said, leading me to the bottom of the stairs. "Holding the rail, take two steps down and then onto the floor."

I did as he asked, again without questioning him. I was determined not to feed that runaway ego of his. He placed the wet hand towel onto the vinyl floor where my foot landed, inspected his work, and led me to the computer lab. We entered and kept the lights off, presumably because of the classroom's glass door. The far wall was also glass, creating a room of metal racks filled with the blinking colorful lights of computer servers and storage drives.

Lock caught me staring. "They wall it off, in part because they keep the room uncomfortably cool for the betterment of the computer equipment."

"I see," I said.

"You're angry because I sussed you out. Don't be. It was a clever puzzle and a decent enough hiding place. It happens I know your handwriting, so sourcing the note was easy enough. The lavatory was about your only choice for a hiding place.

Process of elimination. And of course I knew you'd arrive ahead of me, which is why I was hiding in the bushes for ten minutes before you showed up. So . . . there's that."

"You know," I said, "it's not that you're smart, practical, and logical that gets me. I actually admire, even respect your abilities. They're uncanny, really. It's that you're a show-off, a conceited boy who gets no pleasure from his own intelligence without waving it like a flag for others to see."

"Yes, I know," he said quite delightedly. "It's annoying, isn't it?"

"If you know that, then why not dial it back a bit? You'd have all the friends a person could ask for."

"I have you," he said bluntly. "Why would I need more?"

"I . . . ah . . ." Tongue-twisted, stammering, blushing, flooded with warmth and alarm, I simply shook my head, shrugged, and worked to compose myself.

"So," he said, "the purpose of the cloak-and-dagger?"

"What's the nearest building to the chapel?"

"Alumni House," Sherlock answered automatically. I pictured his mind like a map; he always knew north.

"The nearest building that counts," I said.

"The dining hall, the building above us, the building we're in."

"The nearest building with a room that locks?" I qualified.

"Point taken. Right here. You think the Bible is here in the computer lab."

"You sound so skeptical."

"Proximity is rarely a player in crimes of this nature. Theft of the Bible from its case in the chapel was premeditated. The thief was not looking for the nearest building in which to hide it. He, or she, had a plan for it from the beginning."

"Precisely!" I said, stumping him. "Who said anything about hiding it?" I waited for him to attempt to join my thought process; I loved being a step ahead of him for once.

I followed on his heels as he walked the towering aisles of ordered shelving holding blinking computer servers. The room was insanely cold; I crossed my arms tightly in defense.

"What are you up to, Moria?" He continued to stroll and observe, his hands clenched behind his back. I appreciated his taking in every little detail no matter how small; he directed my attention to things I hadn't seen: wires connecting devices; a timer; a candy wrapper. He saw it all. He peered through the glass wall into the joining room that held a number of computer terminals—keyboards and screens—on a central table. Around the edges were more tables supporting various devices.

"What's that big one?" he asked, seeing through to the largest of the machines. Leave it to Sherlock, I thought, to know exactly what this was all about. "The one . . . the Kirtas Technology thingamajiggy?"

"You're warm."

"I'm freezing!"

"It's an expression," I said. "It means you're close. Very close."

"A wasted word is 'very,'" he mumbled. "Oh, that's precious!" he said, directing his intensity onto me. "Clever, clever, girl!"

I hoped I didn't look too proud. I was ready to burst.

"To each its own purpose. Yes?" he said.

"Yes," I answered.

We both stared at the darkened contraption in the connecting room.

"The thief didn't intend to steal it but to copy it! To digitize it! The Kirtas is a book digitizer."

"I remembered a school newsletter of Father's," I explained. "How proud the school was to have been given a machine that could archive its rare books collection, yearbooks, things like that.

The thing turns the page automatically and takes pictures two at a time. It can scan a three-hundred-page book in less than thirty minutes."

"Been reading up, have we?"

"I thought you might quiz me."

We laughed. It felt exceptionally good to be able to release the excitement I was experiencing.

Sherlock theorized. "The thief transports the Bible here to the computer lab and begins scanning. But why? A Bible is a Bible. If, as it has been proposed, the volume contains the genealogy of the Moriarty family, then why not just photograph the first few pages?"

"Intriguing, isn't it?" I said.

"It's speculation, dear girl. Do not get too smug just yet."

"'Just' is a wasted word," I said, attempting to sting him, "*just* like *very*."

"And 'got' and 'a lot.' Yes, yes. Shall we debate vocabulary and linguistics?"

"No, we shouldn't," I said, motioning to the computer terminals. "We should find the file containing the scanned pages and see what we're missing."

"There's a piece of the puzzle missing," said Sherlock.

"Only one?"

"You're feisty this evening," said he. "I like it."

He stared at me in a way that made me rubbery and afraid of something. I wasn't sure what.

"What?" I asked, my voice warbly.

"May I kiss you, Moria?"

I directly recalled it being cold in the room—cold to the point of freezing—and yet I was suddenly boiling hot. I nodded. "Yes. I may not be any good at it."

"You can't go wrong," he said, bending at the waist, taking my hand, and kissing the back of it. "See? Easy enough."

That was it; that was all. A gentle kiss to the back of my hand. I think I'd been expecting something from the movies, but on second thought, Sherlock probably didn't watch movies; he struck me as more of a reader. This expression of appreciation, tender and kind, affected me so deeply that I felt myself about to cry. Or shout. I wasn't sure which. At this point, barring the departure of my mother, this was the most unexpected moment in my life, and somehow also the most important. I thanked him in a soft, uncooperative voice. He made a little head bow and I noticed his neck was a violent red. He was embarrassed. I liked that most of all.

"Well," he said, slipping into the plastic chair fronting the computer screen, "I suppose the file itself will be difficult to find and password protected once we find it, but it may yet reveal secrets the creator of the file did not intend. Computers hold far more information than we think." He began typing; from what I could tell, things weren't going so well for him.

I suddenly dared to reveal information he wouldn't know I possessed. "First Jamie headed off to the headmaster's house. Then eventually you."

"You followed both of us?" He seemed devastated.

"Not exactly followed, but I saw you walk over there, and you never saw me," I gloated.

"I may have missed it," he conceded.

"Look, I just wanted to apologize for my brother reporting you. He isn't himself. I don't know what's wrong, but he's different since coming here."

"We're all different, I suspect."

"I delivered the second clue as you asked."

"Thank you for that." I wasn't sure if I'd ever heard Lock thank anyone for anything. "Did he solve it?"

"He read it. I helped him along some. After Headmaster's house he was shaken, I think. Not sure why. From what I saw, he never went to the library that night, which is baffling."

"He must find that third clue. My sense is that

time is of the essence. It was a drastic move for the headmaster to reprimand me."

"Did he? Reprimand you?"

"Actually, I think of it more as baiting me."

"How so?"

"He said he doesn't want me helping James *find the Bible*. I was under the distinct impression he knows that's not what I've been helping with. It's the clues. I think he was hoping I'd contradict him and mention the clues."

"But you didn't."

"I did not. I can spot a trap, especially when I'm led into it by the nose ring."

"What exactly does he want you doing?"

"Nothing. He'd rather I do nothing to help James in any way. How do you find that?"

"Interesting," I answered honestly.

"Contradictory!" he proclaimed. "The school promotes teamwork at every turn. As head of the school, the headmaster is bound to that dictum, that policy. Yet, with me and your brother he makes an exception. One has to ask why."

"Why?" I said.

"Haha. Very good!"

"Thank you. He's testing James?"

"I haven't sorted it out," he said. "But Crudgeon's interest, his apparent role in this, is intriguing, confusing, befuddling."

"There you go, showing off again."

"Am I? Apologies. Diarrhea of the mouth."

"That's disgusting!"

"May I remind you," Lock said, "that of particular interest is his mention of your family Bible? Clearly there's something to it beyond its value to the school as an heirloom treasure. Now, we suspect someone may have scanned the thing page by page. Any idea what it may contain?"

"Honestly, I didn't know we had one, much less that it was here at Baskerville, much less what's in it. But a family Bible? Birth records, baptisms, that sort of thing. Right? Like we said." I recalled James saying this nearly verbatim to Natalie, me, and Bret Thorndyke.

Sherlock nodded. The fun thing about being around him was the energy his thinking produced; it was like standing next to a nuclear reactor— particles flying in every direction, dangerously volatile, ridiculously powerful.

"I believe," said he, "the two to be mutually entwined, the clues and the Bible. Entwined, but not connected. The nature of that relationship has yet to be worked out, but it can't be coincidence that one arrived on the heels of the other."

"So the clues lead to the Bible?"

"Are you listening? No! I might have thought so at one point, but now I have my doubts. The head-master advised me to leave James on his own. To stop helping him. Does that mean Crudgeon knows about the clues, I wonder. If so, how could that be? And why should he care about some hazing ritual, which is what this feels like? If not, is it merely Crudgeon's fear that James might find and touch the Bible—something he's warned us against—or is it more involved than that?"

"So he is testing Jamie. Why?"

"I think Dr. Crudgeon knows a great deal more than he lets on about everything that goes on in his institution. Never underestimate the resources of a strong leader. They have spies, technologies, and treasure at their disposal."

"You are very strange," I said, without meaning to.

"'Very' is a wasted word. We've touched on this. It has no strength or meaning. I advise removing it from your vocabulary at once, along with 'just' and 'a lot.'"

"See what I mean?"

He laughed. Arched a brow in an insightful way. "Yes, you keep saying so! Guilty as charged."

I laughed with him. He was having no luck getting past the computer's opening password prompt.

We heard it together: someone slipped and fell at the bottom of the stairs. Now I understood Sherlock's putting the wet paper towel on the floor by the stairs. He'd made a slippery spot, a way to slow down and announce an unwanted visitor.

Sherlock and I ducked beneath the table, balled up, arms around our shins. The lights in the big room switched on.

Proctor Sidling, coach of football and wrestling, wore XXL gym clothes around campus, and carried himself like one of those army generals in a World War II movie. His wiry mustache was broken by a thickly curving harelip scar; he wore a permanently twisted smile to one side of his face. A math proctor, he had a head for numbers and ran the computer lab. It seemed conceivable he had followed one of us—unlikely Sherlock, since . . . he's Sherlock. I cautioned myself to be more careful in the future—if I had a future at Baskerville after this.

Sherlock pulled us knees to knees to make us smaller in front of the chair so our shadowy form might blend into it. I'd not seen Sherlock scared prior to this moment.

Proctor Sidling disappeared into the shelving of the computer servers. He reappeared at one end or the other—I didn't have the greatest view of the other room. He was looking for something. The two of us, I figured.

He patrolled efficiently, being the general that he was. When that effort led him to the glass door of the terminal room in which we were hiding, I held my breath. He tested the doorknob and found it locked. That seemed to satisfy him. He returned to the lab's main door, switched off the light, and let himself out.

Sherlock breathed for the first time in minutes.

I scooched out and started for the door. Sherlock tackled me and we lay on the floor side by side, his arm across me to keep me still.

The lab door opened quickly, sharply.

Proctor Sidling had played a trick on me. He leaned his head in and switched on the lights, hoping to catch me. I could imagine the man looking around. At last, he switched off the light for a second time and shut the door.

Sherlock released me. I whispered, "Thank you."

"No problem."

"How did you know he'd do that?"

"It's what I would have done," he answered, whispering in the dark. "We can get to the bottom of this, Moria, but only if we can trust each other with our secrets. Any sharing of those secrets will bring this thing to its knees and us along with it. There's something going on here that's bigger than James, bigger than you or me, and involves people at the very top of the school. Do you understand the importance of the reliability of our alliance?"

About all I heard was: *our alliance*. I was feeling a little light-headed as it was; this didn't help any. I nodded. Never mind that he couldn't see me well given the dark; I had a feeling he knew I was with him.

CHAPTER 21

RIGHT FOR ONCE

"Is that another?" Sherlock asked James as my brother struggled to stuff the red envelope into his top drawer. The dorm room smelled of athletic socks and chewing gum. James failed to notice that Sherlock was sweating from our close encounter with Proctor Sidling.

"No. An old one."

"I don't believe you."

"Suit yourself."

"Do you want to know why I don't believe you?" Sherlock said, rhetorically, for James was not to escape the answer. "I was working on that paper for Cumming's class, 'The Rise of Tyranny in the Twentieth Century,' and I was in the library, in Reference, up on a stool. Sound familiar?"

"Don't know what you're talking about."

"There it was: a red envelope poking out from the pages of a volume titled *Secrets in Society and Secret Societies*. I didn't remove it, nor did I open it, as I'm on direct orders from Crudgeon not to help you."

James sat up straighter. "Why?"

"I thought you might know."

"No clue."

"Telling, don't you think, that it was in that particular volume? *Secret Societies*? Clearly, he wants you to find these things," Sherlock theorized. "Doesn't want me to offer any help. But I suppose if I were napping," he said, climbing onto his bunk and lacing his fingers behind his head of oily black hair, "and you were ruminating aloud, I might dream we were actually discussing the contents of the latest clue."

"I don't need any help."

"Well, there you have it!" Sherlock said. "So I'll just have a much-needed nap."

"I'm tired of these stupid clues," James said.

"They are only stupid if they're smarter than us. Ironic, don't you think?"

"I don't need your help."

"Crudgeon would agree. Let's look at the bigger picture, then, shall we? Do we assume the clues are leading you to the Bible ahead of everyone else?"

"Then why not give me one clue?"

"Precisely! Why indeed?"

"Did you do this, Sherlock? Is this some sort of sick joke you're playing on me?"

"It is not. I swear. I have nothing whatsoever to do with the clues. Someone is manipulating you. As for me, I've been instructed to take a step back, so it's all yours now, James. That said, only a fool would ignore someone's efforts to help. And you're no fool."

James shot a glance in the direction of the bunk.

Sherlock continued looking straight up. "Doesn't it intrigue you at all that someone has singled you out and is likely trying to help?"

"I'm not so sure about that," James said.

"Is your self-esteem so low you can't see someone taking the time to help you out? James, you are a direct descendant of the founder of this school! Your anonymous guide could be a faculty member, the headmaster, Chaplain Browning. How can you ignore that?"

"I'm not ignoring anything," James said. "I'm just tired of being run around like a bull in a bullfight. You know what they do, right? The matador keeps sticking knives in the bull to tick him off and make him charge. That's what I feel like! If someone wanted to help me, then the first clue would have led me to the Bible."

"It is a reasonable deduction," Sherlock said.

"I thought you said you're done with it."

"You reported me to Crudgeon," Sherlock said, rocking his head to the side for the first time. The two boys locked in a staring contest. "Why would you go and do that?"

"You annoy me."

"Bully for me! Because I'm smarter than you, or because you're lazier than me?"

"You're a righteous jerk, Sherlock Holmes. A stuffed shirt. Where do you get off acting so superior to everyone?"

"I *am* superior to most everyone. You and your sister, I'm not so sure about, which is why I like you both. It's why Crudgeon picked us to room together. Is there any question about that?"

"So you know it was arranged."

"It's intriguing. I assume I am to tutor you."

"Other way around."

"I doubt that very much."

"Crudgeon told you to stop tutoring me."

"Indeed. Most interesting."

"Stay away from Mo."

"I like her. We're friends."

"Leave her alone. She's just a kid."

"Au contraire! She's a bright young woman who wants to help her older brother, who adores her older brother."

"I said, leave her alone."

"You and Crudgeon have every right to ask me to stop assisting you with these clues. Accepted. As to Moria, she can think for herself. I have no intentions beyond an intellectual discourse. She stimulates me."

"You are using all the wrong words. I ought to crush your face."

"Provoking fisticuffs or taking out your aggression on my person will only endear me to her, James. If you want her to forget about me, stop making me into a victim and try being nice to me. Try working with me, and by that I'm referring to sharing the most recent clue."

"No thanks. I thought you were all done."

"Yes . . . well, I find I have a difficult time separating myself from mystery. I find clues, quests, puzzles most invigorating."

"Find something else to invigorate you. These clues are just running me around in circles."

"And here we are."

"Okay. I agree that you and I have to get along, or this year is going to stretch on forever."

"Moria has told me what a good brother you are, James. I'm sure we can work this out."

"If you would just keep out of my business, it would work out better."

Sherlock rolled away. "Ouch." He spoke to the concrete block wall. "What if the latest clue is the last clue? What if whoever's sending them has merely wanted to make sure it's you looking for them? I stick my nose into it, Crudgeon hears about it—which is interesting—and I'm reprimanded."

"You really think it's the last clue?"

"No idea. But it could be, which would make it a pretty irresponsible time to stop figuring them out, wouldn't it?"

"That's your only interest? A mystery?"

"I love a good mystery," Sherlock said. "Whether someone's trying to help you or mislead you, the person's identity is of keen interest to me."

"I guess I hadn't looked at it that way." It was a rare admission for James. Sherlock took it as a bold step forward in their friendship. "I suppose you're right."

"This once," Sherlock said, rolling back over and offering a smile to James.

James grinned and nodded. "Yeah, this once."

CHAPTER 22

TAKING SIDES

WITH SHERLOCK FINALLY GIVING UP AND heading down the hall to take a shower, James took a moment alone.

The note read:

copper copper everywhere

He reread it several times. Police? he wondered. "Coppers." Pennies were made of copper. Some roofs. Some gutters. What else? He was studying the clue curiously, eating a protein bar and tipping back in his chair, when he knocked over a squeezy-box of lemonade and spilled it across the card. He instantly snagged it, shook the spill off, and watched in amazement as within the stain ghostly letters appeared. He examined the card more carefully. He couldn't read the letters, or any words, but there was no denying something was written.

He conducted a web search for "invisible ink." The Wiki page listed lemon juice as a developer for some invisible inks. The juice he'd spilled! He read on. Copper sulfate was one of several legit chemicals used to create early spy-level invisible inks. The copper sulfate could be developed by one of four chemicals: sodium iodide, sodium carbonate, ammonium hydroxide, or potassium ferricyanide.

"Sodium carbonate." James spoke aloud. He knew exactly where to find it on campus.

Study hall hours forbade third-form students from leaving their choice of study areas for any reason other than a bathroom break. Because of the added missing-Bible curfew, following study hall hours all academic buildings except the library were off-limits, some locked—including the chemistry lab. School regulations did not allow the wearing of hoodies, but sports caps were okay. James slipped on his Boston Bruins cap, opened the window further, and climbed outside into a brisk autumnal night.

It was nearly a straight shot to the art building—but he would have to cross the playing field for field hockey. He could be easily seen from any rooms facing the playing fields and gym, including apartments belonging to the hall masters of all four Bricks. He could try his best to look like an upper classman, but the truth was he was a few inches too short, a few pounds too skinny.

That was when he spotted a maintenance department golf cart parked outside the door to Bricks Lower 3, the ground-level dormitory adjacent to his own.

Knowing maintenance, he thought, the key was probably still in the ignition; if not, he'd jumped his father's golf cart on Cape Cod multiple times. It was a matter of crossing two wires. He climbed back into his room and located a paper clip.

Minutes later, a dark green golf cart with a canvas awning top motored along the sidewalk that bisected the two playing fields in front of the gym. James parked the vehicle to the side of the gym so it wouldn't lead to him. Below the curve of the hill, he made his way along to the back of the art building and let himself in on the ground floor, where the sculpture and glass arts studios were located.

The glass arts studio roared with the sound of

two kilns that ran around the clock. Two girls worked at one of four stainless steel tables. They wore heavy aprons, gloves, goggles, and had their hair tied back with kerchiefs. Glass being a fluid medium, they didn't so much as glance toward James. One spun a long metal punty rod and blew into it while the other pinched the growing mass of glass with what looked like a giant pair of scissors.

James located the bags of materials and chemicals at the far end of the studio and sorted through the labels. He found one marked as sodium carbonate and quietly thanked his father for taking him on a tour of Dale Chihuly's glass studio on the canal in Seattle a summer earlier. Their guide had explained the chemistry of glassblowing.

He collected a cupful of the white powder and approached the studio's soapstone sink, where he mixed it with water. He used a ratio of a cup of the agent to a liter of water, mixed thoroughly, and carefully dipped the corner of the card into the plastic bucket.

"Help you?" one of the girls called out.

"I've got it!" James answered. "Science homework."

The girl returned to her work, unbothered. James lowered the angled card slowly, worried that he could easily ruin everything if he'd guessed wrong. As the line of sodium carbonated water reached the middle of the card, the quality of the coloring changed. And then he saw the first black line. He nearly squealed with excitement.

The glassblower hadn't been offering to help James. This was the mistake he'd made—assuming the world revolved around him and only him. The offer had been to me.

"What have you got there?" I asked, startling him.

"Mo? What are *you* doing here?"

"Nice to see you, too."

"It's past curfew."

"It is, isn't it? So you can imagine my curiosity at seeing my brother cross the JV field after hours in a stolen golf cart. What is that on the card, Jamie? A key of some sort?"

The chemical had rendered a previously hidden image that looked like something one might draw in art class, only a lot better. It was a pen-and-ink sketch of a key with a tree growing out of its end.

"It's the third clue," James said. He added proudly. "I just solved the third clue."

James took me forcibly by the arm and dragged me to the door of the glassblowing studio.

"Hey! Let go of her!" one of the other girls called out.

"She's my little sister! Shut up!" James shouted.

The one with the metal tongs rushed to the door. She held up the implement at James, looking like a lobster. "I said: Let go of her!"

"It's all right," I said, "he's just being annoying."

James loosened his hold on me, though only slightly.

"You sure?" the girl asked me, eyeing James suspiciously. Now the tongs looked more like the mandibles of a trap-jaw ant.

"Positive," I answered, "but thanks. I appreciate it, really."

He led me outside and laid into me in a grating half whisper, half shout. "Why are you spying on me?"

"I told you: I saw you. I was curious."

A panicked James looked back and forth between me and the studio.

"Explain yourself," I said. "What do you mean this is the third clue?"

"Invisible ink."

"That couldn't have been easy to figure out." Boys respond well to boosting their egos. My early

Baskerville education wasn't for nothing. "Can I see?"

He explained the lemonade spilling.

"Bravo." I wondered if Sherlock had had anything to do with making the connection. Not much got past Sherlock.

James reluctantly showed it to me: a small skeleton key with a tree growing out of the top. I now saw the numbers below it as well.

921737

"What's it mean?" I asked.

"Whatever the answer is, it's the hardest of the clues so far."

"I heard you went over to Headmaster's house."

James recoiled at my mention of it. "Where'd you hear that?"

"There's not a lot anyone does here at Baskerville that everyone doesn't know about within five minutes, James. If you haven't learned that yet, it's worth taking note." I hadn't directly answered his question, but by going on the offensive I'd kept him from noticing.

"There was this guy. He knew about the clues."

"What guy?"

"A guy. He told me to forget the Bible and follow the clues. He basically said, why be like everyone else?"

"So, you're sticking with the clues. That's good," I said, pointing to the red notecard.

"Is it? How do we know that's true?"

"The clues are obviously important. They're getting harder, like you said."

"I don't know!" he snapped at me. "How should I know?"

It was the first somewhat civilized conversation we'd had since coming to Baskerville and I didn't want to ruin things. I had my brother back; I didn't want to lose him again. "Sorry!"

"Why send them to me?" He sounded troubled, close to tortured by the thought. The light from the studio windows played on his face, a mixture of yellow from the kilns and the bluish ceiling lights. He looked almost sick. "Why does some creep attack me in the dark and make it seem like he's about to kill me?"

"Wait! What?"

"A guy. Two, actually. The first was a proctor, I think. He grabbed me one night in the dark by Bricks Lower One. That breezeway area. I never got a look at him. I had this creepy feeling he'd been following me, you know? Like it wasn't coincidence, his surprising me like that."

"And the other guy?"

"Yeah . . . well, he was scary. Flat-out terrifying. Told me the clues are all that count. There's something weird going on in this place, Mo."

I was about to sting him with sarcasm when I thought better of it. "Why are you so mean to Sherlock?"

"You have to ask?"

"He wants to help."

"I know that. He wants to prove how smart he is. Guys like that are all the same. Remember Donnie Hinchman? Guys like that."

"He's nothing like Donnie Hinchman! Donnie was arrogant and stupid. He *thought* he was smart. Sherlock actually *is* smart. Way smart. What's wrong with that? Smart is good."

"It's a guy thing."

"He can help us, Jamie." I hoped by using "us" I might soften his resolve.

"Please don't call me that! I've asked you not to call me that! I don't need his help. I've got Clay,

Robby, Bret, Evan. What do I need stinking Sherlock Holmes for?"

"And I thought you were good at math."

"What's that supposed to mean?"

"The four of them don't add up to one of him. Why would upper-formers spend time with you anyway? That makes no sense."

"I'm such a nice guy," he said, though sarcastically.

"They're using you—us—our name."

"Wrong."

"Then why?"

"I mean, sure, that's what probably got them to at least acknowledge I existed. But you know what I think, Mo? I think some of us are meant to lead and some to follow, regardless of how old we are or what grade we're in. I came along at the right time. They need me as much as I need them. It's like pilot fish and sharks, soldiers and generals. It's prehistoric or something."

"How can they possibly need you?"

"Thanks a lot!"

"I mean it! What do they get out of it?"

"They want the Bible found. They want study hall over. They think the clues are part of that, and that's fine with me because I can use all the help I can get."

"But not Sherlock's help."

"You have a crush on the guy. What do you know? A British accent doesn't make you smarter, it just makes you sound smarter."

"I do not!" I spoke a little too adamantly, even for myself. Did I have a crush on Lock? "He's just smart."

"There is no 'us.' Not in this, Mo," James said. He might as well have stabbed me in the heart. "I'm the one getting the clues, not you, not Sherlock. As long as you're on his side, you're on his side."

I wanted to point out how stupid that sounded. I didn't. "There are no sides until we create them! Don't you get that? You're making trouble where there doesn't have to be any! You're excluding someone who can help you!"

"On this one, I don't need him, Mo. The guy who basically attacked me on the way back from Crudgeon's . . . ?" He left the sentence half-spoken as if wanting me to beg him to continue. But I'd stopped playing that game a long time ago. "He has a key *just like* this, tattooed under his arm."

"What!?" I shouldn't have let myself sound so stunned.

"You can't tell Sherlock! Not any of this! Not if you want to be my sister."

"What's . . . that . . . supposed to mean?" I felt

my throat tighten, heard it choke off my words. "That's awful!"

"Between the invisible ink and this? It's a secret society. Has to be. What else? Remember, Mo: I never wanted to come here to school. I practically begged Father. Now, here I am: trapped. You know what a cornered animal does, Mo? It attacks. If I'm going to be stuck here, I'm going to fight back. I'm going to own this place in another year. Two years from now, I'm going to be the general and Crudgeon is going to have to deal with me."

I couldn't swallow my reaction quickly enough.

"Laugh all you want. My new friends are loyal. There's only a few of them at the moment, but there will be more, I know it. Whoever that guy was with the tattoo, he was talking to me as a Moriarty. I felt it. I know it. We've been coming here for generations. Why? There's something about us, there's something about the Bible, there's *something going on* here that no one's telling us. We—you and I—have a lot more power than anyone's letting on. Crudgeon's afraid of me—of us—believe it or not. He thinks if he intimidates me he can hold me down. But that *ain't gonna happen*."

"We just got here a few weeks ago!" I said, exasperated by all I'd heard. "What are you talking about, Jami— James? You sound paranoid. Are you okay? They say the first couple months at boarding school are the hardest."

"See? You don't believe me. They've gotten to you already."

"Who? Who do you think's gotten to me? You see how paranoid you sound?"

"The system here is designed to make us all *like them*, Mo. Don't kid yourself. That's what it's all about. It's a factory where they stamp out adults just like them. Look like them, act like them, you'll have a life like them. Nice little job. Two cars. A couple children. They're trying to hypnotize us into that kind of . . . life. It may be fine for them. Not for me. I'm not buying into that wear-a-uniform, walk-like-me, think-like-me kind of thing." He tapped his chest. "I'm thinking for myself. There are going to be changes to this place, and I'm going to be the one making them. Just because something looks the same it doesn't mean it is the same."

"You're scaring me, James."

"You can be part of this, Mo, but you have to be on my side."

"There aren't sides, James. It's just a boarding school."

"There are sides to everything, and you know it! It's a choice we make, Mo. It's your choice to make. If you make the wrong one, it won't be pretty for you or your friends."

"You're threatening me? I'm your sister!"

He hung his head and breathed deeply. "No."

"Who . . . are . . . you? I want my best friend back."

"Come on, Mo! It's me!"

"I'm beginning to wonder who 'me' is."

"Jamie," he whispered.

"So the threat is meant for Sherlock?" I spoke angrily: "He can help us, James. How stupid can you be?" That was the wrong thing for me to say, and I knew it the moment it left my mouth. This was a different Jamie, to be sure, but my brother was not and would never be stupid.

"Let's just see about that." I'd upset him horribly. He turned away from me and ran at a jog toward the language arts building. It looked like he was going to take the long way back to the Bricks—circling half the campus to avoid having to cross the playing fields and risk being seen.

I followed.

CHAPTER 23

A MOST IMPORTANT VISITOR

"In here," a familiar voice called.

James paused, having just stepped through the door to Bricks Lower 3. He thought maybe I was right, maybe he was overly paranoid. Why else would he be hearing *Father's* voice? The vestibule shared by Bricks 3 and 4 included a custodian's closet, the domain of Brunelli, a tired, hunched man with oily breath and dandruff. If anyone was calling him from the closet it was Brunelli, and yet it sounded like . . .

James froze in place, realizing he was all alone. The vestibule smelled of an industrial disinfectant used throughout the dorms and schoolrooms. To James it was the disgusting artificial scent of Baskerville Academy. Even some of the food tasted like it.

"James!" Definitely from Brunelli's closet. The door was cracked open. A single eye stared out. James recognized that eye.

"Father?"

"In here." The door opened, revealing his father dressed as usual: shirt and tie, pressed trousers. Yet he didn't look himself. Not at all. He looked frightened.

"My room's just—"

"In *here*." Father's tone of voice made James's legs move. When the door was shut, the two of them were forced snugly together by a rolling bucket on the floor and mops and brooms clipped to the walls. James reached to hug Father, but the man spun to switch on the overhead bare bulb. The closet was barely wider than the door.

James had never seen his father look like this. His clothes were basically the same as always, but the man wearing them, entirely different. It looked as if he hadn't slept in a week, his face lined with worry and fatigue. He was thinner and he'd lost some of the Cape Cod tan that typically stayed with him through Halloween.

"Really, Father, my room is—"

"Quiet!" his father hissed. "Not another word. Follow me." He rolled away the bucket and hoisted a heavy metal plate in the floor that James hadn't noticed. It was on hinges. He laid it open gently, quietly. Another light switch revealed a concrete pit with large pipes running left to right. His father climbed down and James followed. It wasn't a concrete pit, as he'd first thought, but a low tunnel that ran several hundred yards toward the Main House.

"We used to take advantage of this place when I was here," his father said, speaking softly. "You can get from Main House to the end of Bricks 4 without being seen."

"Awesome!"

"Nice little trick to know about."

"Dad?"

"You're wondering what's going on."

"Just a little."

"And why the secrecy," Father added.

"Well, yeah. Truthfully, you don't look well."

"Been better." They hunched over as Father led him a short distance down the tunnel. To the right were large and small pipes. They ran continuously as far as James could see. There were bundles of wires. Valves. "We'll be safer here."

"Safer?" Ten feet underground in a utility

bunker that stretched hundreds of yards seemed a bit of overkill for safety.

"You must be careful, son." Father's forced whisper ran chills through James. "Baskerville was tricky for all Moriartys. It's more so for you. The slightest misstep on your part . . ."

"Why? What kind of misstep?"

Father looked pained. He nervously checked up and down the cramped utility tunnel. "I promise, son, soon, very soon, no more secrets."

"Secrets?" James asked.

"Things will be asked of you here. In short order, your life is to change. You will follow in my footsteps. But the path of those footsteps will change if I'm successful."

"I have to get through this place and college first." James tried for a lighthearted moment.

"No, James. Much sooner than that. Much. Though we need to delay it as long as possible. You mustn't put your sister at risk through your actions. I fear it won't be you who suffers, but your sister. Do you understand?"

"Not at all!"

"Women in the Moriarty clan tend to . . . end badly, in case you haven't noticed."

"What? Why do you say that? Mother? What happened to Mother?"

"It's your sister we're discussing!"

"If you're so worried about her, why's she even here in the first place?"

"Because you need each other, and I need you two together in the same place."

"You're freaking me out! What's wrong? What's going on?"

"There are forces at play. Destiny. Fate, some would call it. Legacy. You and I, son, we're part of something by birthright. Firstborn sons. This place. The family business. It's all interconnected. It's all centered here at Baskerville."

"We make money off this place?"

"No! Of course not!"

"You lost me."

"Have the clues started?"

James looked like a fish out of water gasping for breath—lips smacking and sucking for air. "How . . . could . . . you possibly—"

"If you take too long with the clues, Moria could suffer. I can see that happening. But too quickly and we're all doomed. The three of us."

James knew his father to be a quietly composed man, bookish and preferring solitude to the lime-light. He'd never been melodramatic.

"Why Moria?"

"You must protect her, James. You must keep a

close eye on her. I believe they will use her as leverage against us both, if necessary. How many clues have you seen?"

"Who will? What are you talking about? Is this more of the hazing?"

"It wasn't hazing. I lied about that. I'm sorry, I had to. Those young men were after something."

"The Bible," James said. He didn't get an answer.

"How many clues?"

"Three. The last was a key that—"

"—with the family tree. No, no, no! Too soon, too soon!" He repeated everything as if talking to himself. Stammering like a child. James scooted away from him and banged his head on a pipe.

"Ow! Our family tree?"

Father wasn't hearing, or at least not listening at the moment.

"Two things, James. First, no matter what happens, you and Moria must remain here at Baskerville. You understand? Don't get any stupid ideas."

"What's going to happen?" James asked.

"Something long overdue. Something that can't be explained just now." His eyes darting, Father's voice cracked. "I've done something. I've shaken things up. It's time for reform. In any event, you must protect yourself and Moria at all costs. You could be used as . . . leverage." A door thumped somewhere above. Voices of students laughing.

"Study hall's ending," James said warily, his eyes on the large pipes and ceiling. "There will be a room check."

"You should go," Father said.

"No way. I need answers, Father. I need to know what the heck is going on with you."

"Has Crudgeon said anything about the Bible?"

"It's missing. He told the entire school. Mo and I didn't know we *had* a family Bible. What do you mean about the key and our family tree?"

"Not the Moriartys. Not *our* family. The Scow—" He caught himself. "No, it's not my place to tell you. You must be as surprised as I was, and my father before me. The initiation. Remember what I said, James. Take your time. Forget the family Bible. You won't find it. It's a dead end. It will take care of itself. You hear me, James? Forget about the Bible. Completely."

"What initiation? I've never seen you like this!"

"Indeed. Yet it's who we are, son. We are part of a bigger whole, you and I. But it has gone afoul, and I will not stand by. I've worked on certain changes, as I've said . . . it has been my life's ambition . . . gosh, it goes back practically to when I was your age. But there's still work to be done."

"Who or what are we part of, Father?"

"I'm so close, but I can't do it without you. You must stall them, do you understand?"

"Not a thing! I don't understand a thing!"

"I need you in lockstep with me, James. I need more time."

"You sent Moria a card from Atlantic City."

"Did I?" Father groaned. "Clever boy."

"Why there?"

"Allies and enemies, son. You must know them both."

"Your traveling has something to do with this group," James said.

"It has everything to do with it. My life. Your life, soon. But I must have more time if I'm to gain the upper hand. They will use Moria against you, just as they did your mother with me."

"Mother?"

"You must protect her. You must know where she is at all times."

The voices of more kids carried from above as they hurried to make their rooms before curfew. Their presence startled Father.

"I mustn't stay. Take good care, son."

He leaned forward, took James by the head, kissed him on the cheek, and scrambled down the tunnel in the direction of the Main House. Away from James, who, squatting on his haunches amid the steam and the dull lighting, felt tears running from his eyes.

CHAPTER 24

AMBUSH

They came at him from two sides. Sherlock stood up as quickly as he could, turning to face away from the altar and placing his attention onto a stained-glass window depicting the story of the Crucifixion.

He'd waited through the day to sneak in here after curfew. He didn't want to share his reasoning with James, given the headmaster's warning.

James and two other boys hurried up the chapel's nave toward the apse. James walked stridently, like a general, trailed by Clements and Ismalin. Appearing from the choir room came Bret

Thorndyke, who stopped and crossed his arms like a bouncer blocking the door.

"What in the world are you doing?" James had a newfound confidence in both his stride and voice. It was like he'd grown up in a matter of twenty-four hours.

"Waiting for you, James," Sherlock said in his usual haughty way. "Am I to assume you're having me watched? Or was it the chapel you were focused on? Do tell!"

"You were sloppy," James said, coming to a stop a few feet from Sherlock. Clements and Ismalin stood blocking the nave. Sherlock admired the precision of James's deployment of his muscle. He'd thought this through; he'd assigned his boys to particular tasks. James had made himself into a leader of older boys as well as those his own age. Not an easy accomplishment. "That day. The first clue. When I entered, our room was like a steam bath. I complained about it, remember?"

Sherlock didn't answer. His eyes ticked from one spot to another, assessing possible escape routes. James was onto him. Rarely, he thought, did such situations represent checkmate, but James had him in a strong check and he had yet to spot the move to defeat it. There was one move—foot on the low railing that separated the altar table; a long leap to the top of the pipe organ console; a difficult jump to the marble floor and straight down the nave at a run to the front doors. The route offered possibility. He mapped it mentally, calculated it at seven seconds. A long shot; he was more likely to break an ankle than get free.

"You had me fooled, telling me you'd just made yourself some tea," James said. "In fact, you'd used the electric kettle to steam open the first clue. That allowed you to seem so superior and smart. You'd already read the thing. You might have gotten away with it if I hadn't noticed the same technique on the latest—the library. You didn't seal it correctly."

"Indeed. I should imagine that aroused your curiosity to no end. It inspired the surveillance. I should have caught on to that."

"You were too busy being one step ahead. I'm not entirely clear on how you solved the third clue's invisible ink, but I'm guessing ultraviolet."

"Who says I solved it?" asked Sherlock.

"Please. Are we going to play these games? After all, we're all at risk by being here after hours. We could be busted any minute. Besides, we both had the same reaction to it: this place, the chapel. Why is that, do you suppose?"

Sherlock considered the escape route for a second time. He didn't like the way this was going. A broken ankle didn't sound so bad.

"Boys," James said.

The troubling part for Sherlock was how obedient the boys were, including the two upperclassmen. That, and the fact that the choreography had been well discussed, perhaps rehearsed. Clements and Ismalin came around James toward Sherlock while Thorndyke—Sherlock did not care for Thorndyke one bit—adjusted his stance to cover any chance of Sherlock attempting escape.

"Empty your pockets and turn 'em out," said Clements. Sherlock did as he was asked. He handed over a crumpled piece of notepaper, three sticks of gum, and the rabbit-foot key.

Ismalin passed the items to James.

"What attracts you to him?" Sherlock asked Clements so that all could hear. "Is it him or what he offers?"

"Shut it!"

"I'm just curious."

"Shut . . . it!" Clements said, "He asks me to tune you up, I will. That's all you need to know."

"Or did someone else offer you something to befriend him? Say, Crudgeon, for instance."

Clements bristled.

James clearly didn't like the suggestion. "Whatever you're doing, you're done. We're done here." There was no argument from his posse.

James had put together a group of supporters. No easy task in a place like Baskerville. Sherlock wondered if he'd underestimated his roommate.

"I knew it," James said, holding up the pencil sketch of the key so the boy who drew it could see it. "Very good drawing. It was ultraviolet, wasn't it? Did you trace it? I think you traced it." James looked around the chapel. "It brought you here. An interesting choice, Sherlock. Why is that? Why here in the chapel?"

Sherlock considered testing how far James would go to get him to talk. He measured the odds and decided to engage rather than withhold. "Why do you think, James? Or am I supposed to do all the thinking for you? Did you boys know the toilets weren't James's idea? Did he claim responsibility for that one?"

The challenge obviously irritated James. "The design of the key, a skeleton key, is very old. Reminds me of my home in Boston. Like a hundred years ago. The chapel is the oldest building on campus by far. My great-grandfather had it brought over from Europe, stone by stone, and rebuilt. It's probably several hundred years old. So a key like that is perfect for a place like this. On top of that is the tree, the branches. They're big and full, and the biggest, fullest tree at this school is just on the other side of that wall. If you look at it carefully—the drawing, I'm talking about—and I have, the two are incredibly similar. I can see this as a sketch of the same tree a long time ago."

"All of which is well and good," Sherlock said, though disparagingly.

"Meaning?"

"You're thinking purely physically. Historically. You're missing the metaphysical, the metaphorical elements. The symbolism."

"Am I?"

"Since early Christendom, the church and clergy realized the value of symbols to help their congregations stay on the path to glory, the path away from sin. The road to salvation. The symbols had to be chosen from what was known so the churchgoers could relate. The church hired artisans to create religious symbolism. Among the most popular—"

"—was the key."

"There you have it," Sherlock said. "The key to heaven. The key to salvation. The key to enlightenment. Marital trust. The keys, quite literally, to the kingdom. So, yes, I thought it wise to start here in the chapel."

"And what have you found?"

"I thought you said, 'We're done here.'"

"We're done when I say so."

"But you just did," Sherlock said, stinging him. "At any rate, you interrupted before I had much of a chance."

"You've been in here . . . twenty-seven minutes," he said, consulting his wristwatch. "What have you found?"

The boy's tone was threatening. Cruel. Clements and Ismalin stood a little taller. Sherlock could feel a beating coming.

"Nothing," Sherlock said. He needed a distraction. "Some interesting stained glass. Images one wouldn't normally expect."

"Such as?"

"This one here. It's the Crucifixion. The two thieves and Jesus on the cross. You look at it, you move on. But . . . if you look more closely, what do you see, James?"

James moved closer to the poorly lit window glass, craning his neck to look up at it. To Sherlock's disappointment neither Clements nor Ismalin took the bait; they maintained strict attention on Sherlock.

"It looks as if the glass in the one on the left isn't as dark. Maybe it broke and was replaced."

"Or maybe it was designed that way."

"What way?"

"The thief on Jesus's left, our right, is named Gestas. It's said that he mocked Jesus's righteousness. Gestas told Jesus that if he was the Son of God then he should set himself free and take the two thieves with him. But the second thief, Dismas, told the other guy to back off, that Jesus didn't belong on the cross in the first place. He's known as the good thief. Jesus blessed Dismas and promised him a place in heaven."

"That is such garbage!" Thorndyke called.

"Quiet!" James called out, condemning Thorndyke. "It's interesting, especially since the good thief is made of lighter glass."

"He's being emphasized," said Sherlock.

"Why would anyone emphasize a thief?" James asked.

"Why did you say we're done, if we're not?"

"Why the thief?" James asked.

"I have no idea. I do, however, take note there is no key in any of these three windows."

"If you run," James said, "we'll catch you. When we do, we won't be so nice."

"I'm not much of a runner."

"Guys . . . check out all the windows. Look for a key, a picture of a key. A door with a keyhole. Anything that looks like it involves a key. You,

Sherlock, stay where you are."

"As you wish, sire," Sherlock said, placing a hand onto an elaborate wrought-iron floor stand that held a massive, unlit candle. As the boys spread out, Sherlock pulled the stand incrementally closer to himself. The metal squealed against the marble. "Sorry! Lost my balance!"

Once more, Sherlock drew the candelabra toward himself. He slid his right foot out of the way, allowing him to cover what he'd been hiding. Inlaid in the white marble flooring was a small skeleton key with a tree limb top.

CHAPTER 25

OFF THE RECORD

Mᴿˢ. Fᴜʀᴍᴀɴ ᴡᴏʀᴇ ᴀ ᴡʜɪᴛᴇ ᴄᴏᴛᴛᴏɴ ᴛᴏᴘ tucked into a Stewart plaid calf-length wool skirt, held closed with an oversized safety pin like a Scottish kilt. Her snakelike, unflinching eyes peered out from black cat glasses.

"Mr. Moriarty. A word, please."

"I'm on my way to class." In fact, half the school occupied the hallways of Main House in a frantic, yet orderly flash mob.

The woman's smile, or what passed for a smile, could easily be mistaken for a wince of pain.

Heeding Father's advice to stay in Baskerville,

he obeyed the headmaster's secretary and entered the classroom. She shut the door behind him, not following inside herself.

Crudgeon stood at the far end, away from the door. "Mr. Moriarty."

"Headmaster." James wondered why the meeting wasn't taking place in the man's office, only two hallways from this room.

"Sit."

James squeezed into the chair, placing his laptop and books on the chair's writing arm. Crudgeon perched awkwardly on the desk at the front of the room.

"Breaking into the headmaster's office will most certainly result in expulsion."

"Excuse me?"

"Being caught in the act, immediate expulsion. In this case, evidence is circumstantial, but it was a poor choice to make, James, especially as I've offered to help you."

"I . . . ahh . . ."

"Your future is here at Baskerville, James."

"Yes, Headmaster. I understand that." He thought back to Father's warning. *I need more time.*

"These kind of wanton acts will not be tolerated. You will find the school a harsh and intolerant place should you insist on continuing with this nonsense."

"Would there be any chance you might believe I had nothing to do with whatever you're talking about?"

Crudgeon appeared to be trying to work a kink out of his neck.

"I didn't think so," James said. "For the record, it happens to be the truth."

"If we were on the record, we'd be in my office and this meeting would be in the books."

"So it's not . . . on the record?" James asked curiously. "That's why Mrs. Furman is out there playing bouncer?"

"I will be calling you to my office for just such an appointment. I will make accusations and you will deny them."

"Because I didn't do it! Why would I confess to something I didn't do?"

"What exactly were you after, James? I can tell you more about your family history than any of those records can. I am happy to do so."

"Headmaster, *it wasn't me.*"

For the first time, Crudgeon appeared to consider the possibility. "Your sister, perhaps . . ." Spoken like a man thinking aloud.

"No!" James snapped sharply. "Moria? No!

Never!" He harkened back to his father's warning of the system making a target out of his sister. Of the miserable history of Moriarty women, most of which James knew nothing about. "She's way too much of a goody-goody, Headmaster. Maybe one of my friends thought they were doing me a favor. I wouldn't know. But not Moria."

"Did you *arrange* the break-in, yes or no? This is the only time you will be offered amnesty, do you understand? Yes, or no?"

"No. And I'd rather be expelled than get someone else in trouble."

"That can be arranged."

James lowered his voice to a whisper. "When I left your house . . . that man. Did you arrange that?"

"What man?"

"I think you know what man. The man who told me to give up the search for the Bible, which is interesting, because I'm not looking for the Bible."

"A man told you this?" Crudgeon was either surprised or a decent actor.

"You said 'not yet,' when I said I wasn't a sergeant." James waited for the man to say something. "Is my father a sergeant?"

That woke up the headmaster.

"More than a sergeant? Colonel? General?"

"What do you know?"

"What do I need to know?"

"You need to know you're in dangerous waters. Tell me what this man said."

"I think you know."

"Do not get fresh with me, boy." Crudgeon's typical demeanor was crumbling before James's eyes.

"Tell me about the initiation." For James it was a wild stab into the dark; he'd heard Father mention it, nothing more.

Crudgeon stood unexpectedly. He was shaking. "What were you after in my office? Now's your chance, your only chance."

"Clues," James lied, having no idea why. *Protect your sister.* "Father's years here. My family's history. Anything that might help me understand why some guy practically in your front lawn didn't want me looking for our family Bible when that's the only way out of study hall. The whole school blames me and Moria, Headmaster."

"Yes. Pity, that. I hadn't factored that in. The social ramifications are regrettable. I can't take it back now, you understand? When I lay down the law, it's just that, the law. Your sister and you will have to endure. These things pass with time."

"There's no reason to question Moria,

Headmaster. Leave her out of it, please."

"No, I won't. Because you're guessing. You don't know the files. You haven't seen them. It's fine to be loyal to one's family, James. Admirable, in fact. But loyalty to a fault makes for scapegoats, and I can't afford for you to go playing martyr on me. Do we understand each other?"

James nodded.

"Say it."

"Yes, Headmaster. I understand."

"You are in over your head, son. Curiosity really did kill the cat, you know? How do you think an expression like that starts? Not with a single cat, I'll tell you that. A summation of so many cats over so much time. Don't make yourself one of them. Speak with your *sister*." Crudgeon leaned on the word. "Find out *everything* you can, and report back to me. And next time, don't be so stupid: let responsibility fall where it belongs. Ultimately we are all held responsible for our own actions. Even sisters."

"Please, Headmaster. Not Moria. She wouldn't do something like this, and if she did, it would only be because she was thinking it would help me."

"I expect great things from you, James, but don't push me."

"No, sir."

"Don't stick your nose where it doesn't belong."

"No, sir."

"What else did the man—this man—say? Other than the bit about the Bible?"

James wanted to say: "That's for me to know, and you to find out," but he didn't. Instead, he lied. "I think I'm being hazed, some kind of hazing. It started at my house, before I ever came here." He studied the man, feeling his stomach turn as he realized this wasn't news to the headmaster. The man had to force a look to appear surprised. James felt sick to his stomach.

"Could be. You wouldn't be the first."

"My father before me."

The look from Crudgeon was at once both mirthful and black-ice cold.

Terrified, James spoke to break the silence between them. "I won't let you down, Headmaster."

"That's yet to be seen. Now, get out of here, and remember: this meeting never took place."

CHAPTER 26

A WOLF IN SHEEP'S CLOTHING

I SKILLFULLY AVOIDED MY BROTHER FOR THE next two days. I'd caught his burning eyes boring into me when passing in a hallway between classes and I sensed he was upset with me, though I wasn't sure why.

I elected the tactic of avoidance. Twice I hid in the girls' washroom to evade him. Several other times I used Natalie and Jamala to cover for me. I spent inordinate amounts of time in my dorm room since boys weren't allowed on our floor without Mistress Grace's permission.

I arrived to meals late so I could pick a table

well away from James, avoided the common room altogether, headed directly to the girls' locker room after classes, and waited for field hockey to start. All in all, it was a highly successful campaign, one that might have continued for a week or more had I not been blindsided by the unexpected.

There I was, leaving my dorm for dinner, late as per my plan, when, while passing Brunelli, the janitor, pushing a mop and rolling bucket, the man reached out and grabbed me. I opened my mouth to cry for help, but a hand was slapped over my lips and my brother's voice said harshly, "Not a word!" He dragged me into the washroom. It wasn't Brunelli. James was up to some new tricks.

I realized immediately several problems with my plan: seeing the janitor's blue coveralls, I'd paid no attention to who was inside them; by electing to go to dinner late each evening, I'd ended up in an empty dorm. There was no one to come to my rescue.

"James? How did you—?"

"Never mind that! You're going to answer me, Moria. You're going to answer my questions—honestly—and if I sense otherwise your life at this school is going straight down the toilet."

With sinks and toilets all around us I was tempted to make a joke about his poor choice of metaphor, but it didn't seem like the best timing.

"So ask," I said, trying to act casually. "I'm kind of hungry and we're both late for dinner."

"You . . . or my nutcase roommate . . . broke into Crudgeon's office."

Decision moment: on the one hand, I thought I could lie pretty convincingly to James. We both had lifetimes of experience as brother and sister. On the other hand, I didn't lie; I pretty much took the path that if you did it, you had to own it; if you can't own it, then don't do it in the first place. As to Sherlock's involvement . . . I would decide on that as I went.

"Fine leather appointments," I said. "Though the artwork is all copies and photographs. He could have done better." I couldn't help my wit; when you have it, you have it.

He raised his hand as if to slap me, and I shied away despite knowing he wouldn't do it. James and I had a history of wrestling, of pinching and pulling hair. We didn't slap. He lowered his hand.

"Sorry. I'd never hit you."

"Let's hope not," I said, "because I won't hit you back and then you're going to feel really awful." The mood changed in that instant—desperate brother, frightened sister. "None of what's been going on makes any sense," I said. "All I want to do is go to school and have friends and play field hockey—most of the time, really poorly. I want my brother back. I want all this clue stuff and Bible stuff over. I thought if I could find out more about what's going on maybe it would be over more quickly. So, yes, I paid a visit to the headmaster, and he didn't happen to be there."

"At two in the morning," James said.

"Something like that. More like four, but yes."

He pursed his lips, trying to conceal a smile. "That's my sis. And?"

"I found some files . . . on his computer of all places."

"You hacked the school's computers?"

"His password is their dog's name—Cairo—followed by the year he became headmaster. It took me all of three tries."

"You little genius!"

I didn't tell him that had been Sherlock's doing. I was more than willing to be labeled brilliant by my brother. It had been a long time coming. "No history. No ancient fable or mysterious clue. I did find, among other files, some blueprints and a legal document. They came up during a search for our last name. I didn't have time to read hardly any of the documents—the folder on us, on the Moriar-tys, is massive—but there's a money thing tying our family to the school. Upon a male heir graduating, a large donation is made by a trust. Also, did you know, for instance, that our great-grandfather paid to have the chapel moved from Europe?"

"A recent discovery. Yes."

"It's like we own this school or something. I don't exactly get how it all works, but you being the male heir is obviously important."

I could see him calculating. I'd known for years the power of my brother's mind. As long as it had been focused on the Red Sox or the Bruins, on schoolwork, it had kept itself contained. In the past two years, since James's voice began to change, his attention had widened. He read the morning paper cover to cover and had detailed discussions with Father about the stock market and politics, stuff I didn't understand or care about. I thought these changes were mostly responsible for Father's sending James to Baskerville. My partial reading of the old legal document had changed that. For James as well. He'd been sent here as part of a generations-old agreement.

"So let's say there's some kind of trigger for our family's financial support that has to do with the male heir—me—attending or graduating. Maybe that agreement or that trigger also has something to do with our family Bible." His voice grew excited. "Maybe I have to swear something using the Bible. Like in court. In order for the school to be paid. 'Do you solemnly swear to abide by the rules of Baskerville Academy, blah-blah-blah.' See? The Bible goes missing, and the school freaks out. Father freaks out. Maybe, even, whoever is sending these clues freaks out. I end up some chess piece in a game that you and I haven't figured out yet, meaning we're at risk. Meaning the headmaster is worried about me, worried about you."

I was nodding so hard I was making my neck sore. "Definitely, almost makes sense."

"Almost?"

"An oath? Really? How could that get them their money?"

"Yeah . . . you're right," he said. "But I feel we're close."

"We" was about all I heard. . . .

"It makes sense they need the Bible for something. They don't want it back just to display it."

"Maybe our great-grandfather was a head case. Maybe there's some rule that the Bible has to be on display."

"That's not impossible. Crudgeon wouldn't tell us that because he'd have to explain that our family funds the school and that would give you and me too much power over him. Interesting."

"It is!"

I'd seen his face get red like that before. Only a couple of times, and they never ended well. He'd nearly killed London one time, strangling the dog and holding him off the ground—London, his favorite. I'd saved London; he was only scared, not hurt. But I couldn't save James. It was like he'd passed some internal threshold where nothing could reach him. It wasn't a bad temper but more like another person had come out from within him. I feared that was about to happen again—and it wouldn't be London he'd strangle.

"It's all right," I said encouragingly.

James took me hard by the shoulders. Truth be told, I nearly fainted. I thought he was probably going to rip me in half without knowing what he was doing. He could dispose of my body in the showers, or in pieces down the toilet. My legs wilted.

"Crudgeon assumes it was you who broke into his office."

"W . . . h . . . a . . . t?"

"If we don't figure this out, he's going to use you—I don't know how—to get to me," he said, his eyes wide with terror.

"The Bible is separate from the clues. The guy with the key tattoo under his arm made that clear enough. Father warned me to protect you."

"You've spoken to Father?" I cried out jealously. "When? Did he call?"

James's face was paralyzed. "Never mind that. We have to guard against anything happening to you, Mo. I'd do anything to keep you safe—"

"Never mind? *Seriously*, Jamie? No, I won't 'never mind.' I *do* mind. I mind *very much*. What about Father?"

He told me about the bizarre underground visit, about the discussion of legacy and how Father was trying to stop someone from doing something but that it was taking more time than he'd hoped. How Baskerville, the family Bible, and Jamie and I were all part of it, but that Jamie didn't know what "it" was.

I knew the sisterly thing to do at that moment was to share the instructions Father had given me while in his study. I didn't share because Father had asked me not to, but I wasn't certain those rules still applied.

"Would you really do anything to save me?" I wished he'd say it a few times more. I felt good all over.

"Power is about leverage," he said, sounding like a grown-up version of James. I think that's when I realized the changes in James would be forever. He wasn't a different James, he was the older variety. "My boys and I will protect you."

"Your 'boys'? You sound like a bad guy in a movie."

"I have a couple guys who help me out, Mo. You know that. Soon, there will be more."

"You're building a posse?"

"Something like that. Don't worry about it. What I need you to do is to cooperate. Co-operate. Operate *together*. You get that? If I'm fighting you at the same time I'm trying to protect you, that's not going to work."

"You make it sound so dangerous."

"You'd understand if you'd seen Father. I think it is dangerous. For both of us. Me, because I'm the male heir and something is expected of me. Like I told you, Father knew about the clues, so they must be a tradition. The scary dude told me to give up the Bible search and focus on the clues. So there's that, too. You, because if I mess this up, they'll use you to get at me. Father was blunt about that. We don't know who 'they' are. I don't know how I might mess this up, which makes it all the more likely I will."

"You know what's weird?" I said. "As weird as this sounds, I actually know what you're saying. I get it."

"So you'll cooperate?"

"One thing: don't ask me to give up Sherlock as

my friend. Do not go there."

"Mo? That kid's trouble. It's you and me. Three's a crowd. I'm not going to tell you who you can have as a friend, but I'm asking, I'm *begging* . . . give it a rest until we figure this stuff out. Please!"

"M . . . O . . . R . . . I . . . A!!? Moria Moriarty?" It was Mistress Grace. "Are you in the dorm?"

I pushed James into the nearest shower and pulled the curtain shut. I wheeled the bucket and mop into a stall and pulled the stall door closed. I headed out into the hall, tugging on my skirt and rubbing my hand—a girl fresh out of the wash-room.

"Down here, Mistress Grace!" She was nearly to the far end of the corridor, well past my dorm room.

I didn't know until then that a person's move-ment tells its own story. Mistress Grace was a motherly, round woman with soft hands and pin-prick beady eyes. A happy woman, she moved around easily and lightly enough to be half her undetermined age. Presently, her face was grim, her walk slow, her eyes downcast.

As she arrived close to me I could see more the details of her worn expression: glassy eyes and streaked mascara.

I'd heard Father use the expression "The devil's in the details." I'd assumed it meant that small details were often the biggest obstacles. But the devil was quite honestly in the details of her face. She was bewitched, overcome. And it had something to do with me.

Of that, I had absolutely no doubt.

CHAPTER 27

NO EASY WAY

"MORIA, I'M AFRAID THERE'S BEEN AN ACCI-dent." Mistress Grace's voice reflected the evidence of her tears. It was as sad a thing as she'd ever spoken.

"James? Something's happened to James?" I tried to look as if all the blood had drained out of me.

"No, dear, not James, thank heavens."

"Sherlock?" His name just escaped my lips. It felt as if someone other than me had put them there. Why Sherlock? I wondered. And why would that same chill own me?

"I'm afraid it's your father, dear girl. There's no easy way to say this: he's . . . gone."

I awoke in the school infirmary looking up at white acoustical tile and hearing the murmur of voices.

"She's awake!" said James.

I sat up, but too quickly. The room swirled and spun.

I opened up my eyes to James's worried and tear-streaked face close to mine. He was holding my hand and sitting in a chair that was lower than the bed, making him seem smaller.

"Jamie," I groaned. "Water, please?"

An arm connected to the school nurse delivered a plastic cup of ice water. "Lucky for you, Mistress Grace caught you, or you'd have really thumped your head."

"Yeah," I said, "lucky me." Tears practically squirted from my eyes. "Jamie . . . is it . . . true?"

He was crying as well. He nodded and hugged me and I think we stayed that way a long, long time. Headmaster Crudgeon stood at the foot of the bed watching. I didn't know how long he'd been there. I would find out later he'd never left my side. The cruel Mrs. Furman was there, as well as Mistress Grace. There was an ice pack on my head and my feet were raised on a pillow.

The infirmary room contained two hospital beds and some equipment on wheels. It was all very antiseptic and spare. I hadn't even known it existed. From the view out the window I placed it as the upper floor of the McAndrews Science Hall.

"Could we have a minute?" Jamie asked as politely as I'd heard him say anything since arriving to Baskerville.

The adults moved into the hallway.

"Is it true?" I asked.

He nodded. Tears rolled down his cheeks again. "He fell off a ladder."

"Father on a ladder?"

"Shh. I know. Listen, Mo, do you remember my telling you he came here, to school, the other night?"

"Of course! I fainted, I didn't go psycho!"

"Hush! Not so loud! Remember? He was all worried about you."

My body shook with grief. I felt twinges of anger, regret, sadness, and a profound sense of emptiness.

"About . . . well, that if I didn't act right it might end up on you. But him? He was freaked out, but I never thought this would happen."

"The ladder."

"Exactly. He was winding the wall clock in the hall."

"Father was? That's Ralph's job!"

"I know. But don't say anything. There's something horrible going on, Mo. I'm in it. We're in it. And we don't even know what it is." He wiped away snot from his nose. "First Mother, now Father."

"What's that supposed to mean? Mother?"

"He was scared. Father was scared."

My breath caught. *Not our father.* That's what Jamie—James, I corrected myself—was saying.

"The attack . . . my bedroom," he said. "What if that wasn't for me? What if they were just using my room to enter the house and—"

"—get to Father," I said. "James! What are we supposed to do?"

"Get you out of here. Get well, Mo. We can't talk here. You get well and we'll figure this all out. But secretly. In private, you understand? Nothing to Crudgeon or the others."

"Of course not."

"It's super important."

"I get it," I said. "I'm better right now. I'm ready."

"You don't have to convince me," he said, looking up. "You have to convince them."

CHAPTER 28

BROKEN TRUST

"I HEARD ABOUT YOUR FATHER. I'M TERRIBLY sorry." Sherlock sat at his desk, a stack of open library books before him. He closed the top three books the moment he saw James.

"Thanks," James said.

"If you need the room to yourself . . . ?"

"No, I'm okay. I don't think I have any more tears left in me." He tried to laugh; it sounded more like a wet cough.

"They're in there," Sherlock said, "and you must trust to let them out whenever they want."

"An expert on grief too?" He lashed out at his

roommate, eyes squinting, his voice strident.

"Sorry to say, yes. Me mum and da, both gone. It's just my older brother, Mycroft, and me. We are like you and Moria, except he's seven years my senior."

"I need you to stay away from her for a while."

"Sorry?"

"Just for a while. No more you and Moria."

"But she needs friends now more than ever. You as well, James."

"Not you, she doesn't. Not me, either."

"I beg your pardon?"

"Bad things happen to Moriarty women," James said, quoting Father. "Father's death. They're calling it an accident."

"And?"

"Moria can't be involved."

"You don't believe it was an accident," Sherlock said.

"I didn't say that. Forget it, please. Promise me you'll give Moria some space."

"The clues? The Bible?"

"You see? There you go again!"

"James, I can help." Sherlock was thinking about the image of the key in the floor that he intentionally hid in the chapel.

"No."

"You're sure this is how you want it?"

"Yes."

"Can we talk about some of this? Not later, but now?"

"I suppose."

"We know a family Bible typically contains birth and death records, James. But is there any reason to believe that's why it was taken?"

"Meaning?"

"Moria and I think it may have been copied."

"Copied?"

"Scanned. In the computer lab. No proof. Just a hunch."

"For what? How can that make any sense? A Bible's a Bible."

"It doesn't make sense. Not unless your family Bible is different somehow."

"A swearing in," James said. Clearly feeling uncomfortable about his doing so, he shared the conversation he'd had with Moria. With the death of Father, he was more desperate than ever to figure things out.

"Interesting," Sherlock mumbled.

"How so?"

"Your father will have left you instructions."

"So say you."

"So say I. In the will, or the trust, or whatever

arrangements he has made for you and Moria. A Moriarty tradition or ritual."

"The *initiation*," James whispered.

"How's that?"

"Something my father sa—" He caught himself.

"You spoke to your father? Recently?"

"Never mind that."

"James. If you—"

"He knew about the clues. I think he'd done them as well back whenever. He said that word, 'initiation,' but it was like he regretted it. Never mind! *Leave it alone!*"

"You're absolutely right. How unkind of me. You need time to grieve and not worry about such things." Sherlock's mind was whirring.

"Promise me."

"Promises are made to be broken, James. I don't make them. I do, however, give you my word in this: I respect your concerns, and I want nothing whatsoever to do with any harm that may come to you or Moria. Nothing could be further from the case. And I will point out the obvious: the headmaster is not to be trusted. I believe you've made the connection we've been seeking, and clearly the headmaster is culpable in some manner or other."

"You're not listening."

"I am not your enemy, James. You may indeed

have enemies, but I am not one of them and it's time you figure that out."

"What connection?" James asked, too curious to allow it to pass.

"Your presence here at Baskerville, the tradition of the clues."

"Mr. Know-It-All."

"I observe. I analyze. And yes, I render opinion as a result of both. But please—"

"Just . . . stop!"

"Very well." Sherlock returned his attention to the pile of books on his desk. "But I think you might consider a visit to your home where . . . it happened . . . before the police muck it all up."

"You're impossible!" James said.

"I try," answered Sherlock.

CHAPTER 29

A SAD NIGHT

Four days passed expeditiously and James and I found ourselves back in our Beacon Hill home in anticipation of a hastily arranged memorial service scheduled for the following morning. Ralph delivered us curbside, where we were greeted by Lois, our prim and proper former nanny. For a while now, Lois had been about as close as we got to a mother. We hugged and wept in the drizzle outside our sturdy brick home, the ground feeling as if it were shifting beneath our feet.

"We will get through this together," she said. Just the kindness in her voice helped. For one brief moment since I'd heard the news, I felt a glimmer of hope. James disconnected from our group hug and pretended he felt nothing. He'd been so quiet on the long drive from the academy. I'd tried but failed several times to engage him in conversation—and let's face it, I can be engaging. Father's death had crippled James. He was keeping everything inside, a recipe for disaster.

I had an important mission: get a few guarded minutes alone inside Father's office. Find the key in the fireplace. Unlock the drawer. Read whatever was there. The existence of the mission helped curtail my grief, made small talk frustrating and even more boring than usual.

There were familiar faces inside, something James and I hadn't planned on. All men, they were engaged around our dining table in what looked like a meeting—papers and pens, cell phones and coffee cups strewn about. A long meeting, by the look of it. They rose, closing journals and calendars, and greeted us lovingly.

A few we knew as our "uncles"—close friends of Father's since James and I had been toddlers. Each was familiar. These were the men who showed up, most often in pairs, to the house at all hours. Two of the men we'd met before—from Father's university? His club downtown? I couldn't remember exactly who they were. Businessmen. Investors. Attorneys. I imagined them trying to sort out our family affairs for us.

They each offered their condolences. They gave me hugs and shook James's hand. One of them, Mr. Lowry, a man with white hair but an athletic build, led James off into Father's study. I tried to follow but was diverted by Lois, who led me into the kitchen.

All I could think about was the ashes in the fireplace and what they hid.

I didn't know what went on in that meeting; James rebuffed my attempts to find out. I assumed it was money stuff, something to do with Father's will or insurance. I think James felt more important because of it, and neither of us needed that. After a while, the men collected their belongings and left, once again taking time with both James and me.

Being back in the house reminded me so much of Father that I could hardly keep my balance, much less worry about such things. I'd never felt such emptiness. It stole my breath, my voice. It cluttered and complicated my thoughts. I cried and I shook. I didn't forget about Father's office, but grief overcame even curiosity.

I'd always found being the only girl in our family to be tricky. Father and I had something special between us that only I shared with him. It had died in this house along with him, and I felt that absence with every painting of my old relatives I passed, every piece of furniture and photograph. I didn't want to be here. I resented being here. I wanted to get into Father's office and then have Ralph take me back to Baskerville. It felt odd, so very odd, that I should consider the school home when I was standing in the place I'd grown up—but Father's death had turned everything upside down. Absolutely everything. Especially me.

Baskerville would now be home for years to come. No more Beacon Hill; too many memories here. The thought made me almost sick to my stomach. My situation was tricky in another way as well. I hadn't told James what Father had told me about the key in the ashes, nor about my assignment from Sherlock to photograph everything I could.

My effort to accomplish both these tasks meant more secrecy. On this night I would be taking another step away from being the perfect sister. And while it added to my already considerably broken heart, it also filled me with a kind of thrill and excitement that I found intoxicating. I suddenly enjoyed the thought of breaking the rules. Maybe I was more like James than I knew.

I set my phone's alarm to wake me at 1 a.m.

and placed the phone beneath my pillow so as not to wake others. I must have fallen to sleep quickly, for I jolted awake from a blank nothingness, maybe the deepest sleep I'd ever had.

My mobile phone in hand, I tiptoed down the stairs barefoot in my athletic shorts and camisole top.

First, I headed to Father's office, by far my most important mission. I passed the oil paintings of former Moriarty men and women looking out at me. The existence of a Moriarty family Bible, the files in Crudgeon's office suggesting James was tied to the school—I had a newfound confusion about these old people in their funny clothes. Their hardened faces, as dry and cracked as the paint that formed them, projected a severity and solemnity that made me actually consider their roles in my life. Father had been an only child; his father, a military man. The Moriarty women were not talked about; I hoped to change that in James's and my generation.

I turned away from the sitting room into and through the library and reached the door to Father's study.

Locked.

Father's study was never locked. I tried it again. The first pulse of energy rising through me was frustration and anger; the second, curiosity.

I wondered why, and on whose authority our father's office door had been locked. No doubt one of the men who'd been clustered around our family's dining room table the night before. Mr. Lowry, Father's attorney, came to mind. But why? And what right did he have? This was followed by my asking myself who might have the key to Father's study, the answer immediate: Lois, who had served Father as a home office secretary since her nannying skills had proved less necessary.

Lois was sleeping over to serve as guardian, as she had done on and off for years when Father traveled without us. I considered trying to snatch her purse and search that cluster of keys I'd seen her handle all these years. But being caught might prevent me from accomplishing Sherlock's assignment, so I hurried through that first.

I was diligent and thorough in making a photographic record of every aspect of the house, and Father's "crime scene," as Sherlock had called it. It was an expression I abhorred. But I had to live with it, as I had let slip what James had not: there was no way my father had been up a ladder winding our wall-mounted clock.

Father was afraid of heights.

James awakened in a foul mood on a foul Boston day of wind, rain, and an Indian summer heat wave. It was as if the heavens had opened up crying over the loss of Father.

He showered and prepared for the memorial just as I did in my room down the hall from him. While I felt guilty over going against my brother's wishes and emailing all the photos I'd taken the night before to Sherlock, James was the one deeply troubled. He shouted for Lois and bossed her around. He demanded breakfast be delayed. He was acting like a brat.

I was still angling for a way to get into Father's office, having chickened out of trying to steal Lois's purse from her room in the middle of the night. Things weren't going well for anyone. It felt as if Father had cast a curse over us all.

It wasn't until much later in the morning, as I was standing by the partially open door to James's room, ready to confess my sins to him, that I saw him pull his suit jacket from the dry cleaning cellophane and start to put it on. I jumped back so he wouldn't see me as he turned to fish an arm into a sleeve. I faced facts: I was too scared to admit to James I was in cahoots with Sherlock, too sensitive to tell him about the assignment I'd been given by Father concerning the key in the ashes. I didn't know how James might react. I wasn't sure I knew my brother any longer. It made me sick to my stomach. In only a matter of a few weeks he had changed considerably. That realization triggered an added sadness to a day already draped in it.

I was about to abandon his doorway when I saw him pat his coat pocket. He tucked his fingers inside and withdrew a thick white card the size of a thank-you note. He flipped it over. I saw some kind of pencil or tower, an arrow or rocket. There was something printed at the bottom—numbers, maybe. James patted and searched the rest of his pockets. As he did, I slowly and quietly stepped back from his door.

I turned my head sharply. Lois stood at the end of the hall, staring at me spying on my brother. As my eyes landed on her, she lowered her head and made for the stairs, wishing to be invisible. We both knew it was too late for that.

Running through my head was, no doubt, what was also running through my brother's: How did a card end up in the pocket of a suit freshly back from the dry cleaners?

The answer was as clear as the question: someone had put it there the night before for my brother to find.

CHAPTER 30

ESCAPING SPIRITS, RETURNING FEARS

I CAUGHT UP TO SHERLOCK ON THE WAY BACK from the mandatory chapel service honoring my father. If it hadn't been Father's memorial service I might have thought it an impressive, even gorgeous event. All students wore school uniforms with black armbands on their left arms. Everyone was showered and groomed, even Tilly Simpson and Grant Pendergraz, two of the more slovenly kids on campus.

Sherlock had been avoiding me for the three days since James's and my return from Boston and I didn't take it kindly.

"So much for friends supporting friends," I said, coming up behind him at a jog.

"Moria."

"You're speeding up? You're seriously going to walk away from me?" Humiliated, I stopped on the sidewalk in front of Bricks 2. To my surprise— and inward delight if I'm being honest—Sherlock stepped off the sidewalk to allow others to pass. He looked back at me. I felt amazing. His eyes cared, his shoulders sagged in resignation. He was fighting something internally. I felt like his mind was telling him one thing, his heart another, and that filled me with the first inkling of joy since Father's passing. I knew at that moment that this boy could get me through my grief—this strange, weird, brilliant, dazzling boy.

"You holding up?" he said softly, having crossed the distance to me. He passed the test—I wasn't about to go to him; he had to come to me if we were to be friends.

I nodded. "I emailed them to you. The photos."

"I shouldn't have asked you to do that." He was about to say something more—I could feel it—but he stopped himself. "I was wrong to ask."

"What is it?" I said. "What's happened?"

"What's happened? Your father has had a horrible accident. You need time to deal with that, Moria.

I can't believe you and James came back so soon."

"We can't sit at home moping. Besides, everything in that place reminds us of him. It's horrible, really. Here, there are much more pleasant memories. And friends." I thought maybe I'd laid it on a little too thick, but Sherlock, for all his brains, could miss the most obvious things.

"I shouldn't have asked you. Let's leave it at that."

"No! I won't leave it at that! You've been avoiding me. Repeatedly! What's with that?"

"Have not."

"Have too!"

"I'm giving you space."

"I don't want space."

"You need time to process what's happened."

"I have a lifetime to process what's happened. I loved my father." I started crying, darn it all. "He was the best . . . most amazing . . . and I'll miss him every day of my life, with every heartbeat." I wiped my nose on my arm. "But he was a fighter. As quiet and reserved, even distant, as he could be, he never quit. He taught James and me to never quit, never give in. 'When the going gets tough, the tough get going.' That kind of attitude. I owe him that, Sherlock. I have to keep swimming. Treading water isn't an option."

He reached out and pulled me into his arms, his chin pressed into my hair. I held him as tightly as a pillow when I'm miserable. I shook in his grasp. He said nothing. For a few long seconds the events of the past few days floated out of me, like spirits trying to escape. I recalled him kissing my hand, as I had a thousand times now. I begged the universe to just let me stay here like this, to let the world pass me by so I could disappear into this hug like hiding under a blanket. But it wasn't to be. Sherlock spotted James approaching. He released me.

"Don't quit on me," I whispered, allowing him to separate us. "There's a note in James's suit coat pocket. It's another clue, I think. Help me, please!"

"You're on your own if you want to continue this . . . nonsense. It's brought nothing but trouble for all of us. I promised James: I'm out." Sherlock didn't wait for James. He left me there, my head spinning, my heart breaking.

"Please!" I called, aware of the futility. Sherlock was not one to waffle. He didn't look back. That hurt most of all.

CHAPTER 31

FAMILY PHOTOS

WE DON'T SHARE OUR SECRETS; THEY WOULDN'T be secrets if we did. I had my own. Plenty, if truth be told. Recently, I'd been places I shouldn't have been, had followed my brother and Sherlock and others. I'd made it a game with Natalie and Jamala. We'd formed a little gang of spies. I knew things I wasn't supposed to know; I'd seen things I wasn't supposed to see. It changed the way I looked at people because I would know when they were lying to me. Knowledge, as it turned out, can damage relationships. I never would have guessed that.

The school mailmaid—yes, that's what we

called her—was nicknamed Madame Mim for her bent chin and sizable wart by her left eye (it looked more like a mushroom). One eye was fogged gray while the other roamed around as if disconnected in the socket. You would catch occasional glimpses of her through the open door to your tiny mailbox and it would scare the shoes off your feet. She was back there stuffing boxes, trying to read names off letters and packages. She wasn't very good at it. McDonald would get mail for McConnell. Doris for Horace. Students spent a good deal of time redistributing mail around the dorms or in the common room.

So it was no great surprise to me that I should receive Priority Mail addressed to my older brother, he of the same family name. It would have been more surprising, I suppose, to receive mail actually intended for me.

The proper thing to do, of course, was to pass it along to James, unopened. I would have done just that had I not caught a glimpse of the sender's name above the return address. Mr. Conrad Lowry, Esq.

The rationale was easy: anything from my father's business lawyer addressed to James was also meant for me. It wouldn't matter if I read it first and then passed it to James, or vice versa. I didn't go as far as to tell myself James wouldn't care. I knew he would. I knew he'd chew me out if I opened it. But I had my excuse at the ready; a strong defense. It would be difficult for him to argue otherwise.

I opened the letter.

The contents, several letter-sized pages folded separately from a cover letter, were printed on heavy, brightly white watermarked paper. Fancy law firm stuff. The cover letter was brief, but telling. Conrad Lowry, writing to James—not James and me, I noted—explained the early autopsy findings were "summarized herein." He had withheld the "more unsavory details" but had included a few photographs he believed our father's child—again, no reference to me—deserved to see.

The letter couldn't have been more than eight sentences, but by the time I finished reading I was foaming mad. Clearly the meeting in Father's office between Lowry and James had made them chums; equally clearly, I was to be no part of any of it.

Secrets.

The thought of being excluded by my brother and a lawyer we barely knew more than to say hello to, the thought that their conspiracy involved my father and excluded me, sent me into an internal tantrum. It galvanized my conviction to get to the bottom of what was going on and to do so using any underhanded means I chose to employ. Not only was I smarter than my brother, I told myself, but more conniving. A woman develops her skills of manipulation from the first moment she gazes longingly into her father's eyes. By the time she's sixteen, that same man is handing her the keys to a new car, buying her a new dress for the prom, and assuring his wife, her mother, that their little girl is all grown up now and knows what she's doing.

Unfolding the photocopied pages contained in Lowry's letter, I saw a picture of what I assumed to be Father's belongings found on his person: wallet, cell phone, key ring, cash. Seeing his beloved fountain pen twisted my stomach and I nearly threw up. Alongside was a plastic evidence bag.

There were photos of the ladder and his body alongside. I turned away from them quickly, just couldn't look.

Next was even worse: color photocopies of the underside of a man's arm, the skin a sickly pale. I wouldn't have recognized the arm or the tiny tattoo if, along with the date and time, my father's name had not been printed in computer type at the bottom of the sheet along with the acronym BPDME (Boston Police Department Medical Examiner) running vertically along the side.

To say any one thing shocked me more than

another would be lying. The arm, the skin, the harsh lighting in the photograph, the fact this was my dead father's arm . . . But the tattoo was of a key with a tree growing out of it.

I took a mental photo of the tattoo—I would never forget it—my stomach threatening to empty. My brother had described such a tattoo on the arm of his attacker. I returned the paperwork to the envelope as I knocked on the door to the post office. Madame Mim answered the door, her chain-knit lavender sweater spotted with food stains, her wandering eye drifting. I explained the letter had been delivered incorrectly and asked her to please place it in my brother's mailbox. She was testy, clearly used to hearing such complaints. She grabbed the letter angrily and slammed the door in my face. Knowing Madame Mim, it would take her a day or two to figure out which mailbox to put it in; I thought that might give me a useful advantage.

The secret I knew that not even my brother did was the secret that Sherlock had been hiding from the others in the chapel on the night my brother and his pack had caught him there.

For what none of the boys had known that night—not even Sherlock—was that a certain girl had been hiding in the chapel balcony. A certain girl had witnessed it all, including what Sherlock had covered up with his shoe.

CHAPTER 32

A REBEL AND A THORN

I'M NOT SAYING I WAS SPYING ON HIM, BUT JAMES
left the Bricks early the morning of September 18th
and, instead of heading to breakfast in the dining
hall along with other early risers, he hoofed it over
to the school sundial. Poised in front of the Main
House and near the chapel, the alabaster sculpture
rose twenty feet in the air, with a winged Mercury
riding the top. Tiered steps encircled it, flaring like
a wedding cake to the lawn's freshly cut grass.

As my brother stood there studying the spire,
he withdrew a card from his blazer's side pocket
that I thought I recognized as the note from his

dry cleaning. He was obviously comparing the two images as he walked around the sundial in a slow, deliberate manner. I had no idea what he was looking for or at, and the tree I was hiding behind was as close as I was going to get to him.

I spotted something that caused my heart to jump. Having no idea if it meant anything or not, I had to make a note of it, or in this case, a drawing. I turned and pressed my back to the bark. Fully hidden from my brother at the sundial, I pulled out a pen. Lacking any paper, I drew onto my forearm. The image was of the sundial and the tall tree behind it. Drawn onto my arm there was no mistaking the similarity to the tattoo of the key found on Father's arm.

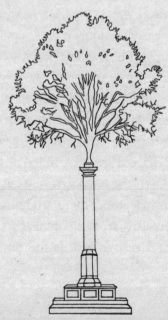

I stared in astonishment; the resemblance was uncanny. Coincidence? Did it mean something? I didn't have long to consider.

Unseen by my brother, the school chaplain approached him. An unusually short, balding man, as thin as paper, Chaplain Roger Browning had the reputation as a troglodyte (cave-dweller) who read in the evenings by candlelight and whose sermons were eerily knowledgeable of events in the Bricks of which even the masters and mistresses remained unaware.

Straining my ears, I made out most of their conversation.

"James."

"Chaplain Browning."

"I wanted once again to express my deepest condolences."

"Thank you for what you said at Father's memorial service. I didn't know you were here at Baskerville back when my father was."

"Oh, yes. I was something of a troublemaker back then. Your father was a rebel, for certain, but nowhere near the thorn that I was."

"Hard to believe."

"I simply wanted to say . . ."

A lumbering trailer truck passed by on the road

beyond the stone wall, obscuring my ability to hear.

" . . . What one sees and what one observes are often different."

"What am I seeing that I'm not observing?" James asked.

"Therein lies the difference between something staying the same, or progressing. If looking to progress, and I believe you are, never take the fast road, as it rarely produces satisfactory results. Fast roads will get us there quickly, but we often miss the most satisfying scenery."

"What are you saying, exactly?" James was cross. "The fast road to what, exactly? You think losing my father is easy? Seriously?"

"Heavens no. I'm saying hello, son, and passing along my condolences."

"What is the scenery thing, anyway? This scenery I'm missing?"

"Beauty is in the eye of the beholder," Chaplain Browning said. "In this case, the details as well."

"Well, that certainly clarifies things." My brother's dangerous temper was surfacing. The chaplain took a step back from James. "What can you tell me about this sundial?"

"What is it you want to know?" Browning continued to keep his distance.

"When was it built?"

"My goodness, I'm not certain anyone can answer that. Like the chapel, your great-grandfather had it brought over from Europe. It was installed here *to his specifications*. Exactly as he wanted it."

"It's marble."

"Italian marble. Yes."

"And the thing on top?" James asked.

He was referring to an X and P mounted at the peak of the sundial.

"It's the Chi-Rho symbol. The first two letters of the Greek *Khristos*, or 'Christ.' To many in ancient times, it represented the constellations Orion and Pleiades. To the Vatican as well. Did you know that seen from satellite, the layout of the Seven Hills of Rome and the Vatican's Piazza are a perfect representation of Orion and Pleiades?"

"Meaning?"

"Meaning it was carefully planned and constructed to mirror the sky. The Key of Solomon unlocks the mystery behind the constellations of the gods."

"A key?" James repeated almost breathlessly.

"Yes."

"Let me guess: Orion and Pleiades."

"Correct. It's all wrapped up in magic and secrecy. The Vatican in those times was filled with ritual and closely guarded secrets."

"Like *The Da Vinci Code*!" James said.

"Yes. That symbol is original to the sundial. Likely a kind of street sign, a marker that the traveler was either protected by a secret society or had arrived to his meeting place."

"And the marker was near the chapel, originally?"

"Oh, yes! Your grandfather had it placed *exactly* where it had been in relation to the chapel. In relation to the compass as well."

"What kind of secret society?"

Chaplain Browning smiled and folded his hands in front of himself. He wasn't going to answer.

James took a step closer.

I tried to remember the contents of the pages I'd seen while in Crudgeon's office. I'd skipped over what had looked like architectural drawings. I now wondered if I'd been too hasty.

My brother looked ready to punch the man in the face.

"James!" I called out, waving and walking toward the men.

"Oh, great. Just perfect," James said upon seeing me.

Chaplain Browning spun an about-face and headed for the chapel.

I had to think of something to explain my sudden appearance. "You going to breakfast?" I asked.

"I am," my brother answered.

"That's the chaplain, right?"

"Duh."

"What'd he want?"

"To tell me how sorry he is about Father. He says they were school chums, which I don't believe for a minute. The guy is the complete opposite of Father."

"You mean, he's alive?" I said, not knowing why I said it. Right now everything was about Father's death. Families ended. Lives ended. Everything ended. Most of them, like Mother and Father, long before they should. "Was that all? You looked kind of angry."

"I thanked him for the memorial service. I wasn't angry."

"I see."

There we were, brother and sister, best friends for life, lying to each other, and at a time we needed each other more than ever. I nearly told him about the key hidden in Father's office, how I'd missed my chance at it, how I felt it more important than any hunt for stupid clues or even the search for our family Bible. How I wouldn't rest until I found a way back to Boston, and into that room.

As it turned out, I shouldn't have been so ambitious.

CHAPTER 33

REUNION

CURIOSITY'S A BLESSING AND A CURSE. FATHER had always complimented me and James on how much of it we displayed, how "critical it is to clear thinking," words that I missed now but finally understood. Why, I wondered, did such valuable lessons have to come too late?

My curiosity was currently keeping me awake. Father used to walk to clear his mind, so in honor of him I decided to try it myself. I threw on some clothes and left the Bricks, headed for the sundial. Any middle student required a pass to leave the Bricks past 10 p.m., a pass I did not have. For this reason I crept around outside like a spy, moving shadow to shadow. I'm not the touchy-feely type; I don't go in for the hippie-dippie "everything's connected" theory of life. I fight off inexplicable coincidences as just that. But stuff happens. It just does. I think about a friend and five minutes later the phone rings—it's her. That kind of stuff.

So, when I witnessed a school maintenance cart being driven poorly, headlights off, bombing across the JV field, I paid special attention to its driver. I did this mainly because I'd witnessed James using just such a cart a week earlier. If not James, then who? Information could be a precious bargaining tool; I was learning things at Baskerville Academy.

To my surprise, it wasn't a maintenance person. It looked an awful lot like Sherlock Holmes.

Natalie's bicycle was one of those road-racing varieties with a million gears, a place for a water bottle, and a gel seat. She'd offered me riding permission and had given me the lock's combination.

As I pedaled furiously around the end of the Bricks, aimed toward the state road, I caught sight of a gray blur that I took to be the golf cart. Two minutes later, I confirmed my sighting. We were both off-campus racing toward an intersection with another state roadway. To the right, the direction Sherlock steered the cart, was Putnam, Connecticut, a nineteenth-century mill town in the midst of a modest revival. It was now home to two Indian restaurants, a good pizza parlor, a supermarket, and some craft shops run by people who dressed and acted like former hippies. I happened to know none of these was of interest to Sherlock Holmes. He was, without question, heading to the bus stop for the last ride to Boston of the night, the 10:42.

When I boarded the bus just before the door closed, Sherlock's eyes practically popped out of his head. I sat down next to him as if we'd planned this all along.

"How did you expect to get in without me?" I asked.

Wordlessly, he dug into his pocket and opened his hand, revealing my brother's key to our Beacon Hill home. "You're sweating," he said.

"Are you going to tell me what we're doing here?" I asked, shivering from a chill at the darkened back door to our house.

"Shh." Sherlock had been treating me like a dog deals with a twig caught in its tail. Snapping at me, not much else.

"What is it you hope to—"

"I think we might have been followed."

"Nonsense! You think someone's watching the bus station?"

"Once we were on foot. Once we hit cobble-stone. I heard someone."

"Cobblestones." I led him to the back of the house.

"I can't see anything."

I took James's key from him and let us in. "The trouble with boys," I told him, "is they have to do everything themselves. Girls are always a last option."

He grunted and closed the door behind us care-fully and quietly.

"Don't worry, no one's here," I said. "Not at night. Not anymore." London and Bath raced to greet us, nearly knocking me over. As I petted them and frolicked with them, I felt my throat tighten. Lois and Ralph were taking good care of them, but they were obviously lonely. I shouldn't have come back here so soon. "What are we doing here, any-way? Why did you get on the bus?"

"The Bible."

"What? Are you crazy? The Bible's hidden at school somewhere."

"No, it's not. It's here."

"That's ridiculous."

"The guys who broke in? The guys he told me about? Maybe they were hazing James as your father told you. Maybe, as James now thinks, they were after your father, but I don't think so."

"I don't need to hear this. And here I thought you were coming here to check out the photos I emailed you."

"In a way you're right. I am investigating your father's accident."

"That's better."

"He was found wearing weekend clothes—blue jeans, a nice shirt, and *formal* shoes. In *two* of the photos you sent, there are framed pictures of you, James, and your father in the background. In both, he's wearing nearly the same clothes, jeans and a casual shirt."

"I know the photos. They're in the foyer."

"But leather Top-Siders, not dress shoes."

"Meaning?"

"He was put into dress shoes to explain his slipping off the ladder. Furthermore, your father was left-handed."

"But how do you know—"

"The stepladder was positioned in a way to favor a right-handed person climbing to wind the wall clock. Your father didn't position the ladder, someone else did."

I couldn't feel my heart beating. "And he hated heights."

"Exactly! We don't know why your father might

have had the Bible, or if he even knew the Bible was in the house, but it's apparently worth killing for, and that's troubling."

"Whatever it contains, there's now a copy," I said, recalling the computer lab.

He missed that I had tears on my cheeks, or he just didn't care.

"We must find it," Sherlock said, "and we must take into consideration the headmaster's warning not to touch it. We can surmise it may be booby-trapped in some manner he deemed significant and therefore worthy of a warning. Do you hear me, Moria?"

"Barely."

"Where would your father hide such a thing?"

"He didn't. You're not right about this."

"I'm right about everything. Is that still news to you?"

"You're repugnant."

"You needn't be pugnacious. I'm not going to spar with you."

I reached for the wall switch. Sherlock caught my hand. "Neighbors. A torch?"

"We'll burn the house down?"

"Flashlight! You call it a flashlight!"

"Oh."

Negotiating the downstairs by a flashlight's

beam was creepy. Shadows moved as we moved. It was like the walls and floor were alive.

"The Bible isn't the most important thing," I said.

"Why not?"

"You need to get me into his office."

"Because?"

"I'll show you if I'm allowed."

"You're not making sense, Moria."

"You see, not everything makes sense."

"That's where you're wrong! You haven't given me all of the facts."

"Get me into his study and I'll give you more facts."

"Show me."

Father's study door was locked, just as I'd found it on the night I'd wandered from bed. I explained that I didn't even know the door had a lock, but that Lois probably had an extra key. That hardly mattered since she wasn't here.

"I thought about the window," I said, "but I'm sure it's locked. The hinges are on the inside. I saw a horror movie once where the killer took off the hinges and the door fell open. Terrifying."

"Fascinating," he said, irritated with me.

"If we break it, they'll know."

"The men who were here," Sherlock stated.

"Yes. It had to be one of them who locked it. Lois wouldn't have."

"Unless your father had left her instructions."

"Which is impossible since he left me instructions to go in there."

"Did he?"

"Don't rush me. Get me inside, genius."

Watching Sherlock work was like watching an art teacher sketch, or hearing a band leader play the trumpet. I began to find myself inside his complicated head as I tracked his eye movement, saw his thumb rubbing his index finger absentmindedly. I'd never had a boy intrigue me as this one did.

"His pants?" Sherlock said.

"What are you asking?"

"The pants he was wearing when . . . you know . . ."

"OK, then, *why* are you asking?" said I.

"His keys, of course. We don't have Lois, but there would have been at least two keys. Quite possibly a third put away for safekeeping in the event one or the other was lost." He paused. "His bedroom?"

I was immediately angry with him. Not because he was asking personal questions about my father but because I wondered: Why hadn't I thought of that? This was the maddening part of spending time with this particular boy: I couldn't help but feel inferior.

"There was a bag," I said. "His keys, wallet . . . the police."

"You know this because?"

"I may have intercepted a letter meant for James."

"May have? Did you copy it?"

"Oops."

"Do not tell me you did not think to copy it."

I didn't say a thing. I was glad it was basically dark so I didn't have to feel the weight of his scorn.

"Amateurs," he muttered. "Where is this bag?"

"The photos were taken at the police station."

"There are photos . . . plural?" He sounded exasperated. He placed his hand to his chin. "His belongings would have been turned over to someone."

"Lowry, our family attorney."

"Quite possible."

"If he didn't keep them, and he might have, then he'd have given them to Lois to do something with," I said. "You're right! His bedroom!"

Together, we followed the steady stream of yellowish light emanating from my hand. Upstairs. Past James's room. I opened the door, but couldn't go in, my shoulders already shaking.

"I've got it," said Sherlock tenderly, easing the flashlight from my white-knuckle grip.

I heard a plastic bag being messed with. The jingle of keys. I nearly squealed with joy. Had Sherlock told me that "most solutions are easy; we just like to make them hard," or had I dreamed it?

Minutes later, we'd sorted through the keys and Father's study door came open. "I need to do this by myself," I informed Sherlock for a second time. "I made a promise." To his credit, he didn't question my decision.

"That's fine," he said. "Just hurry, please."

I'd forgotten about his hearing someone following us.

I stepped inside.

CHAPTER 34

UNLOCKING A SECRET

FATHER'S OFFICE SMELLED SHUTTERED, THE AIR still and stale, my favorite scent of wood oil and leather slightly faint, as if Father had taken the goodness with him. Provoked by Sherlock's urgency, I directed the beam of light to the back of the fireplace and, switching hands, aimed the flashlight as I dug into the fluffy, dry ash.

Contact with the key sent electricity through my arm, into my chest, warming my heart. Father was the last to have touched this key, I thought. We had a tangible connection.

I hurried to his desk chair, catching my foot on

a rug and nearly face planting. Sherlock called in to me. I answered I was fine.

I was not fine: my heart was jumping around in my chest.

The key in my hand was all too familiar.

A gorgeous thing. A work of art, really. The tree leaves and limbs were tiny, threadlike wire. They were flat, not three-dimensional; they tickled my palm. A single gold wire wrapped around the tree trunk, adding a spark of color and making it even more exotic. It felt surprisingly heavy for such a small thing. Something more elusive emanated from it: power. It was as if the key had been struck by lightning and a good deal of the charge still remained. It connected to the man who'd challenged James near the soccer field, to Father, to the invisible-ink clue. I sensed it truly was the key to all of this.

It fit into a single drawer, that which Father had pointed out: the top-most drawer to the right. I turned the key. The lock mechanism was fluid and smooth. I slid open the drawer and aimed the light.

Inside was his passport. I took it out. It bulged with added visas and weather-warped pages.

"Lock . . ." I mumbled. "Lock, come in here, please."

Standing behind me, he nudged my hand for the flashlight and placed his head practically inside the drawer.

"Nothing," I moaned. "Only his passport. He traveled a lot, but believe me, James and I already knew that. Do you think it was Lowry or maybe one of the other mystery men who emptied it?"

"It's not exactly empty," Sherlock announced in that annoying tone of his. "It simply doesn't happen to have anything inside it."

"Not now, OK? Sometimes that stuff's cute, but not right now."

"Think, Moria. If Lowry had emptied it—if anyone had!—then why leave the passport and why return the key to the ashes? That is illogical to the point of absurdity. In point of fact, he left you something on the back panel. Here, help me." He handed me back the flashlight while he deciphered how to release the drawer from the guides that secured it. The drawer came free and he plunked it down onto the blotter. As I moved the beam of light, I saw it: words had been burned into the wood of the drawer's back panel, like with a branding iron.

whenallthat'sleftisright

Sherlock grabbed a piece of notepaper from Father's leather desk organizer. He wrote down the message, carefully checking it for accuracy. Then he turned the drawer over, pulled on each panel, tried everything in the world to make the thing come apart, and returned it to the desk.

"What are you doing?" I asked.

"You're going to lock it and return the key."

"That's all?"

"Do you have a better idea?"

"What's it mean? We have to do something."

"We did something," Sherlock said. "I wrote it down. That's something." He pocketed the note-paper.

"But *what's it mean?*"

"I don't know any more than you do. Another

puzzle, another clue. We will make sense of it, Moria, but not here, not now. We're taking too long. We need to find the Bible and get out of here."

"The Bible isn't—"

"Don't start with me! I humored you, now you humor me." Sherlock left the room. A minute later I found him wandering the foyer. He peered into the blue sitting room, the dining room, and finally the library. I followed Sherlock through the kitchen. He moved around effortlessly, as if he knew the place. "His study is too obvious," he said. "You knew the man. So where would he hide it, Moria?"

"Don't scold me!" I heard something outside the front door and I shushed him. "Did you hear that?" I whispered.

"I'm not scolding," he said, also in a whisper. "And I didn't hear anything, but as you know, I'm concerned we may have been followed. I don't want someone finding two more ladders."

"You really are an awful boy."

"Insensitive of me, admittedly. Apologies."

"Not accepted."

"Understood."

"I don't have any idea where he might have hidden it," I said.

"Others will have looked for it. Searched top to bottom. Carefully. Efficiently. Perhaps they've found it, but for now we will assume it remains in place. For one thing, having made the search public, the headmaster would likely call off the hunt the moment it surfaced."

"How would he know any of this?" I asked.

Sherlock said nothing, but looked at me funny.

"Crudgeon's involved?"

"Most certainly. Motive, unclear. Degree of involvement, unclear. But involved? Yes. Little question of that. Is there a cellar?"

"It's damp. Father wouldn't put any books down there, no matter how carefully wrapped or packaged. He treats books with the utmost respect. Mind you, I think you're wrong about this."

"Did he have a home safe?"

"I hate the past tense."

"Sorry. Someplace he locked up important documents?"

"Not that I know of. And if he d . . . did . . ." I stuttered, "I wouldn't know the combination anyway. James might, I suppose."

"I think he'd want you and James to be able to find it. 'When all that's left is right.' He would have thought ahead. Where would he think you or James might look?"

"You know what, Lock? You scare me."

"I don't mean to."

"Not that kind of scary. Scary-smart. He's always told me and James that the best place to hide something is out in the open. The thing is, we never asked him about such things. He would just randomly bring it up at dinner. And not just once, either! It got to where James and I would kick each other under the table when he started into it." The memory clenched my throat.

"So, something missing, or something added," Sherlock said. "The genius is that only a family member would know such a thing. Brilliant! It's an unbreakable code." He wandered the foyer. "I am positive your house has been searched. No wonder it wasn't found."

"Again, so confident."

"For the same reasons I just told you. I'm right about this."

I looked around with fresh eyes. It was strange to see my family home and everything in it as a kind of stranger.

"It might be a painting. A rug. A piece of furniture. It might be something that's been moved from one room to another. It's here, and he's left you a clue to find it."

"Don't get weird about this, okay? Just let me look around." We wandered the ground floor. I was in the lead, with Sherlock a step behind. The family portraits, the Charles River landscapes, the marble-top dressers, the stained-glass lamps. Everything in its place. The kitchen had never been made modern, other than some new appliances. Miss Delphine worked in a space that hadn't been remodeled since the 1970s. The decorative copper pots were where they'd always been, the wall clock. Nothing fancy. Nothing changed.

"I'm not sure what I'm looking for," I confessed to Sherlock.

"It's okay, Moria. You're doing great."

We were prowling the downstairs library—yes, we had two libraries in our home—when I stopped. A distracted Sherlock bumped into me and stepped back. "What?"

"Oh, dear," I said.

"What?" he said more anxiously.

"See the theme?"

"I'd be blind if I didn't!"

Our downstairs library housed a coffee table fashioned to look like three gigantic books stacked flat. Each spine opened as a drawer. There were bookends of the same leather-bound look. There was a box made to look like a stack of fake books that Father used as a catch-all for pencils and rubber bands. A credenza with leather spines facing out.

"That lamp," I said, pointing. "It's new." It stood on a small French table at the side of a vast leather chair where Father read in the evenings. The lamp's design was similarly themed: a wrought-iron stand, a large book facing out contained in a wrought-iron cage, and a lampshade of animal hide. It was a gorgeous thing, but I'd never seen it before.

Sherlock craned his lanky frame over to read the title. "*On the Origin of Species*, Charles Darwin."

"Fake as well," I said. "See? It's wood. Painted like gold-edged pages."

"But it's new?"

"It is to me," I said.

"Then," Sherlock said, reaching for the wall plug, "we must take it apart."

"What? No! Why?"

He worked quickly, toying with the brass "rope" used as a pin to lock shut the cage surrounding Darwin's oversized book. "How clever," he said, unscrewing the "rope." "This design, this knot, is called a monkey fist. Get it?"

"No, I don't get it," I said caustically. He was growing tedious on me.

"Darwin's theory of evolution involves apes and man. Monkey fist."

"Ha ha," I said, bored.

"And think of this: if it was locked with a real padlock, then it would draw more attention to itself. But this is just a pin, easily opened, so how could it be hiding anything important. See?"

"Just get it over with, would you? It's late, real late, and I'm not enjoying being back here."

Sherlock muttered excitedly, something about how the lamp's construction hid the wiring inside the cage. "Meaning the book is free and clear, Moria. Usually, the wires go straight up through a tube to the bulb. Why the more elaborate design? I'll tell you why—"

"There's a surprise."

"So one can remove the contents. That's why." Either the wooden book was heavy, or Sherlock weak. He carried it with some difficulty to the floor, where it thumped onto Father's oriental carpet. He stood it up, examining it from all sides.

"It's a big piece of wood, Lock. Nice try." I wasn't sure he'd heard me, so intense was his concentration.

He didn't look up as he spoke. "Magnifying glass on the dictionary, far corner."

I looked over behind my father's desk, astonished to see a large magnifying glass lying on the page of the open dictionary. I wondered what else this strange boy had seen that I'd missed. I delivered the glass to him, knowing that he was instructing me like a servant. He held his eye to the lens, distorting his face, and then lowered it to the upright wooden book. He mumbled and muttered and spoke to himself. I didn't understand a word. "Yes, yes, yes," he eventually said. "Clever. So very clever."

"What is it?"

Still without looking up or acknowledging me he issued another order. "Paper clip." He held his left hand out, palm up and open.

"Yes, master," I said, annoyed with him. But I did as he asked. Just before I dropped it into his hand he spoke again.

"Unfold it! What do you think I want it for?"

"I have no idea what you want it for!" I protested.

"The tiniest, the smallest of holes, just at the corner here. Some glue or wood putty sealing it. The color is off only fractionally. It's a very good job of it."

"A nail hole?"

"Think, Moria! Think! A reasonable deduction, but flawed. Why only one? If the entire piece is glued and done so by a true craftsman so the lines are nearly imperceivable, then why a single nail hole?"

"I was asking, that's all."

"Then he must have been counting on James to

find this, not you."

"James took wood shop."

"Well, there you have it. Makes me all the more confident."

"Of?" Having carefully unbent the paper clip, I handed it to him.

Magnifying glass in hand, Sherlock lowered the paper clip like a pin. It came to rest and he pushed once, hard. I heard a pop.

The lid of the box opened just like the cover of a book.

I reached for our family Bible.

CHAPTER 35

WAKING TO A NIGHTMARE

"You're making this a habit," James said, sitting on the edge of an unfamiliar bed. Then I placed it: the school infirmary.

"What? Where?"

The nurse came to the foot of the bed. "Ah, there we are!"

"What do you remember?" James said. I heard the deep concern in his voice, and I considered trying to drag out his sympathy.

"He was shouting at me not to touch it."

"Who? What?"

I realized I had better figure out what was going

on before volunteering too much information. I had no real memory, just fireflies orbiting my head. "Or was that a dream?" I said, trying to cover my mistake while I gathered my senses.

"You were found passed out by the sundial."

"Was I?"

"Natalie found you."

"Sekulow?"

"Who else? Yes. She was worried about you. You weren't in your bed when she woke up from a nightmare at three o'clock last night. She didn't report you right away—see who got the good roommate? Once she found you, she called for help. You're lucky."

"The sundial?" I remembered Sherlock's face. Had there been a box? I wondered. Sherlock had shouted a warning at me right before everything had gone dark. But not like unconsciousness—more like a sack being pulled over my head. That was it! I recalled faintly. A hood. My hands slapping something soft. Or was that just my imagination?

"I couldn't sleep," I said.

"So you violated curfew?" James said. "I told you I would protect you!" He sounded so angry. "How do you expect me to protect you if you go wandering around campus in the middle of the night?"

My head hurt. The nurse saw me reach to my forehead.

"I have some ice water," she said, moving it to my side table. It bought me a moment to think. My mouth tasted like I'd eaten a sandalwood candle, not that I was in the habit of eating sandalwood candles.

My room held two hospital beds and a window that looked out onto the gym. A metal end table held a pink plastic vomit-dish and my water cup. I felt queasy looking at that color pink. No wonder people vomited. "So Sherlock didn't care enough to stop by?" I tried to sound like a jilted teen. It wasn't that difficult.

"He's AWOL. He's toast. He'll be suspended, no question. Maybe expelled." James sounded far too satisfied by the prospect of that outcome.

I sat up sharply. My head ached horribly. I thought I might throw up. "What's wrong with me? I feel horrible."

"There, there, child." The nurse eased me back and fed me a straw. The water tasted of the plastic cup. It was delicious, nonetheless. "Easy . . . easy . . . that's enough for now."

I'd been found by the school sundial. Sherlock was missing. What was going on?

"Why can't I remember anything? It was dark.

There were trees. Blurred trees."

I saw Sherlock's face lit by pulsing light. He'd been with me. I spoke without thinking, my headache owning me. "Lock never made it back to your room?"

"What's that supposed to mean? He was with you?"

"It means . . . you're saying he missed curfew?" I'd spoken too quickly and James picked up on it.

"What do you mean by 'back to' our room? Was he with you?" he repeated, a dog recognizing a scent. "Where were you two? Did he talk you into meeting him somewhere? I'll bash his head in! He hurt you and then fled campus?" Every muscle in James's body tensed. I'd never seen him quite like this. For a moment, for an infinitesimal amount of time, I actually considered lying to my brother to see what he would do to defend me and my honor.

"James! No! Nothing like that! I have no memory of anything. I have no idea how I ended up here. Sherlock did not invite me to anything. Believe me, I'd remember that! James, do you hear me?" I waited, terrified I'd unintentionally wronged Sherlock. I realized how only a few words had gotten James thinking all the wrong things. "I'm just *concerned* about him," I said, trying to look embarrassed by the admission. It didn't take much.

"I like him, James. You know I do! Don't be like this!" I could see his anger brewing. "I don't want him suspended. I don't want him in any trouble."

For once, I wasn't lying to my brother. I had no idea why I'd been found by the sundial, or what, if anything, Sherlock had to do with it.

Looking down, I saw a bandage on the inside of my elbow. James saw me looking.

"They're testing your blood, Mo," he whispered as he leaned in as if to adjust my pillow.

"Why?" I asked, equally confidentially.

His eyes softened. "They think maybe you touched the Bible. Remember Headmaster's warning us?"

"The Bible? Jamie, I'm scared. I've never been unable to remember stuff before. Do you think that's possible? Do you think . . . our family Bible?"

"No clue. But they think so." He stroked my hair. "Don't worry. I'm going to figure this out."

"Sherlock is innocent, James."

"Sure he is." He took my hand. His was warm, nearly hot to the touch.

I reached for the pink bowl.

CHAPTER 36

A MOST WELCOME VISITOR

THE NEXT TIME I OPENED MY EYES, THE WIN-
dow looked hollow, black with night. My room
glowed in the frightful pallor of tube lighting. I
heard rats scratching the floor. I dropped my jaw to
release a shriek when a head popped up. Sherlock,
with a long, bony finger pressed to his lips. "Shh!"

"You about scared me to death!" I said, too
loudly for his liking. Only then did I process the
smudges of dirt on his face, his tousled hair and
bloodshot eyes. "You look horrible."

"Quiet, please." He moved toward the door,
glanced carefully into the hallway, and eased the

door shut, leaving it open an inch.

"What . . . is . . . going on?" I asked.

"I'm not officially here. Not exactly on campus," he said hoarsely. "You might say I'm visiting."

"James said you didn't come back to the room last night. Was it last night?" I'd lost all track of time.

"How could I?" he asked.

I must have offered a blank expression.

"You don't remember?" he said. He followed with a brief explanation. "The Bible? Your father's house? I escaped. You weren't as lucky. I did everything I could, Moria, but I was outnumbered. There were at least three of them. My only choice was to run. I felt horrible. Your driver saved me."

"Ralph!"

"Yes. First he tackled me, then he saved me."

"Tackled?"

"I ran out the back door. I set up for an attack, but misjudged. The abductors removed you from the house out the front door. Bold of them, I might add. By the time I could get myself straight, you and the Bible were gone."

"The Bible? It was at our house?"

"You honestly don't remember *any* of this?"

I shook my head, embarrassed by the tears spilling down my cheeks. Sherlock took my hand and squeezed. "It's all right. It's all going to be OK."

I doubt my expression altered. Holding my hand, he noticed something or was looking for something. He turned my wrist and studied my fingers. "Excellent! Exactly as I'd suspected." He gave my hand back to me. I appreciated such spontaneity and enthusiasm; members of the Moriarty family were not allowed to show such emotion.

"Why were you crawling around under my bed?"

"Not exactly crawling around. Collecting evidence. Investigating."

"Investigating what?"

"What have they done with your clothes?" he asked.

I hadn't noticed that I was wearing a hospital gown. I pulled up the sheet. "How would I know?"

"One moment." He checked the drawers of my end table. Not finding any clothes, he spun around searchingly and approached the sliding doors to a small closet. "Found them!" he said.

"You stay out of there! Keep away from those!"

"Shhhh! There's a nurse on duty down the hall!"

"I'll scream for help if you don't shut that door at once."

"Moria!" He pulled out a sleeve to my uniform shirt and . . . he buried his face in it, *sniffing*. Few things have disgusted me as much, embarrassed me as much. It was a creepy, unsettling moment and as desperately as my brain wanted to listen to him, my instincts took over.

"STOP THAT!" I shrieked.

Both of us froze with my outburst. I regretted it immediately. In a panic, he shut the closet, headed for the window and—

The door to the room swung open, revealing a nurse.

He might have dived or flown. He'd vanished. I supposed that diving out a third-story window would either kill you or land you back in the infirmary. But he deserved it. When I felt my mattress sag, I realized he was under my bed, hanging from the mattress's springed support.

"Moria? What's wrong, sweetheart?" Made frantic by my crying out, the night nurse looked around the room, spotted the open window, and shut it. "That's odd," she said.

"I . . . it must have been a nightmare," I said. "Someone put a sack over my head . . ." It didn't take much to start me crying.

She said comforting things to me, helped me with my pillow. If a pen had not slipped out of her dress pocket, she wouldn't have noticed the damp grass clippings on the floor. With a few clippings pinched between her fingers as evidence, she spoke quietly. "Boys have no business visiting you after hours, Moria. I know at this age it feels like you can't stand to be apart for a single minute, but if I catch *any student in my infirmary after hours*"— she intentionally raised her voice—"he will face disciplinary action." She hesitated. "I'll return in a moment to inspect your room thoroughly. I suspect you might need a minute to collect yourself. I'll only be a moment."

Assuming I had a visitor, she was generously giving me a chance to get my "suitor" out. Sherlock seized the opportunity, coming out from under my bed, kissing my hair, and climbing out the window onto the roof.

His invasion of my privacy rattled me. I'd had time to settle down. Sherlock had been looking at my shoes, sniffing my clothes, and . . .

I pulled on a string and switched on the light. I looked at my fingers, just as Sherlock had. I gasped as the nurse returned through the door. Slipping my hand beneath the covers, I wondered why my fingertips were stained a copper brown.

CHAPTER 37

OVERPOWERED, UNDERPREPARED

Some of what follows I had to be told twice, as my memory continued to play tricks on me. My experience had put me in a delicate state—something I was ashamed to admit to others. I learned soon enough that it is best to be honest about one's health and feelings, that you can't be helped if no one knows you need helping.

I so enjoy having people depend on me. You have no idea! You also have no choice now but to trust me when I tell you what happened next:

In need of fresh clothes, Sherlock headed toward the Bricks immediately. His visit to the infirmary had caused him no end of worry about being caught, but he needed clothes before he left campus. His few discoveries about me and my condition had also thrown him into a state of agitated excitement. He elected to circumvent the open playing fields and hold close to the Bricks, hunching beneath the lower dorm windows so as not to be seen. Stepping inside the lower entrance to Bricks 3 and 4, he spun around to ease the door's panic bar in order to shut it quietly.

He was instantly lifted off his feet and dragged backward while simultaneously being blindfolded and having a pair of athletic socks stuffed into his mouth. Clean socks, thankfully.

A door was closed. The smell of disinfectant wafted. He knew at once he was inside Brunelli's janitor closet.

"We're good," a boy's voice said. Sherlock recognized it as belonging to Bret Thorndyke.

Grit scraped beneath his shoes. The odor changed to one of overheating, like a basement room where the ironing was done. The boys pushed, dragged, and lowered him through a hole. For a moment he feared they were burying him alive. But no. He found himself sitting on what felt like a large pipe.

He began talking, the sock making things difficult.

"I'm going to remove the sock," James said. "You scream and you'll wish you hadn't. Nod, if you understand."

Sherlock said nothing.

"I said: nod."

Sherlock spit the socks out without any help. "I'm not a screamer," he said. "I find it vulgar. As to the blindfold, it's completely unnecessary. There's Mr. Richmond, Mr. Thorndyke, Mr. Knight, and you, James. We are confined in a subterranean utility area of some sort—interesting, I must say—that's accessed by Brunelli's closet."

One of the older boys said a cuss word.

Sherlock continued. "Allow me to explain, as you don't believe I could possibly know any of this."

"No thanks," said James.

But Sherlock wasn't to be quieted. His adrenaline had him feeling frantic. "Mr. Thorndyke spoke, so he was easy. Mr. Richmond wears an overpowering sports deodorant that's more like perfume. There's not a student in the school unfamiliar with its stench. Identifying Mr. Knight was more difficult. It's down to process of elimination, previous sightings, and odds. Could have been Ryan Eisenower. But I'm quite certain I'm right. May I remove the blindfold, please?"

"Go ahead."

Sherlock looked around at four angry faces. The tunnel's existence interested him more. He drank in the details. "Of course," was all he said.

"You nearly got my sister killed."

"Incorrect, James. I have followed our agreement to the letter."

"Liar."

"Rarely. Occasionally, when the situation leaves me no choice. This is not one of those, I promise you."

"You're going to tell me everything you know about what's going on. Then you're going to stay away from my sister and pretend this meeting never happened."

"You've been watching far too much television, James. Might I suggest a good book instead? You're speaking in clichés."

He spoke unkindly to James.

"But since you are steeped in the lore of motion picture," Sherlock said, "allow me to reference *A*

Few Good Men and its most memorable line, 'You can't handle the truth,' which in this case happens to be spot on."

"Try me."

"Oh, James. Really . . . Look, partial truth is poison. It has urged many a person in the wrong direction only to realize, too late, they should have waited for all the information, not acted on a poor sample. I'm close, James. Until I know the whole truth, I'd be hurting, not helping."

"Waiting."

"Moria is a curious one, something I cannot help. You know what they say about the cat. How well do you trust these cretins?" Sherlock took in James's gaggle.

"You can speak."

"Your father's fall from that ladder is likely so much fiction. Staged, is a more promising explanation. I'll know more soon. When the Bible is announced as having been found—and it will be announced soon—you should insist on viewing its contents. With gloves, of course. It is your right to view it, as a member of the family, is it not? Furthermore, I think the administration's reaction to that request would prove most informative."

"Speak English," Thorndyke said.

"Shut your trap!" James said, chiding the upperclassman.

Thorndyke accepted the rebuke, again informing Sherlock of the leadership position assumed by James.

"I'm listening."

"The others are not. What say we make this between the two of us, James? Being as we're roommates and all."

"Go," James directed the three. "Quietly. We'll meet upstairs in Three's lounge."

If looks could kill, Sherlock thought.

When Sherlock and James were alone, Sherlock lowered his voice and carefully chose his words.

"Your father took back what was rightfully his— the Bible—and hid it in your Beacon Hill home."

Only a few weeks earlier, James would have interrupted his roommate, this odd British student, would have contradicted him at every opportunity. James was no longer that same boy.

Sherlock had expected such an interruption, was taken aback when it failed to occur.

"He," Sherlock said, "was involved in something either dangerous or secret. Do you know the nature of that, James?"

"No idea." Again, James didn't question

Sherlock or react disapprovingly.

"I surmised as much about your father, and took it upon myself to investigate both the situation as explained and also in terms of the evidence. Unfortunately, Moria followed me. You must believe me, James; I had no idea such a thing might be possible. I took every precaution. But there she was, climbing onto the bus last night. We reached Boston, and Moria called your driver. We asked to be dropped off away from the house. We entered the house from the garden and were careful to not switch on lights or make any indication the house was occupied. After some time I had confirmed some of my suspicions about your father's accident, namely that it wasn't an accident. I can go into more detail if you like."

"Room check's coming up. We have to hurry. But yes, of course I want to know. Tell me about Moria."

"She and I located the Bible. It was hidden in the library."

"Unbelievable . . ." James uttered softly.

"Oh, you must believe me!"

"It's an expression, Holmes. Hurry it up!"

"Someone had followed us. I would question the loyalty of your driver, but—"

"Impossible. Ralph's family!"

"Yes, he would later prove himself to me several times over."

"Come on!"

"We were attacked. As Moria reached for the Bible, I tried to stop her. My attention waned, I'm afraid. She grabbed hold of it just as a hood was placed over her head. A hood was intended for me as well, but I have studied the Eastern defensive arts—have I shared that with you? I'm only a yellow belt, but it proved enough to avoid the intentions of this lout. I escaped, took up hiding, and misjudged my opponents. They used the front door, not the back. I missed my opportunity to rescue your dear sister."

"Do not call her that!"

"I encountered Ralph on my way out the back. We returned to where Ralph had left the car and he generously offered to return me to school. One thing I must make note of at this juncture, James: at no time did Ralph suggest we should alert the authorities to those cretins absconding with your . . . sister."

"The cops. You're saying he didn't suggest calling the cops."

"Precisely so."

"Ralph, Lois, they are like family, and they

know how the press thrives on stories of the wealthy. Like it or not, my family is rich. Father avoided all the press. He was obsessed with it."

"Yes," Sherlock said.

"What's that supposed to mean? As if you knew him!"

"I meant no disrespect. Apologies. What I can tell you is this: Moria was not to be found upon my return. Ralph remained on standby . . . he was so concerned. I called him just now."

"You . . . what?"

"I promised to call when I found her."

"And?"

"That's it. Honestly, there's nothing more."

"I know you, Sherlock. There's more."

"Speculation, entirely."

"So? Try me."

"All right, but keep in mind, it's only so much fiction until proven."

"I got it."

"The Bible plays a bigger role than a family record keeper, or, if that's all it is, then there are records of your family within it that might tarnish the family reputation, including that of Baskerville. People have broken into your house, not once but twice, in order to regain control of it."

"What people?"

329

"Unclear. As I said, something dangerous or secret, or both. Great efforts have been taken, and at great risk. I believe the Bible to be protected by a chemical, a drug if you like, that renders the handler semiconscious and, later, with little recollection of events of the hour or hours leading up to and following contact. A chemical amnesia. Again, this supports the seriousness of its contents. Moria was taken to a confined space following her abduction. This I know. She was possibly questioned, and likely had little or no defense against speaking the truth."

"A truth serum? This isn't a game!"

"Not a serum—the same substance on the Bible that renders one amnesic and semiconscious makes the victim subject to speaking the truth. I remind you: entirely speculative on my part."

"I'd say. And the clues?" James sounded worried and distraught.

"I can't imagine how this must be for you, James."

"Will you shut up? I don't need mothering."

"It's called friendship. We've talked about—"

"Shh! Listen!"

Someone was inside the janitor closet.

James switched off the tunnel lights.

"We separate," he whispered. "At least they'll

only catch one of us." James moved in the direction of Main House. Sherlock stumbled through the dark in the opposite direction—Bricks 4 and the end of the dorms. The tunnel lights came back on. James ran, making himself smaller and smaller. Sherlock used the light to climb atop the pipes and wedge himself under a wire caddy. He lay on his side, facing out.

"What in tarnation is going on down there?" Brunelli's gruff voice. Sherlock wasn't the kind of boy to be scared of others—he considered himself so superior—but the janitor for Bricks 3 and 4 was no one to mess with. "Who's down there?"

Sherlock's chosen position was no accident. The location of the light nearest him would help blind a person looking up at him.

It took the old goat over a minute to climb down into the cramped tunnel. Sherlock could imagine him looking in both directions. James wouldn't be recognizable, and Brunelli would have no chance to catch him. Sensing another boy was involved, he moved toward Sherlock's position.

"It ain't properly right for you boys to be down here! You hear me? It'll get you tossed sure as Sinbad. I ain't reportin' you this time, but final warning: boys been trying to sneak around in this here tunnel for long as I can remember, and you won't see none a them names in no yearbooks. Mind my words. You'll be going home you do this again." The lights switched off. The trapdoor clomped shut.

Sherlock didn't move in case the man had a surprise in store. He waited a full forty-five minutes before leaving his perch. He worked his way in the dark all the way to the end of Bricks 4, where another trapdoor found him in a janitor closet. He took the exit outside.

"Well! What have we got here?" It was Mr. Cantell. He stood smoking a cigarette.

"I didn't know you smoked," Sherlock said.

"You make too much of your own intelligence, Mr. Holmes. What you know and don't know is lost on you because you convince yourself you have no match. In this you are delusional and sadly mistaken."

"What will Headmaster think of your habit?"

"Headmaster enjoys a fine cigar himself on Saturday nights when the wife's otherwise engaged. That, along with a brandy or two. You see what I mean, Mr. Holmes? Do not attempt to threaten a person such as myself until and unless you know you possess the requisite material or evidence to support such an effort."

"I'll remember that. And so should you, Master Cantell."

"You see? Another veiled threat!"

"Not veiled at all," Sherlock said.

"We will visit Dr. Crudgeon, you and I," he said, dramatically twisting the toe of his shoe onto the cigarette. "Wipe the cobwebs out of your hair and make yourself at least somewhat presentable. You know how Headmaster appreciates decorum."

CHAPTER 38

DECODING

"SHERLOCK!" I SAID, AS NASTILY AS I COULD given that I was whispering. "What are you doing in there? You scared the wits out of me!" He was pressed between my favorite navy blue skirt and a top I'd given up on because it showed my middle. "Get off my shoes! Those are expensive!"

He stepped out of my closet. "I'm glad you're better," he said.

The thing about friends—real friends—is that you pick up a conversation as if you've never left the other's side. Sherlock and I had crossed that threshold at some point. We didn't spend a lot of time dancing around the topic at hand. In this case, there were many topics to address, and we both understood our time was short.

"What were those stains on my fingers?" I asked.

"I need your assistance," he said.

"I heard you were expelled."

"Suspended," he said, correcting me, "until Monday. Most unfortunate. An interesting punishment that makes so little sense except to draw attention to itself. Why do you suppose Crudgeon wants me off campus for the next four days?"

"And my clothes. Why'd you smell my clothing? That was strange, FYI, but I'm going to give you a chance to explain yourself."

"And I would if I could, but I can't. September twenty-first. Nine-two-one-seven-three-seven. The numbers below the sundial on the note placed anonymously into James's pocket? You see? Sunrise on September twenty-first—that's today—is six thirty-seven a.m."

"I don't see . . . no."

"Nine-two-one. September is the ninth month. The twenty-first day: two-one. Today. Sunrise is . . . was at six thirty-seven. The note calls for exactly one hour later: seven three seven. Seven thirty-seven a.m. I have"—he checked his wristwatch, an old battered thing—"twenty-one minutes to be in disguise."

"Disguise?"

"I'm suspended. I can't very well walk around campus looking like this."

"Walk around?"

"I have these," he said, producing some balls of hair. "Borrowed them from the theater department." The pieces uncurled in his hand. A beard and mustache, I was guessing. "But I know little about the application of cosmetics. It's something I must study, apparently. Could you?"

"I'm in my pajamas, in case you didn't notice," I said. "I have an exam this morning."

"It's early yet."

"Did you sleep in there?"

"Maybe just a catnap," he said.

"I don't like boys sleeping in my closet."

"It's wildly uncomfortable, if you must know. I can't see it becoming a thing."

"Get out of there this instant." I pulled him out. "Stay here. I have to warn Natalie and Jamala there's a boy in our room. They're showering."

I took off, in part to clear my head. I warned off my roommates, borrowed a neighbor's robe, and returned to the room.

"What about your costume?" I asked as I used some watered-down glue to stick on his facial hair. I used both eyebrow pencil and gray eyeliner to give him fans at the edges of his eyes and worry lines in his forehead. I made his cheeks slightly hollow—not tricky on such a skinny boy—and his mouth to turn down into a frown.

"Theater department. I hung it up in your closet. The college professor, mad-scientist look."

"I sleep too heavily."

"Natalie snores," he said.

"Tell me about it." I cut him off before he actually did, though I could listen to that accent of his for hours. "It's an expression!"

"Ah-ha! Right! Eleven minutes."

"Don't do that! You're making me nervous. I'll have you looking like an ogre."

"Just as long as the ogre doesn't look like me, I'm all set."

"Voilà!" I held up my hand mirror to his face. He scrunched his nose, squinted, frowned. Smiled. Turned his head this way and that.

"Excellent job, Moria."

"Of course it's excellent," I said.

"Careful now. Imitation is the most sincere form of flattery."

I wanted to kick him. Instead, I held up my hand. "My fingers. You were interested in the stains."

"*The Name of the Rose*," Lock said. "Great book. You should read it. Monks. Murder. What could be better? Headmaster warned us, warned us all, not to touch the Bible. It wasn't ink on your fingers, it was some kind of amnesia drug."

He told the same story I would later hear he'd told James. The more I heard the more vulnerable and afraid I felt. I didn't appreciate blacking out for an entire twelve hours. Ick.

"You're better now, that's what counts."

"But why smell my clothes? That was perverted! And crawling around to look at my shoes? What was that all about?" I asked.

"James," he said. "It's about James. I will explain, I promise. But now, if you'll turn your back, I need to change into my suit."

A visiting professor with full facial hair walked across the school lawn toward Main House as the tower clock neared 7:37 a.m. James was standing at the base of the school sundial looking lost. Technically, the sun had risen exactly an hour earlier, but at the moment of the autumn solstice—an hour past sunrise—the sundial cast its shadow forward, down its steps and onto the surrounding marble pedestal. There, a single gray, rectangular stone was inlaid, seemingly out of place until the moment arrived.

"Morning," the older guy said.

James nervously regarded the passing stranger, several yards off. "Morning."

The professor nodded and continued on his way.

In front of James, an unusual phenomenon was occurring. The sun caught the ancient symbol—the X and the P—atop the sundial, throwing a most unexpected shadow onto the errant gray stone. It formed a perfect cross intersected by what looked like a key.

But more unique, the shadow covered up enough of the odd stone to leave only a discolored area of the stone showing: an unmistakable arrow pointing to the chapel.

Seconds later, the images crept forward and dissolved, absorbed by the grass.

Sherlock stayed the course, still heading for the Main House. At the last moment, as James opened and then pulled the heavy door closed, Sherlock sprinted for the chapel. His mustache flew off his upper lip. He pulled the chapel door open only inches and slipped inside, immediately crossing the vestibule, and ascending the stairs into the balcony. He saw James turn and look back toward him. Believing he'd been spotted, Sherlock nearly called out. Then it occurred to him to pivot and look behind him. There, the chapel's enormous rosary window glowed as if divinely illuminated. Its colors shone like never before. Sherlock couldn't take his eyes off the window exploding in colors.

Perhaps a minute passed before a shaft of light broke free from a disc of glass at the window's perfect center. The beam strengthened and shifted, traveling with the movement of the sun, first a knife blade then a full-fledged spotlight. Its brightness caught the millions of flecks of dust in the air, swirling like snowflakes. It bored across the distance of the chapel, above the nave, concentrating its focused, blazing energy onto a center wooden panel behind the altar along the chancel's curving back wall.

As quickly as it had arrived, it was gone.

Sherlock watched as James looked down. He heard him gasp as James spotted the inlay of the key in the floor stone. Sherlock had a decision to make. Worried for James, he moved quickly down the stairs, and up the nave.

"You're meant to open it," Sherlock called out, disguising his British accent in favor of a gravelly Brooklyn drawl.

James watched the older professor shuffling toward him. "I saw you outside! Who are you?"

"A friend. The center panel will open, I think you will find." Sherlock stopped far enough away to maintain his anonymity. Another yard or two and James would certainly spot the boy beneath the disguise.

James didn't appreciate the company. "What's it to you?"

Sherlock didn't answer at first. "It won't be easily found," Sherlock said in his own voice. "The key is the key."

"Is that you? Seriously? What the heck?"

"The door will lead to the organ pipes." Sherlockian voice again. "A play on words, you see? Music has keys. If you will allow me, I'd like to help."

"You don't quit."

"No, regrettably. Not in my nature. It's for Moria I'm doing this, not you, James, if that's of any consequence. Not sporting the way they dealt with her. I'd like to get this all behind us. Please," he added, finding the word difficult to say.

"I don't need help."

"I never said you did. I'm offering it."

"Well," James clearly didn't know what to say to that. "You look stupid dressed like that. I can't believe you said hello to me and I missed it was you."

"I'm rather enjoying myself."

"You're weird."

"A majority opinion, to be sure," said Sherlock.

"You think it's the Bible? In there?"

"I'm not sure. I think . . . no, I know . . . that this is where the clues end."

"Father didn't want me finishing them."

"Say again?"

"Said he needed time, more time. He didn't say what for."

"On the odd chance we're successful . . . wait here one minute, will you?" Sherlock returned with two pair of white cotton gloves used by altar boys to clean the chapel silver and handbells. "Why are you being nice to me?" Sherlock asked.

"You're annoying, but you're helpful. I need you."

Sherlock nodded.

"I believe what you told me in the tunnel. I'm on a mission, here, Holmes. It may or may not include you. For now it does. That's me being honest, in case you don't recognize it."

Sherlock laughed aloud.

"How . . . why do you think . . . how can you always be so sure of yourself?" James sounded at once both impressed and upset.

"I lay no claim to anything found," Sherlock said. "The clues were intended for you, James, not me. They end here. Now. Through that door."

"Okay, then. Let's get this over with."

CHAPTER 39

OF FRIENDS AND ENEMIES

Failing to find a latch to open the wall panel, Sherlock stepped back to examine it from a distance.

His frustration palpable, James commented again that he was ready for "it to be over."

"Sadly, my boy," Sherlock said, "I sense it's only just beginning."

"How do we open it?"

Sherlock moved the wrought-iron candle stand aside and placed his weight onto the toe of his shoe. He had to point his toe like a dancer in order to deliver his weight only onto the keystone. It moved down under the pressure. The wood panel sprang open. The size of a narrow door.

"That was a lucky guess," James said.

"An educated guess, but yes. Tread carefully, my friend," cautioned Sherlock. "We've arrived to the end of the road, and sometimes that takes the shape of a cliff."

Inside the cloistered space, hundreds of metal organ pipes stood like soldiers from short to tall. Row after row of them. Stair-step landings provided access to the rows of pipes on either side. The only light came through acoustic fabric panels that during services allowed the organ music to reach the chapel's interior. A quick look around failed to reveal much of anything.

"Maybe more of a dead end than a cliff," said James.

"Look for a key or tree branches carved into one of the wind boxes or perhaps the pipes. I'll take this side, you take that."

"More clues?" James groaned.

"They didn't make it easy for you."

"Me? I doubt that."

"Yes, you, James. Legacy. The family Moriarty."

Less than a minute passed. "It felt better when I hated you," James said. Sherlock joined him to see the key-and-tree emblem engraved below the air hole in one of the medium-sized pipes.

Sherlock dropped to his knees and grappled in the semidarkness. The wind box beneath the marked pipe had been customized.

"It's hinged. Stand back," Sherlock said.

James stepped aside.

Sherlock yanked the organ pipe. It moved like a lever, and as it did a section of the landings on the stairs lifted and opened. Flickering yellow light came out of it.

Sherlock sniffed the air. "Ah," he said. "That explains it."

"Explains what, exactly?" James sounded frightened or excited. It was hard to tell which.

"Your sister's clothing . . . last night when she disappeared . . . I saw her today and smelled it in her hair . . . at least I thought I did. It proved to be in her clothing. I deduced she'd been taken someplace closed. I thought perhaps a church in Boston, one that uses incense. I was wrong. It's here. That's the smell."

"They took her here?"

"To question her, I imagine, which makes this place all the more dangerous to you, James. I have protected myself to some degree. We must accept that the clues may not lead to a prize. I suggest we turn around while we still can."

Something struck Sherlock's head. A club or metal pipe. It hit him from behind. The yellow light dimmed. Sherlock saw the papier–mâché face of a raven head and beak. Then, his mind went blank.

CHAPTER 40

ONLY IF YOU'RE LUCKY

James was urged down a set of steep stone steps by a cloaked raven behind him.

"You hurt my friend," James said, amazed to hear himself calling Sherlock his friend.

"Silence, please."

As he reached the bottom, James flinched as two men stepped out of shadow to wrap a purple cape around him. The two men wore horrid gargoyle masks obscuring their faces. Judging by their height, they were either sixth form or adults.

"I don't like this. I'd like to go back."

"There is no going back."

James was encouraged lower through the narrow stairway. Torches burned. He turned to the right and entered into a large space with earthen walls encrusted with enormous tree roots. There was a ceremonial altar behind which stood three figures, the center of whom wore a red gargoyle mask the color of old blood. Torches stuck out from the dirt walls, illuminating the space in a flickering dance of shadows.

On a stand in front of the three was a large leather volume that he knew had to be his family Bible.

James sucked for air.

Standing shoulder to shoulder, twenty or more figures surrounded the room, all in full costume.

"James Keynes Moriarty!" thundered the central figure. "You will bow before this tribunal and, on this day, the twenty-first day of September, the autumnal equinox, be presented with the rules and requirements to be initiated as a journeyman in the Fellowship of Scowerers, like your father and his father before him."

James was led to face the three. He was moved by the raven onto one knee and his head was pushed down to bow in submission. He shook with fear.

"In two days you will be offered the opportunity, one time and one time only, to have your name inscribed into this Bible. Tonight, you will be schooled by the fellowship as to our ways, though not our secrets. Those will only be revealed if and when you say the words." The voice from the red mask sounded deep and rich and, somehow, vaguely familiar. Crudgeon? he wondered. "You may refuse us at any time in the next several hours. So be it. You will remember nothing of this. We will see to that."

"Like Moria!"

"Silence! Your friend upstairs and you will know nothing of this place. For you both, the clues will stop at the sundial. Only then, if you're lucky. You will be forever puzzled by what they may have meant."

James lifted his head slightly. The Bible was only a yard away. He looked down at his gloved hands.

This moment was what Father had seen coming. The clues had led Father just as they had led James. Father had lost his chance at whatever he'd needed more time for. James knew it had something to do with this place, and these men and this Bible. He would not leave his father's death without more answers.

"I accept."

CHAPTER 41

IN AN UNEXPLAINED HURRY

WHILE THE STUDENT BODY'S ATTENTION WAS on Headmaster Crudgeon and Mrs. Furman at the front of Hard Auditorium, I took a moment to search faces, hoping I might see Sherlock in disguise.

"Quiet please!" Mrs. Furman clapped three times sharply, reminding me of elementary school. The audience went silent.

"Students!" Headmaster Crudgeon called out in a voice that barely needed the microphone he held. "It is my pleasure to announce that the Moriarty family Bible has been found and therefore mandatory study hall for all forms is hereby suspended!"

A roar went up that may have cracked the building's foundation. I hadn't found a single face that might be Sherlock. For me, there was nothing to cheer about. Natalie, who was sitting next to me, looked at me with sympathy in her eyes, believing my lack of enthusiasm was a carry-over from my internment in the infirmary.

Crudgeon raised his hand. Mrs. Furman took one step forward and the place went as quiet as if we'd all been slapped in the face.

"You may be pleased to know you have the efforts of one particular student to thank for the Bible's recovery."

I felt a sudden heat flood through me, pride and gratitude that Headmaster would single out Sherlock despite his suspension. That, I realized, was why I couldn't see him anywhere. No doubt Crudgeon had commuted his suspension and had him waiting in the wings of the stage to come out and receive the recognition he so deserved. Things actually did work out in the end, I thought. For the first time in what seemed like a long time the sting of Father's death lessened, if only a fraction.

"James, would you please stand up," Crudgeon said.

Sitting in the second row, my brother came to his feet, basking in the outrageous volume of cheers and applause that erupted. Kids thundered their feet on the floor, turning the entire auditorium into a kettle drum. James waved like the queen of England.

We met eyes, he and I, and I felt a pain in my gut as if I'd been stabbed. It was as if his eyes had turned into black cinders. My brother was gone; I didn't know this boy.

I couldn't take it. I hunched and moved past knees and reached the aisle and, as the student body rose to its feet in adulation for my brother, I fled the auditorium.

Mistress Grace followed me out and caught up to me.

"Moria, dear, whatever is the matter? Are you not feeling well? Should we get you back to the infirmary?"

"No . . . no. Thank you, though." I tried to think of a plausible explanation for my departure. "I was claustrophobic, that's all."

"We need to get you to the infirmary, dear. We're going now, before the students are released. Off we go."

"Really, I'm fine!"

"It's not up for discussion." She took me by the arm. I considered resisting but she was acting so strange—so buddy-buddy—that I didn't have the heart.

Adding to the oddity, laidback Mistress Grace was in a hurry. And it wasn't just her physical movement; she embraced me with an urgency that put me on edge. I didn't need guiding; I knew how to reach the infirmary.

We scurried across the back lawn toward McAndrews Science Hall and rode an elevator to the third floor.

"You go into room 4, dear. I'll let the nurse know we're here."

Tired and upset, I was more than happy to follow her instructions. I had little desire, but perhaps great need for rest.

I opened the door to room 4, looked inside, and turned quickly to catch sight of Mistress Grace facing me. She'd been waiting to see me go inside.

"I can buy you five minutes, no more," she said.

"Oh . . . thank you sooooooo much," I said to her with tears in my eyes.

In the room's far bed lay a sleeping Sherlock Holmes.

CHAPTER 42

THE DUMPSTER QUESTION

"Before I came to your room I consumed seven raw jellyfish. Not easy to find, but there's a health food store in Putnam that sells them frozen. Awful-tasting creatures. Do you know why I ate them?"

"I thought you were asleep," I said. "You have a bandage on your head."

He rolled over and looked at me. He was more pale and drawn than I'd ever seen him. His eyes had sunk farther into his head amid what were either two black eyes or one tired boy.

"Don't cry, dear. All's well."

"Don't call me that! It's patronizing. You're not my father!"

"Jellyfish has been discovered to help in memory retention, ergo, the best defense for whatever it was on the Bible they used to put you into your stupor."

I would have told him to slow down, but I was joyous at being in his company and I thrilled to the challenge of keeping up.

"You were attacked," I speculated. "Drugged."

"Mind you, the jellyfish were a bit like bringing a glass of water to a three-alarm fire, but I dashed their efforts at least somewhat, if not significantly. They clubbed me on the head. Very likely administered the amnesic concoction shortly thereafter, and left me by the Dumpster behind the dining hall, which is important to us."

"Is it?" I wasn't following all of what he said, not by any means. But I didn't really care. I heard "us." It rang in my head like the chapel bells. I liked this boy. I adored him.

"So it's bits and pieces, I'm afraid," Sherlock said. "A slideshow that moves too fast. A raven mask made of papier–mâché. Boys, or men, wearing capes. Flames. Torches? I'm not sure. The smell of earth and incense."

"Why is the Dumpster important?" I asked, latching on to that for no particular reason.

"Not the Dumpster, but the rear of the dining hall. It must have been close, you see? They couldn't go lugging my body all over campus, now could they? I'm not as light as you, and besides, you were moved long after the entire school was asleep."

I enjoyed being called light. I appreciated that he'd noticed me in that way. "You've figured this out while recovering from being given a concussion and drugged? I couldn't even think the first twelve hours I was awake."

"I'm quite something, aren't I?"

"Just shut up!" I said, laughing.

"It's not all done and dusted, but I do have a plan. That roar I heard just now? Crudgeon announcing the discovery of the missing Bible?"

"Gee whiz," I muttered. "Who are you?"

"Did he say it was found in the ceiling of the computer lab by Proctor Sidling?"

"James," I announced. "He said James found it."

"Oh, dear."

"Not you, not me, James."

"It's not the credit for the thing, Moria, that is troubling. The best things we do are often those for which we receive the least credit. Not to worry. It's the implication of the thing that's troublesome. It's bigger, more widespread than I thought," Sherlock said.

"What is?"

"We'll get to that, perhaps. The thing of it is, Crudgeon is deliberately, overtly, enhancing your brother's reputation here. He's king-making."

"My brother's a king?" I used my voice to let him know how ridiculous that sounded. "I think you need more rest."

"Your brother is being groomed, positioned to be well liked and trusted by his peers. He has the support of the highest administrator in the institution. What does that tell you?"

"That you need a sedative. Should I call the nurse?"

"Ha-ha!" Sherlock looked at me disapprovingly.

"It tells me you've thought a lot about this. It tells me that Father is connected to Crudgeon, and possibly what happened to him . . . if it wasn't an accident . . . and that James is now being groomed for something."

"You did well," Sherlock said from his position on the hospital bed. "I'm glad for that."

I thanked him for the compliment, as they were rare. My throat tightened, and I'm afraid I scowled, if only just a little.

"What is it, Moria? Please!"

I spoke softly. "It's what I just said. Father. I need your help, Lock."

"The cause of your father's death," he said.

"How is it you're always a step or two ahead?"

"If I wasn't, would you want my help?"

I laughed.

"Is James with you on this? We would need James, Moria. It's his father, too."

"I think we can bring him around," I said. "I believe that with all my heart or I wouldn't ask you."

"Even with James onboard, I'm not sure how I can help," Sherlock said.

"Oh, but I do!" I said confidently. "You'll be my private detective."

Sherlock's entire demeanor changed. It was as if some internal light switched on, all pain or traces of headache vanished, replaced by a sense of purpose and a visceral excitement.

"Splendid!" he said, sitting up smartly. "I very much like the sound of that, Moria." Lock reached out his cold hand to me.

We shook hands vigorously to consummate the deal.

He looked at me eagerly. "Are you any good at papier-mâché, my dear girl?"

"What?"

"There's work to do. First things first, we need to get me out of this dress they've put me in. It's barely better than an apron, I'm afraid."

CHAPTER 43

SPIES, TOGETHER

"WHAT IF YOU'RE CAUGHT?" I ASKED SHER-lock, moving a branch of a bush out of the way in order to see him.

"I won't be."

"How do you know this will work?" I was holding the papier-mâché mask Natalie had made at my request. Sherlock had described what was needed.

"I don't," he said. "Not at all. But I've put my theory through innumerable tests and proofs and I must say this is the most logical explanation. I'm his roommate, don't forget. You're his sister. You tell me something is up, I believe you. We're a team.

"Crudgeon doesn't think I know," he continued, "because Crudgeon thinks I'm still quarantined in the infirmary. Safe and sound. Out of the way. You and Mistress Grace have helped continue that ruse. Why is it you think she's helping us, anyway?"

"She likes me," I said. "I'm a Moriarty, too, and she's something of a feminist and doesn't think James should be getting all the attention. She's sore about that. So she tells the nurse she's reading to you and lets you escape knowing you're trustworthy enough to return. It's worked three times. Let's just hope it can work once more."

"It's lovely of her, I must say. Perhaps some flowers or candy is in order?"

"Where do you come from?" I said, before thinking to stop myself. "Never mind that!"

We occupied a space between honeysuckles in Mr. Hinchman's side lawn, enveloped by a moonless night's sky. Across the access road was the back of the dining hall and the infamous Dumpster near which Sherlock had been deposited. Our attention was trained not onto the dining hall, but the alumni building, one of the original Colonial houses on campus that dated back to the school's origins in the late 1800s.

"How did you know they'd come?" I asked.

"Your clothes smelled of incense. One of the few memories I've been able to preserve from my . . . incapacitation. I detected a similar odor coming off the thug as he clomped me on my bean. Ergo: the chapel. If there's to be an initiation—your brother let that slip and tried to make it go away, but it was something your father had mentioned to him—then where better than in an ancient building brought over stone by stone by your ancestors? Hmm? You see? You have to know something about secret societies: they are steeped in ritual, often superstitious, and extremely protective.

"And so here we are," he said. "Here they are, arriving one by one at the start of curfew. Which reminds me: you must start writing down number plates from the vehicles." He reached under his cape and handed me a pen. "Help straighten this for me, will you please?"

We were risking a great deal breaking curfew, but we were risking it together. I adjusted his robe. Six cars had arrived over the past twelve minutes, each exactly two minutes apart. Men and women, always only one to a car. Each driver had entered the back of Alumni House.

"So it's in there? This meeting?"

"In a manner of speaking."

"I'm waiting," I said.

"The key. Recall for the image, if you please."

"A skeleton key with a tree atop it."

"Definition of a key?"

"What? I don't know. A thing that opens a door." I didn't need a vocabulary lesson. I wanted to help my brother.

"There are some fifteen definitions for the noun, one of which is the central building block at the top of an arch. I'm afraid we focused on other aspects of the thing. Some of them paid off, I will give you that. But the fact is, the tree is the key. That tree, there. The oldest tree on campus."

"It's the key? What does that mean?"

"It's the top of the arch, Moria. It sits over a structure. These people aren't in the Alumni House. But I know where to find them."

"You'll be careful. Tell me you'll be careful."

Sherlock said nothing.

After a total of seven more vehicles—exactly twenty-four minutes—the perfectly timed arrivals stopped. Sherlock stood, took the papier–mâché mask in hand, and tucked it under his arm. A hyena, its teeth bared.

He hurried across the road, his robe flowing behind, and climbed the steps. He disappeared inside.

CHAPTER 44

THE INITIATION

Sherlock located the tunnel he was looking for in the basement of the Alumni House. A cupboard held by a piano hinge was pulled away from the wall, revealing a torch-lit opening.

He wore the mask and robe, allowing him to slip past a similar-looking sentry guarding the entrance.

Walking down a stone corridor felt like a step back in time to the era of castles and dungeons. He felt a chill that had nothing to do with the cool temperature of being below ground. The tunnel admitted him to an earthen room also lit by torchlight.

He gaped at the tree root–entwined walls and ceiling, the dirt floor and the pageantry of the masked members. They roamed as if at a cocktail party, talking casually. Sherlock stood with his back to two thick roots, studying the costumed members. A fox. A warthog. A boar. Carnivores, all.

Sherlock heard two claps. The attendees moved nearly in unison to stand around the perimeter of the room, facing in.

The attendees began to hum. Sherlock quickly picked up the chant's melody and added softly to the chorus. Three individuals—one in a red mask—stepped up to an altar table, their costuming more formal. The third man proved to be holding a large book in gloved hands. He placed it in front of the altar table on a stand. The Moriarty Bible. Sherlock gasped, then coughed gently to disguise his surprise.

There was movement at the top of the stone stairs at the far end of the room. James descended, escorted by two others, a leopard head and some kind of fish.

Sherlock couldn't be sure, but his roommate looked hypnotized or under a spell. He wasn't walking right. He stopped. The one in the red mask spoke.

"James Keynes Moriarty. You have successfully completed the Clues of Confidence, demonstrating a willingness to complete the tasks put before you without questioning them; leadership; and curiosity and conviction. Through these qualities we seek a united society and it is to these qualities to which we turn when in need. Do you understand? You will answer, 'aye' or 'nay.'"

"Aye!"

The humming continued.

"James Keynes Moriarty. You come bearing the blood of our founders, the blood of our leaders for nearly two centuries. You therefore come to us as royalty. Through your training in the years to come here at Baskerville, as well as outside its walls, you will be made to undertake bold actions, to develop skills essential to your position, and to eventually lead men and women of all ages in the endeavors of this society. Do you understand and accept these conditions?"

"Aye!"

"James Keynes Moriarty. Should you fail to uphold the strict secrecy of this society, or to deviate from our path, you will be conditioned or rendered, according to the strictures of our charter, in a way to inhibit your memory or end your life, as the governing committee sees fit. Do you understand?"

"Aye!"

"And knowing this, do you willingly, of free mind, consent to this agreement as you have read it, and wish to continue with this initiation?"

"Aye!"

Sherlock's heart would not stay in his chest. He felt for certain those around him must be able to hear it beating furiously to be free of his chest. *End your life* . . . Was this an agreement James's father had consented to as well? Was that why he had wanted James to buy him more time? He had known that he was in violation of rules, the punishment for which could end his life.

Sherlock wanted desperately to grab his friend and take him from this place, but it occurred to him that James was answering yes to all the questions. He wondered if the agreement James had read was contained somehow in the pages of the Bible.

"You, here, who have gathered as witnesses of this moment, how say you? Are we to induct James Keynes Moriarty into the brotherhood of the Scowerers? All in favor, say aye!"

"Aye!" came the chorus. The humming stopped.

"All against?"

Silence. Only the spitting of the torches.

An eagle's head was put atop James's shoulders and he was led to a chair in the middle of the space. It was a glorious shoulder mask and looked to be ancient. He was made to sit as a costumed attendee stepped forward to a table holding an unrolled cloth bearing stainless steel medical tools, dishes, and bottles.

The humming restarted.

James was helped to raise his arm amid the same calming melody. He reached high overhead. He wore no shirt beneath the robe. One of his escorts stepped forward, took James's arm, twisted it, and laid it across the table.

The tattooing began. There were no electric machines, just the patient hand holding a needle that was repeatedly stabbed into James's skin. James flinched, but did not cry or speak. The artist continued his or her work for at least twenty minutes.

Sherlock felt proud he had helped to solve the string of clues; in many ways it should have been him in that chair, though he wasn't much of a society man. He felt less pleased that he and Moria, as a team, had unearthed the Bible, realizing its presence was to play an important part of James's initiation. That part of the ceremony was yet to come; but come it would.

Again, Sherlock processed the facts. James's father had wanted James to take his time solving the clues. He'd known that the clues would lead to this ceremony. Had the father wanted to stop James from taking part in the initiation altogether, or delay his son's participation, or had it been something more personal that needed doing? Sherlock didn't merely want the answer to that question, he needed it. He would seek it, regardless of the personal cost to himself, for the answer might also explain the death of a man beloved by his two children and reveal those responsible. There was work yet to do.

The tattoo being applied high up under James's arm was difficult to see at a distance. Given the time involved in its creation, it had to be extremely detailed for something so small. The more he studied it, the more Sherlock realized it was no bigger than a key.

CHAPTER 45

IN THE MIDDLE
OF THE WOODS

A MONTH LATER, SHERLOCK AND I WALKED IN the woods between the school and the old estate. The colorful leaves were so deep they danced at our shins and made crinkling noises as we trudged through. Chickadees and gray squirrels made noises above. Halloween had come and gone, taking any chance of a warm day with it.

"Are you going to tell me?"

"No more than I have."

"That it's secret for a reason."

"Yes. Exactly that."

"It's selfish of you and terribly unfair," I said.

"No doubt."

"You're scared for him. For James?"

"I'm scared for us all," he said. "We need to find out who killed your father, and why. And to do that, we need to come to understand this secret group."

"Way to make me feel better."

"My role is not to make you feel better, Moria. My role is as your private investigator. Your words, not mine."

"I was expecting a report."

"My report is this: we have your family's Ralph on our side; also Mistress Grace."

"Will they know about the Scowerers?"

"I only told you that much because I trusted you to never repeat it."

"We're in the middle of the woods."

"Never! Regardless of how safe it may seem. I do believe we would be in some danger were we or anyone heard to utter that name outside of the council itself."

"OK. I'm sorry. Never again." We walked another fifty yards. "You mean like what happened to Father. Real danger."

"Oh, yes. That's spot on. That kind of danger, indeed."

"It doesn't seem we have much, not so very much to go on."

"'Very' is a—"

"Worthless word. Yes. I'm sorry."

"We do have a few things they don't have."

"Such as?" I inquired, sounding doubtful, I admit.

"Trust," he said, causing me to turn my head and look at him, not the bed of leaves.

"Is that so?"

"And each other," he said, reaching down and taking my hand in his. Our fingers interlaced. I tightened my grip and he returned in like fashion. I briefly shut my eyes, allowing him to lead me along like a seeing-eye dog. The air smelled crisp and alive. The empty branches rattled overhead musically. My hand was approximately two thousand degrees. My heart soared.

I smiled, the first real smile since I'd had news of Father's fall.

I don't know if Sherlock saw my eyes closed, or felt my hand as warm as I did, or if he watched my face turn into that smile, or if he was simply being Sherlock, something he had so much trouble avoiding. Whatever the case, he made me smile even wider with what he said next.

"Walk upright, Moria. Clear-eyed and strong. There's adventure yet to come."

ACKNOWLEDGMENTS

This story is an imagining of how a boy descended to a darker place to become the world's greatest mastermind, my brother, James Moriarty. I have devoured every short story written by Sir Arthur Conan Doyle. It is only with the greatest admiration and respect that I dare to exploit my brother's transgressions. I beg Sir Arthur's indulgence.

Without the help of David Linker, Nancy Zastrow, Jen Wood, and Miranda McVey, I would have been without my magnifying glass. Without my cousins, Storey and Paige, and their mother, Marcelle, I would have been without a heart.

Yours,
Moria Moriarty,
BOSTON, MASSACHUSETTS

THE MYSTERY CONTINUES WITH BOOK 2.
TAKE A SNEAK PEAK!

CHAPTER ONE

Awakened by the sound of an outboard motor coughing to a start, I threw my legs out from under the down comforter, toes searching for the fuzzy lining of my slippers. As I stood and headed for the partially frosted window, I pulled a throw off the corner chair, accidentally dumping one of my Christmas presents, a novel, onto the plank flooring. Wrapping my shoulders, and reaching for the pair of binoculars that I'd been given four years earlier on my eighth birthday, I trained the glasses onto the churning waters of Nantucket Sound.

The waves collided, thrown into a gray-green

chop topped with white foam like a latte. The condition had something to do with currents and tides and a lot to do with wind direction and speed. Among the swells moved a flat-bottomed white fiberglass skiff called a Boston Whaler. The whaler threw foam and spray to either side as it cut its way atop the rough waters. I recognized its single occupant, the boy driving, as my brother, James. He wore a blue knit cap over his brown hair, a yellow foul weather suit, and over it, a bright orange life vest. He worked the wheel with his left hand and the throttle with his right. Oddly enough, the binoculars didn't reveal the falling snow. Only as I looked with my naked eye could I see it as a fine white confetti blanketing the seascape.

The sky held an elaborate mix of colors: aqua, gray, pink, and purple. A painter's sky. Our mother had been a painter, a good painter. A fine artist, she was called. She'd hung shows in banks and the library and sold well at the Provincetown summer craft fair, where I remembered her in a straw hat, bright lipstick, and sunglasses. We all smelled like suntan lotion in summers, and hamburgers, and fresh-cut grass. Ice cream doesn't smell or we would have smelled like that as well. I didn't remember my mother clearly, but it's all that's left of her: memories. Father, too. Life stops. Life goes on. As a twelve-year-old I found it hard to wrap my mind around it all. James wasn't doing much better at fourteen. (He looked and acted older—sixteen; seventeen if he wore a necktie—but inside I wasn't sure if he had an identifiable age.) He'd changed in the last few months, during our first semester at Baskerville Academy, a boarding school in northeastern Connecticut. I suppose I had, too, but it takes others to see change in yourself, and I had few others around anymore. There was Lois, who'd been Father's secretary, and then our nanny, and now was our surrogate legal guardian. Ralph had been Father's driver, and maybe his closest friend. He felt like our uncle. It was odd to spend Christmas break with your family's house staff, in your family's Cape Cod compound that had been in the Moriarty family for three generations.

Tragedy had brought us together; tragedy had torn us apart. The four of us existed in a kind of limbo, feeling halfway between blood relatives and unwanted second cousins. Thankfully, neither Lois nor Ralph had tried to play the father or mother card. Nonetheless, there was no getting around the awkwardness that these two adults were now employed by my brother and me.

The skiff survived the chop to reach a sailboat that had arrived quickly from around the point that formed Lewis Bay to the west. Its white sails suddenly made to luff; I watched them flapping and knew the deafening sound of it. I watched shivering as James threw a bow line and was pulled to. A stern line pulled him parallel. He climbed aboard.

The binoculars lacked enough power to reveal any faces. It was more like watching a stage play from the back row. I took away the general gist of the story: two adults—men, by their size—met James and led him into the cabin belowdecks, while the crew dropped a pair of bumpers between the whaler and the sailboat. There was someone in foul weather gear at the large wheel at the back of the cockpit. There was a sense of urgency on the part of all, even seen from this distance.

James came back out of the cabin exactly five minutes later—I timed it. The same two men accompanied him back to the rail, shook hands with him, and saw him safely over the side. As the outboard engine started, it burped purple fumes. Lines were cast off and the skiff headed back toward shore. I confess to feeling something of relief. The ocean had no respect for humankind. I wanted James, the last of my living blood relatives, home safely.